BLOOD AND TEARS

Book Four of the Kelsey's Burden Series
KAYLIE HUNTER

This book is a work of fiction. All names, characters, places, businesses, incidents, etc., etc. are the imagination of the author, and any resemblance to actual persons or otherwise is coincidental.

Copyright 2016 by Kaylie Hunter

Cover design by Melody Simmons

All rights reserved. No part of this book may be used or reproduced in any manner without the written permission of the author except when utilized in the case of brief quotations embodied in articles or reviews.

KELSEY'S BURDEN SERIES:

LAYERED LIES

PAST HAUNTS

FRIENDS AND FOES

BLOOD AND TEARS

LOVE AND RAGE

Chapter One

Arriving at the Demon Slayers' clubhouse in Biloxi, Mississippi, Maggie and I stepped out of my SUV and into the steamy afternoon sun. I stretched my back and shoulders, trying to free the bunched muscles from the long drive from Florida.

Renato and Nightcrawler walked out of the clubhouse. Renato nodded in friendly greeting to me before appraising Maggie. Nightcrawler stood back, tense and remote.

I met Renato and Nightcrawler a few weeks back while at a bar in Michigan. Two days ago, I reached out trying to locate the family of a young girl who was murdered, and I discovered it was Nightcrawler's niece Elly. We agreed to meet up on my way to Louisiana.

"Renato, this is Agent O'Donnell with the FBI, but to everyone that knows her, she's just Maggie. Maggie, this is Renato, President of the Michigan Demon Slayers motorcycle club. And, that's Nightcrawler," I said.

"I'm sorry about your niece," Maggie said, directing her attention to Nightcrawler.

He nodded but didn't speak.

"We don't generally allow cops in the clubhouse without a warrant," Renato said, directing the statement to me.

"I wouldn't have anyone that runs 'by the book' riding shotgun beside me," I said, staring back at him.

Renato thought about it a moment before a slight grin split his lips. "I believe you, but it'd be better if we talked out here," he nodded to a nearby picnic table. "Do you want anything to drink?"

"Rum and coke would be great," Maggie answered, reinforcing the fact that she wasn't here in a professional capacity.

"Ditto," I agreed.

Renato ordered a prospect to run inside, and we had barely settled at the picnic table before the eager kid returned with two beers and our cocktails. Nightcrawler glared at the kid before he turned tail, jogging back into the clubhouse.

"We need a name, Kelsey," Nightcrawler growled in a low tone.

"Darrien Pasco," I said taking a sip of my drink. "But you can't get to him, and as much as you want to argue that point with me, I'm telling you, it's in your favor to leave him alone."

"He killed my niece!"

"Yes, he did," I said, watching him closely. "And, she wasn't the only one. There was another victim that suffered a much worse fate. That girl's father is in a position to make sure that vengeance is served, and believe me, Pasco *will* suffer."

Nightcrawler dragged his hands over his closely shaved head.

"Your word, Kelsey," Nightcrawler growled, staring at the table.

"You have it."

Renato placed a brotherly hand on Nightcrawler's shoulder.

I pulled my sunglasses from my shoulder bag to shield my eyes from the intense sun.

"Is there anything we can do?" Renato asked.

Looking around, I saw several other club members, but they weren't close enough to listen to our conversation.

"Can you tell me about Elly's disappearance? Did she run away or was she taken from around here?"

"She ran. She left a note that she was leaving with a boy she barely knew and just disappeared with a bag full of clothes and no money," Renato answered as he rubbed a hand over his tired eyes. "We tried looking for her, but couldn't find her. The boy turned up dead, overdose, in Miami a month later."

"Then most likely, the person that was responsible for grabbing her and selling her to Pasco was a man named Max. There's no payback to be found there," I said, shaking my head.

"You arrested him too?" Renato asked.

I hesitated and looked at Maggie. I hadn't come clean yet with what had happened to Max. And because I was withholding information, I didn't want Maggie putting her career on the line to protect me.

"I'll go back to the car and make some phone calls," Maggie grinned.

As I waited for her to walk out of earshot, Nightcrawler chugged half of his beer.

"So? Did you arrest him?" Renato asked again.

"No, not exactly. I intended to question him, but he tried to escape and ended up jumping off the boat, and the sharks ate him," I said, visibly shivering at the memory.

Renato and Nightcrawler stared at me intensely.

I shrugged and put my arms up in a 'what can I say' gesture.

Nightcrawler broke out in loud laughter, his body shaking from the effects, as he leaned forward. Renato clapped him on the back a few times, smiling at me.

I offered a few more details to Nightcrawler on the demise of Max, and another round of drinks were delivered. Nightcrawler grinned through the entire macabre story, which would have been disturbing if it weren't for the fact that it satisfied part of his need to hurt those that hurt his niece.

Maggie rejoined us at the table a few minutes later.

I looked at Renato and took a deep breath. "I need to call in my marker."

He took a long drink of his beer and nodded at me to continue.

"My son Nicholas was kidnapped a few years ago by Nola Mason, an associate of Pasco and Max's. Taking them down was part of the plan to flush her out, but I hear she set up camp closer to New Orleans. I need the word put out with her description and my son's. But it's a search and report information only job. I can't risk my son being caught in any crossfire."

"He's alive?" Nightcrawler asked.

"Yes," Maggie answered for me. "As of a little over a week ago, he was still alive."

"Why? Why would she keep him alive if she's involved with human trafficking?" Renato asked.

"Nola's taunting me. She's using Nicholas as a weapon against me."

Renato moved a hand on top of mine, but I pulled mine back. I needed my emotions to stay buried. I needed to be able to think logically, like a cop, if I was going to save Nicholas.

"Send us the information, and we'll spread the word," Renato nodded.

"I asked Tech to email you everything you need," I said to Renato before turning to Maggie. "Can we have another minute?" I asked her.

"Sure," she grinned, replacing her empty glass with my full one and walking back to the SUV with my cocktail.

"She's not your typical Fed," Nightcrawler grinned, watching her ass as she walked away.

"Not even a little bit," I grinned back at him. "One last thing — the shipments that you may or may not have with Mayfair Shipping need to stop. Keep it on the down-low, but Mayfair's been compromised."

"By who?" Renato asked concerned.

"By me," I winked.

• • •

I heard Nightcrawler's laughter all the way back to the SUV.

Chapter Two

It was dark out by the time we checked into a hotel just outside of the French Quarter in New Orleans. We ordered room service and worked on our laptops until Maggie called it a night and went to her room. I continued working through the data that both Genie and Tech had sent to me.

Around two a.m. I received an instant message from Tech on a property twenty minutes outside of town that looked like a possible hiding spot for Nola to keep Nicholas. I briefly thought about waking Maggie but decided against it as I checked my weapons and grabbed the SUV keys.

I parked a half of a mile away and walked the rest of the stretch on foot. The area was populated with abandoned homes, damaged by hurricanes. Homes that once had been filled with families now housed an assortment of creatures that called out into the night.

In the distance, I heard an owl. My mind wandered back to the message that Nicholas had sent to me through the other boy that had been in Pasco's dungeon. The boy had told me: *Nicholas could sometimes hear trumpets where they keep him. But the sound of the bugs at night is really loud and usually drowns them out. He can also hear an owl nearby.*

I listened closely, and on the edge of my hearing, past the echoing noise of the cicadas, I could barely make out the sound of jazz music playing.

My heart beat faster. This is where she's keeping him.

I increased my pace, pulling my gun as I walked down the long driveway that weaved around a section of marshland. I listened as I approached the dark house. No sounds emanated in the darkness other than the quieting of the night creatures as they sensed my presence. Not a single light was on in the house or on the grounds. No cars were parked in the driveway.

I heard a splash of water from somewhere deep in the woods and assumed an inlet was nearby. I slowly circled the outside of the house, checking the entire perimeter before returning to the front door. There was no sign of any movement. I slowly and quietly moved up the front porch.

I paused, moving my hand over my bracelet to rub the locket for good luck before turning the door knob and stepping inside.

Wait, I thought. Something's not right. The door shouldn't be unlocked.

The moonlight cast a bluish glow over the interior rooms and furniture. I moved down the hall, noting three doors. One was a small bathroom. A second was a bedroom that had been vacated, evidenced by the empty open dresser drawers.

The third door was closed, but the newer style deadbolt on the door was unlocked, and the door pushed easily open. Inside was a ransacked mess of toys and boy's clothes. A small bed was pushed to the corner of the room, and heavy bolted brass locks on the windows reflected off the moonlight.

Turning on the light, I confirmed what I already knew—this is where she had held my son.

And he was already gone.

Flipping the lights on, I made my way back to the front rooms in the house. Now standing at the entrance of the living room, the room brightly lit by the ceiling fan light, icy chills racked through my body as I looked around.

My breathing became labored, like trying to suck air through a wet towel. Blood coated the living room carpet in a widespread stain. Streaks of reddish-brown sprayed up the wall and across the ceiling. The couch was shoved back several feet on one side with a blood-soaked cushion laying half on the floor. The recliner chair was overturned during the obvious violence that had occurred. I grabbed my chest, trying to force the air into my lungs as the images of what must have happened in this room ripped through me.

I sensed Maggie entering the front door and reached out to grab her arm. Trying to anchor myself to the here and now.

"We don't know anything," Maggie whispered, rubbing a hand up and down my arm. "We'll get a crime lab here, and until they test everything, we don't know anything."

She was trying to reassure me, but I couldn't listen to it. I turned my back to her, walking to the bedroom, my mind spinning, my stomach tumbling, and my skin burning with intense fire.

I sat on the bed where Nicholas had most likely slept night after night, waiting for me to rescue him. Every emotion that I had tried to contain over the last few years boiled just below the surface. I leaned over, inhaling his scent on the pillow. It was my undoing. Sobs racked my body as I collapsed in a heap on the tiny bed.

Nicholas was gone.

Again.

Chapter Three

The noises of other people moving about in nearby parts of the house woke me. I looked around the room, wiping the crud from my eyes. The toys that scattered the floor were in various stages of destruction. I envisioned my son smashing them, ripping them apart, angry at Nola, angry at the world, angry at me.

In sharp contrast to the broken toys, a nearby bookshelf was filled with rows of books, all neatly aligned. Each book was specifically placed and arranged by subject: math, science, history, etc. All except one.

Oliver Twist was centered on the middle shelf between two math books. I pulled the book from the shelf and opened it. A few pages in, handwritten messages began to appear in the margins of the book. I leaned up against a nearby wall, sinking to the floor, book tensely gripped between my fingers and began to read.

I'm okay, Mom.
The man that was hired to watch me isn't so bad.
And Nola isn't here.
I miss you. Find me soon.

My heartbeat raced as tears spilled. I flipped ahead a few chapters seeing that most of the pages had notes.

Do you hear the owl? It sounds like a wolf.
Do you remember Aunt Charlie reading me that story about the girl who cried wolf?
I don't cry much anymore.

My hands shook as I skipped ahead again.

Nola gave me a picture of you today, but only for a minute.
You were laughing. You looked happy.
Have you forgotten about me?

I gasped, raising my hand and pausing it on top of the words that tore the crater in my heart open further.

Nola's mad today. She said you were bad.
I don't know what you did, but I'm glad you made her mad. Thanks, mom.

I flipped to the back of the book and read the last entry. I had to know. I had to know what his last message was to me before he was once again ripped from my life.

Larry says I have to pack.
I don't know where they are taking me.
Find me, Mom. Find me soon.
Nola's here. I have to go.
Nick

I wasn't sure how long I sat there clutching the book to my chest before I registered that Maggie was squatted in front of me trying to talk to me. She pulled me up from the floor. Taking the book from me, she tucked it inside my shoulder bag before handing the bag to me.

"We'll search through everything in the room and go through the rest of the books. I'll let you know if we find anything," she said as she moved me down the hall.

I was numb, running on auto-pilot. I paused at the front door and looked back at the blood painted room behind me. Lab techs were carefully collecting evidence.

"Maggie, it's not all his blood," I said turning to her with tears threatening again. "They told him to pack. He's still alive."

"I believe you," she whispered while briefly hugging me.

Several Agents looked away. They wouldn't believe me, but I didn't care. Maggie believed me. My family would believe me.

And, Nicholas was counting on me.

Maggie led me onto the porch, and I was swallowed in large arms that lifted me off the ground and held me close. I wasn't sure who held me. I only knew that the embrace was safe and warm, and I didn't have to think anymore. I closed my eyes and cried myself back to sleep again.

I only woke a few times during the trip back to Michigan, between boarding and exiting planes and occasionally Grady forcing me to eat or drink something. The rest of the trip was wrapped in nightmares that darkened my mind and caused goosebumps to etch my arms.

By the time I was awake enough to interpret any form of reality, I was in my own bed, in my own house.

Charlie slept next to me with her arm wrapped around me, clutching me close. Grady slept in a nearby chair, hunched up in an impossible position for a man of his size. Reggie and Jackson slept on the atrium couches where the early dawn light danced along the walls.

I slipped from the bed, and walked barefoot out of the bedroom, down the hall. Hattie greeted me in the dining room with a plate of eggs and fruit. My coffee was already sitting on the table.

"Good Morning, Hattie," I said, kissing her on the cheek.

"Good Morning, Sunshine," Hattie said, holding my face for a moment in her hands, staring at me with concern before releasing me. "You need to eat. Grady said he couldn't get you to eat or drink much yesterday."

"I'm not really hungry," I said pushing the plate to the side and reaching for the coffee.

Hattie walked into the kitchen and poured herself a cup of coffee before returning to the table.

"You told Maggie that Nicholas is alive. Is that true?" Hattie asked.

"Yes. I don't think Nola killed him," I said, taking a sip of my coffee as my stomach curled at the memory of the blood-soaked room.

"Then you need to stay strong for him. You need to eat. You need to catch up on your sleep, and you need to find your son," Hattie scolded.

I was lucky the day I met Hattie and hired her to work for me. She kept me grounded when the craziness got too real. Her caring nature soothed me.

I looked back at the plate, and despite the protests from my nervous stomach, I forced myself to eat some of the eggs and cantaloupe. Hattie returned with a piece of toast coated with a thin layer of peanut butter, and I ate as much as I dared before pushing the rest away.

"Hattie," I said, before my voice cut off, choked out by unshed tears.

"Enough, Sunshine," Hattie said as she embraced me. "You have to be strong for just a little longer. We'll find him."

"And, if I can't?"

"You will. And, you're not alone," she said as she pulled back from the embrace. "Look around, Sunshine. You're not alone."

Looking about the room through flooded eyes, I saw Anne, Katie, and Whiskey standing on the stairs. Sara was climbing up onto my lap. Donovan held Lisa by the front door with Alex standing beside them. James, Chops, Candi, Bridget, Haley, Sam and Tyler watched from the living room. Charlie, Grady, Jackson, and Reggie stood at the entrance to the hallway. Carl, Tech, Dave, and Steve stood at the top of the basement stairs.

I looked back at Hattie.

• • •

"See. It's going to be okay, Sunshine. Now eat some more of your breakfast," Hattie said, kissing me on the forehead before returning to the kitchen. "Alright, everybody. Since you all decided to get up at once, I need volunteers in the kitchen to help me cook breakfast."

Everyone moved in different directions, and soon the chaos of the morning helped slow my mind. I wrapped my arms around Sara and kissed the top of her head.

Hattie was right. I had more friends and family than I could have ever hoped for. They would help me find my son.

For two long days, true to their word, I wasn't alone as we sifted through every scrap of intel we could find to search for Nicholas. With Lisa's wedding the next day, I had sent everyone away earlier in the night, and by 3:00 a.m., frustrated and angry, I grabbed an empty box and started to remove the property searches from the corkboards around the room.

Other than the house outside of New Orleans, we had hit a dead-end on all the rest of the sites. We needed a new lead.

I heard the security panel at the end of the hall buzz followed by heavy footfall. I didn't have to turn to know that it was Grady. He had kept his promise and stuck by my side to search for Nicholas, even secretly driving to New Orleans to be close by if I needed him instead of flying to Michigan with everyone else. I was glad he had been there to drag me home.

"The wedding is later today. You need some sleep," he said coming up behind me and massaging my shoulders.

"I know," I sighed.

I started shutting down laptops as Grady shut down lights.

"What are you doing still up?"

"I took a night shift watching the house. Tyler just relieved me."

"Did you save yourself a bunk bed somewhere?"

"No. I'll figure it out."

"I heard Reggie and Jackson arguing earlier which means Reggie is most likely camped out in my bed. If you don't mind sharing with him, then I can sleep on one of the atrium couches."

"How about I sleep on one of the atrium couches, and you bunk with Reggie," Grady grinned.

"Fine by me," I smiled while buzzing us through the security door into the gym. "I like sleeping with Reggie. He's all warm and cozy, and I don't have to worry about wandering hands."

Reggie was technically my ex-brother-in-law, but the way I see it, I divorced Wild Card, not Reggie or their father, Pops.

"I'm all warm and cozy," Grady grinned.

"And, the wandering hands?"

"Might be an issue."

We slipped quietly up the stairs, down the hall, and into my bedroom suite. I turned the bathroom light on, with the door half closed so we could see inside the room. Reggie was curled up in a ball sleeping with a grin on his face and an arm thrown over a sleeping Donovan.

Grady and I both pulled out our cell phones and took pictures.

"What the hell?" I laughed.

"Lisa's parents arrived tonight and are staying at her house. Must be Donovan was thrown out," Grady grinned.

"I'm sure when Donovan stole my bed, he never thought that it would include cuddle time with Reggie."

I looked over at the atrium couches and realized they were both occupied as well. James slept on one and Goat slept on the other. My house was beyond full if all the bunk beds and other couches were already occupied.

I pulled blankets and pillows from the nearby closet and made our beds on the atrium floor. At least the carpet had a thick pad so it wouldn't be too horrible. Besides, I was sure I wouldn't sleep for more than a few hours, so it didn't matter.

We both sat on the floor and removed our boots. I undid my jeans zipper, but that was as far as I was willing to go with all the extra eyes around. Grady wasn't so modest and stripped down to his boxer-briefs. *Damn.*

"You said that out loud," he chuckled.

"Shit," I grinned and buried myself in my set of blankets.

* * *

He laid on his own makeshift pallet and turned on his side to face me. "Why didn't you tell anyone else what you found inside the house in New Orleans?"

"Because no matter what the DNA results show, Nola didn't kill Nicholas. It was staged to freak me out, and I'm ashamed to say it worked."

"You don't think they'll believe you?"

"They'd believe me. But why tell them? I'm already stealing so much attention from Lisa and Donovan's wedding celebration. I don't want their minds on whatever happened in that house. And, I don't want them more worried about me than they already are."

"They offered to postpone the wedding."

"Until when? In two more months, it will have been three years since Nicholas was kidnapped. Charlie and I altered our lives around that day. I won't ask anyone else to derail theirs as well."

I rolled onto my side to face him.

"Besides, everyone is wrong," I grinned at Grady. "I *am* a little scared of Lisa's father, and I really don't want to be around when he finds out Lisa's already knocked up."

Grady laughed, rolling onto his back. Lisa's father was the godfather of New Jersey; a fact Lisa shrugged off as no big deal. The rest of us only held the knowledge that was portrayed in the movies about mafia families, and we had no wish to be swimming with the fishes.

Chapter Four

It's my opinion that the only nice thing about Michigan winters is that sunrise doesn't hit until around 8:00 a.m. It's especially important when you sleep in a room with a mostly glass ceiling, and it blares at you, daring you to try to sleep through its presence.

Trying to be grateful for the five hours of sleep I managed to bank, I threw back my blankets.

"No, just a few more hours," Grady groaned from beneath me, turning his head away.

I realized I was laying on top of Grady, in all his heated skin glory and on his responsive body parts.

"Shit," I laughed and dragged myself off him.

"I wasn't complaining," he grinned as he squinted my way.

"And your hands? Did they stay to themselves last night?"

"They may have wandered a bit," he chuckled.

"You two need to shut up," James groaned from the couch. "I'm trying to think of only pure thoughts over here so I can lose the morning wood and go get coffee from Hattie."

"I'm thinking I need to call Dallas," Goat chuckled from the other couch.

"Oh, no, you don't, Goat," I scolded, getting up and straightening my clothes. "Last time Sara almost caught the two of you in the garage." I gathered my share of the bedding and stuffed it haphazardly into the linen closet. "The time before that, Hattie caught you both in her kitchen pantry. Do you know how much food she threw out? If you need relief, either drive to Dallas's house or—," I grabbed a box of tissue off a nearby stand and tossed it at him, "—go outside and work the issue out for yourself."

Goat chuckled as I made my way through my bedroom, grabbing my phone from my dresser. I noticed that the bed was vacant, but my shower was running. I followed the smell of coffee down the hall, into the dining room. My favorite chair was the only one open, even though several people stood or leaned against walls. I grinned and took my seat as a fresh cup of coffee was placed before me.

"Good Morning, Hattie," I grinned.

"Good Morning, Sunshine," she grinned back before sashaying back to the kitchen.

I saw Reggie and Jackson were in the kitchen helping Hattie cook. And, if Reggie was here, that must mean that it was Donovan that was using my shower.

I pulled my phone from my back pocket and slid it across the table to Tech. He picked it up and looked at me.

"Are you done with the slide show Lisa asked you to put together for the reception?" I asked.

"Finished it this morning," Tech nodded.

"Think you can add a picture or two?" I grinned and nodded at the phone.

Tech flipped through my recent photos and grinned. "Yeah, I think I can squeeze in at least one or two more."

Reggie walked over and set a breakfast plate in front of me. It had a small scoop of eggs, a small scoop of cut fruit and a giant mound of butter fried potato slices with a visible coating of salt on top. He winked and set the ketchup in front of me.

I smothered my potatoes in ketchup as the front door opened and in walked my cousin Charlie. As everyone hollered their greetings and exchanged hugs, I started to scoop the fried potatoes in my mouth as fast as I could.

Charlie threw her purse and coat toward the coat hooks and came racing over, pulling my plate away from me and stealing my fork right out of my hand.

"Oh, I'm so hungry," she grinned as she scooped a mouthful of *my* potatoes into her mouth. "Thanks, Cuz," she mumbled, walking into the living room.

"Good Morning to you too, Kid," I laughed. "Tell me again why we invited you?"

"Be nice," Hattie scolded, setting another plate in front of me. The new plate had a bigger pile of eggs and far fewer potatoes. "And, quit pouting," Hattie chuckled.

I sighed and accepted the new fork Hattie handed me.

"So, what's the schedule today look like?" I asked the room in general while I forced myself to eat my eggs.

"Hair and make-up at 10:00, dressed and pre-pictures at noon, and wedding starts at 2:00," Anne said from the other side of the table. "And, no, you can't start drinking alcohol yet."

"Seriously?"

"Consider yourself lucky," Donovan said, entering the room. His hair was wet, and he filled the room with the scent of aftershave lotion. "The guys have to be ready for pre-pictures by 11:00."

The men all groaned throughout the room. Anne and I shared a grin.

"The CAKE!" Hattie screeched from the kitchen.

I jumped up and ran over to her. She looked ready to pass out, and her hands were shaking.

"I forgot to order the fucking cake!"

"Shit," I giggled.

"Don't you laugh! What the hell am I going to do?"

"We can fix this, Hattie," I continued to giggle.

"How the hell am I going to fix this? Lisa wanted a six-layer strawberry and butter cream cake! We only have six hours before the wedding!"

"Anne, call Tammy. Tell her we have a code red on the wedding cake. We need emergency baking assistance."

Tammy was Dave's wife and a baking guru. She had dual commercial ovens installed in her kitchen for her birthday last year and kept each of us just on the verge of needing to go on a diet with her baking delights.

"Yes, sir," Anne giggled.

"Everyone else," I said, turning around and pointing a finger to everyone in earshot, "Vow of silence. No one under any circumstances is to tell Lisa."

"Kelsey, promise me that my bride is not going to be bawling later today over a damn cake," Donovan grumbled.

"I promise she won't cry about the cake, but that's as far as I am willing to go," I grinned.

"I have Tammy on the line," Anne said. "She needs a few supplies but already has her ovens preheating. And, she'll need to move the layers over here to decorate after they're baked."

"Give me the phone," Bridget ordered, taking the cell phone away from Anne. She started writing down a list and hung up a few minutes later.

She stepped over to the credenza, picked up a nail file and jacked the lock on the far drawer. She removed a stack of cash and stuffed it in her bra before closing the drawer and jacking the lock again. "We are going to need another set of hands," Bridget grinned, grabbing her coat.

Katie stepped over and tested the credenza drawer. Sure enough, it was re-locked.

I just grinned and winked at Bridget.

"I'll go with Bridget," Jackson offered, hanging up his apron. "It will be fine, Hattie, promise," he assured her, kissing her forehead before running out the door.

Hattie turned to look at me. Her lower lip trembled, and her eyes floated in moisture.

"No! Don't you dare Hattie," I warned playfully. "After everything this family has been through, you do not get to cry over a damn cake."

"What else did I forget?" Hattie asked.

"What else were you in charge of?" I giggled.

"Last night's dinner and breakfast this morning."

"Then you got two out of three," I grinned.

"Shit," James said, jumping up from the table. "I forgot to pick up Bones from the airport."

We all laughed as James ran out the door.

"See. It's all good. James forgot a groomsman!"

Hattie settled back into her morning routine, and I rejoined the dining room table.

"Can I get an update of the security schedule today?"

"I'll be working with the security guards on the outside surveillance from ten until six and then we have another team taking our place led by Bones after that," Charlie said. "You're in charge of the inside of the store after pictures. We've had security inside and out for two days to guard the place."

"Good, what about the houses?"

"I have guys set up to patrol the outside of the houses around the clock. I had to cut the per-person bodyguards down to one guard per three people, but I figured with you back, that would be okay," Donovan grinned.

"I've got the girls covered up until the ceremony, so that's fine," I nodded. "I think Katie needs a break from her guard anyway."

I grinned over at Katie, and she flipped me off.

"I can guard Katie for a while," Tech winked at Katie.

"I think we'll be good," I laughed. "What about the video surveillance?"

"Reggie, Tyler and I are rotating so someone is always watching the footage," Tech said.

"Anyone have any concerns?"

"The woods," Grady said. "The woods are too close to the houses and store. It's our biggest security concern."

"I agree. I'm going for a run and will do a search on my way through. I know the properties and should spot anything out of place. Warn the security teams that I'll be out there. I don't want to get shot by friendly fire."

"I'll go with you," Grady offered.

"Me too," Donovan said.

We changed into running clothes and shoes and met up in front of the house to stretch. Charlie came galloping out of the house to run with us.

"Thought it would be good to familiarize myself with the properties before my security shift. Besides, if there are four of us, we can span out a bit."

"Sounds good," I nodded. "We have four running trails on the West property, and then they align into one trail around the backside of the field to the East property. On the East side, it's just one trail but follows the perimeter all the way around and is about forty feet inside the tree-line. Keep your eyes open. If I was a sniper, I would be sitting in a tree above that trail."

We checked our guns before slipping out into the trees in a slow jog.

The West woodlands were my favorite running trails. The birds were so used to Donovan and I trampling through that they didn't bother to even pause in their morning songs as we split off onto the four trails. I took the outer perimeter trail which was also the longest. Grady took the second to last trail, Donovan the second trail and Charlie took the interior trail. Donovan and Charlie would get to the backside of the field a good ten minutes before us. It would work out well to have two teams going through the East property.

On the far side of the West property, I noticed a makeshift burn pit and a few beer cans near a dead-end dirt road, but other than that the property appeared undisturbed. Finishing the last jaunt along the backside, I passed by Alex's house and joined the trail that ran behind the field. Grady was up ahead, but ran in place, waiting for me.

I was breathing heavy in the cold winter air, and though there was no snow covering the trails, the ground was frozen, causing a heavy impact on my calves and feet.

"Shit, I'm not going to make it," I said to Grady as I passed him on the trail to take the lead position.

"Here," Grady said, passing me a scarf.

I wrapped the scarf around my face and nose to filter the cold air. It helped, but my lungs were still overworking.

Turning to the left at the other end of the field onto the East property, I tugged the snap off my holster and pulled my gun, running with it pointed downward at my side as I slowed my pace.

It was dangerous to run with a loaded gun, but this stretch of woods always made me nervous. There were too many hiding spots. The trees and brush were too dense. Too many shadows hovered along the path's edge.

"You okay?" Grady asked in a low hush.

"Just being cautious," I whispered back.

I continued down the path, but slowed my run to barely a jog, splitting my attention between watching the path so I didn't stumble and watching the tops of the trees for any signs of disturbance.

I was about two-thirds down the length of the property when I stopped. Grady stopped behind me and stepped up close.

"What is it?" he whispered, pulling his own gun.

"I don't know," I admitted scouting around. "I'm going to take the deer trail, deeper into the woods. Stay on this path, but walk the rest of the stretch. Be ready."

I backtracked down the running trail about fifteen feet to where a narrow deer path lead deeper into the woods. Gun out, I passed the thorny brush following the deer path. My spidey senses were tingling but not full-out screaming at me that there was a danger.

About thirty yards into the woods, I heard a noise ahead. I looked over to the right and saw a man sneaking through in the direction of the store.

"Freeze. Don't move," I yelled turning my gun his way.

He startled, looked at me, and darted in the opposite direction. I holstered my gun and followed in pursuit, leaving the deer trail behind and thrashing directly through the thick brush.

"What is it?" Grady yelled from somewhere unknown.

"One man. Running East!" I yelled back as I continued the chase.

Grady would have to pull off a miracle to catch up. And, I was getting further and further behind as my body was tiring, and the brush and tree limbs dragged me back.

The man ahead of me must have found another deer trail because I watched in frustration as he suddenly picked up speed, gaining more distance.

"Damn it," I yelled, jumping over a fallen tree, and turning onto the same deer trail.

My feet beat against the hard-packed ground. I could no longer see him in front of me as the brush and trees forced the trail to weave around them. I kept running, knowing that I would soon be coming out the other side of the trail.

I sped up again, giving it my all as I blew past a startled Charlie and flew out into the clearing. Charlie quickly recovered and was on my heels running behind me.

Crossing the clearing and dashing around the nearby neighboring business, I came into view of the parking lot at the same time a green truck squealed its tires out of the drive.

"Shit," I said, leaning over to place my hands on my knees.

"Did you get the plate?" Charlie asked mimicking my position.

Both of us were gasping to gain control of our breathing as I shook my head no. Grady and Donovan came running up behind us.

"What happened?" Donovan asked.

I looked up to see Donovan and Grady, still running in place, both fully controlling their breathing, and not a single drop of sweat visible. I looked back at Charlie, and she looked as bad as I felt. I pulled the neckline of my shirt up and wiped my forehead off.

"One guy, no idea what he was up to. Could have been a trapper or hunter who was just trespassing. I spooked him, and he got away."

"What's your gut telling you?" Donovan asked.

"My spidey senses seem quiet, but I'd like a grid search of the East property to be safe. Can you and Grady cover the store until the rest of the security team clears the woods? It will cause us to be short on coverage for about an hour, but I think it's worth it."

"Agreed," Donovan said. "Grady and I will go set it up."

Grady and Donovan turned back to the woods and started running again. I looked over at Charlie.

"Fuck no. I'm walking back," she grinned.

I chuckled, and we turned toward the road and followed it back to the store.

A police cruiser pulled into the store parking lot as we were walking across. Steve and Dave got out and joined us.

"You two look like shit," Steve grinned.

"My Miami lungs can't take this damn cold," Charlie chuckled, still breathing heavy.

I had finally managed to control my breathing, so I passed Grady's scarf to her. Donovan walked out of the store and jogged over to us.

"We have the grid search going. We pulled fifteen guys, and they're starting from the road and working South," Donovan said.

"Problem?" Dave asked.

"I spooked a guy in the woods. Not sure what he was doing back there."

"What can we do?" Steve asked.

"There are three clear accesses to the East woods. Can you see if we can get some patrol cars set up for tonight? We have security covered for the houses and the store, but I don't want to pull anyone to cover the outside of the woods."

"We have a full staff on patrol tonight, so we should be able to cover it. What about the West woods?"

"Clear except for a small fire pit on the Northwest corner. Looks like teenagers are using it as a spot to drink and smoke."

"Well put a car out there too. With all the security, I wouldn't want some stupid kids trespassing through the woods tonight."

I nodded my agreement.

I turned, feeling eyes burning into the back of my skull. Bones glared at me as he approached. Charlie stepped closer to me. Dave raised an eyebrow and glanced in my direction.

"Grid search is about halfway through the woods. So far, they've found two hunting stands. They've removed both, but neither stand would've had a visual of the store," Bones updated Donovan.

"Let me know if they find anything else. The city police are going to sit on the outskirts of both properties tonight and help keep watch," Donovan said.

Bones nodded and walked away.

"Did the temperature just drop?" Steve chuckled.

"He's a little pissed at me," I sighed.

"Tech filled me in. You made the right call. He'll get over it," Donovan said, slapping me on the shoulder.

"Kelsey!" Anne yelled, pulling alongside us in my SUV. "Get your ass in the car! You're late, and you haven't even showered yet!"

"I'm just the bouncer tonight. Why do I have to do my hair and makeup?" I grumbled getting into the truck.

Anne didn't answer as she hit the gas and pulled out at lightning speed.

Chapter Five

As Anne dragged me through my house, she yelled at Hattie to get over to Lisa's and stop fretting over the damn cake. I barely caught a glimpse of the entire dining room table covered in cooling cake layers as I was pulled down the hall and pushed into the bathroom.

"You have three minutes to shower," Anne ordered pulling out towels and starting the water up.

"Seriously, Anne?"

"Yes, now move it. I'm dragging you over to Lisa's by 10:00 sharp whether you still have soap in your hair or not. It's my only assigned job today."

I laughed but played along, getting undressed and rushing through a quick shower. After drying off, I put on the underwear and bra that Anne had left for me and then wrapped up in the robe hanging on the back of the door. I barely stepped out of the bathroom before Anne propelled me across the room and out the atrium door. I was barefoot, and the cement below my toes sent shivers up my body as I tried to turn back to my atrium, but Anne pushed me from behind right to Lisa's front door, which opened to a smiling Lisa who pulled me inside.

"Damn, you people are nuts!" I laughed.

"You did it, Anne! Thank you!" Lisa laughed and hugged Anne.

Anne jumped up and down in excitement claiming she still had thirty seconds to spare. You would have thought she just made the team winning touchdown.

I was physically moved from one location to another for the next hour having myself properly plucked, primped and styled. I fell asleep at one point, but the stylist working on my up-do hit me on the back of the head with her brush to wake me up.

Sara had somehow managed to achieve the fast-forward version of getting ready and was allowed to get dressed and escorted to the store, where she said she had a project to work on. I stuck my tongue out at her as she left. Sara of course, giggled.

Still, in my robe, I snuck off to the kitchen as soon as the coast was clear to steal a cup of coffee. Phillip, Lisa's brother, grinned from the other side of the breakfast bar sliding a fresh cup to me.

"You look like you need something stronger, but Lisa would kill me."

"If I started on liquor now, I'd definitely get fired from my bouncer gig later," I grinned, accepting the coffee.

Antonio Bianchi, the head of the New Jersey mafia family and Lisa's father, strolled into the kitchen.

"Papa Bianchi!" I jumped up and hugged him.

"You are a smartass," Antonio grumbled, pushing me away gently. "I don't know why my Lisa likes you so much."

"You going to let your bodyguards have the night off and kick-it on the dance floor?" I asked.

"No."

"You going to party likes it's 1999?"

"I do not know what that means, but no."

"You going to shake your booty?"

"No, to all your silly questions. Now, tell me about security," Antonio said crossing his arms over his massive chest and giving me 'the look'. The one that probably instills fear into most but reminded me of Pops and made me giggle.

"You shouldn't laugh at me," Antonio warned.

"No, you should do that all on your own," I said, pulling out a stool.

Phillip turned and opened the refrigerator, ducking down to hide his own laughter.

"Security is excessive and under control. The local police are covering the other side of the woods too, just as a precaution. We had a trespasser in the woods this morning, but security did a grid search and didn't find anything out of the ordinary."

"Good, now tell me why so many men," Antonio said, leaning forward.

It was an order, not an ask.

"Well, you see...," I stalled trying to come up with something that wasn't the truth but wasn't an outright lie either.

Phillip heard my hesitation and looked back at me with concern.

"I know this look Papa. We better sit for this one," Phillip said pulling out barstools for both of them.

"Okay, I'll tell you both, but first let me repeat, we have security covered," I said holding up my hands.

"But there is a threat?" Phillip said.

"Yes. And, this time, it's all my fault. I have a son who was kidnapped almost three years ago by his crazy biological mother. And, by crazy, I mean she's a psychopath. She was working with a human trafficking group in Miami. I managed to take down her partners, but I wasn't able to find her or my son. She's out there. And, she's pissed."

"I heard about the arrests in Florida. I also knew about your son's kidnapping," Antonio said. "But I thought he was dead?"

"The people that faked his death were also arrested. For years, no one believed me that the body wasn't his. Not until I took down the dirty cops and the medical examiner."

"We postpone wedding. Too dangerous," Antonio said.

"Well, there is another piece to that puzzle that has to be considered," I said.

Phillip laughed and ducked his head.

Antonio gave Phillip a curious look before glaring back at me. "Talk," he ordered.

"Lisa may be a bit pregnant, so we didn't want to stall the wedding," I admitted and jumped away from the breakfast bar.

"La mia bambina sta avendo un bambino?" Antonio said, standing.

"I don't know what the hell that means, but yes, I said she's pregnant," I cringed.

"Oh, what splendid news," Antonio grinned.

He walked over to me and gave me a big hug, picking me up from the floor in the process.

"I'm going to be a Grand-Papa!" he laughed.

"Um, I'm glad you're excited?? But can I go now?" I asked.

"Si, Si, run along, little Kelsey. The wedding will continue as planned," he grinned.

Phillip was laughing as I tore out of the room and up the stairs to join the rest of the women.

"Holy shit," I said, running into Lisa's room, closing the door behind me.

"What's wrong?" Lisa asked.

"I had to confess to your Papa about the security threat and then explain about your bun in the oven," I fully admitted out of breath.

"What did he say?" she asked with a look of concern and one hand held protectively over her belly.

"He's pretty damn geeked. He forgot all about the threat and was laughing."

"My dad?" Lisa asked with a raised eyebrow.

"Oh yeah, same guy. Scared the shit out of me when he started laughing. And then he *hugged* me!"

"My Papa? Are you sure? Anne—did you let Kelsey start drinking?" Lisa asked.

"I swear. I'm running on pure caffeine. He's really excited," I grinned.

• • •

"Thank you," Lisa smiled and hugged me. "I was so worried about him finding out."

"I'm glad you feel better. But, let's keep Donovan sweating over it until at least after the wedding?" I grinned.

"Sure," Lisa said, rolling her eyes.

Chapter Six

The entire dressing processes took forever with Lisa only allowing one of us at a time into the other room. And, while they all looked beautiful, with Lisa in an Italian lace off the shoulder gown and everyone else in various shades of blue in styles that fit their shapes and personalities, I was completely done in with all the girly gibberish.

Finally, it was my turn, and I went to the next room where Reggie was waiting. I saw my black boots were sitting on the floor and Reggie held up a garment bag.

"I get to wear my boots?" I grinned.

"Yup. And wait until you see the dress!" Reggie grinned back.

With Reggie's help, I fixed my tear damaged makeup and re-entered Lisa's room. I hugged and thanked her as I stepped in front of the mirror. My dress was a midnight blue with a spray of tiny rhinestones across the low scoop neckline, and the form-fitting blue satin wrapped around my body in swirls to end mid-thigh. My boots had been decorated with a removable run of matching rhinestones that swirled down the sides. And, the best part, I had a matching midnight blue holster decorated with rhinestones for a small Glock to wear on my thigh. I was so in love with my bouncer-gown that I started to cry again.

"I'm so happy," I laughed. "I get to carry a gun!"

"Oh, and check this out," Lisa grinned, handing me a wedding program.

There, at the bottom of the wedding program listed, Kelsey Harrison, Official Bouncer for the Bride, followed by one of Donovan's partners as Official Bouncer for the Groom.

"What do you think?"

"I love it. I think you're a nut, but I love it," I laughed.

"The only reason you're not standing up next to me is because I knew you'd be too worried about security. And, I love you for that. You've protected me since the day I met you," Lisa cried.

"Stop! No more tears! I don't want Reggie to yell at us for messing up more of our eyeliner!" I giggled.

"Picture time, ladies," Reggie said opening the door. "Damn it—you all need to quit crying!"

Reggie continued to scold us as he fixed our makeup. Alex entered wearing a strapping blue suit with blue satin lapels. Lisa must have had it custom made just for him.

I stepped up on my tip toes to place a kiss on his cheek.

"Mr. Alex, you make a very studly Man of Honor," I grinned.

"I just hope the Best Woman can keep up on the dance floor," Alex grinned.

Alex would stand up for Lisa, next to Katie, the designated Maid of Honor. Bones' sister would stand up for Donovan next to Grady, as Best Woman and Best Man for the groom. Alex was excited to be in the wedding party. His diamond earring sparkled as bright as his smile as he escorted us out to the awaiting cars to switch locations.

"Where's your mother?" I asked Lisa when we were all re-assembled inside the store.

"Napping," Lisa grinned. "She was a bit stressed yesterday, so Phillip and I stole a bottle from your wine collection and kept filling her glass. She had a bit of a headache this morning."

"I bet she was a lot less stressed," I grinned.

I quickly scanned the room as I led the women back to the former Bridal & Gowns department where they would waste away the time in-between activities.

"Ok, I'm going to do my bouncer thing for a few minutes while you guys get ready to start the pictures."

The salesroom floor had been cleared of anything store related and was covered in white lights, silk flower arrangements, and tall potted trees. A band was set up in the back corner, and track lighting had been hung over the designated dance floor. Tables and chairs were arranged in the center of the room, with pressed white tablecloths and blue linen napkins. From the former Bridal department to the front windows ran a white satin aisle, lined with short pillars covered in silk ivy. The aisle ended at the front windows where a large raised platform with an oversized archway was set up. The arches were streamed with tulle, lights, silk flowers and silk ivy. If I wasn't wealthy, I might be worried about all the expenses.

"Fancy, aye," Charlie chuckled walking up next to me.

"That's Lisa," I grinned. "The wedding platform?"

"Yeah, it made me nervous too. I already crawled under it and inspected the underside. It's all clear," Charlie nodded.

"I want the blinds closed for the whole room. It will still look nice with all the damn twinkle lights everywhere."

"Lisa okay with that?" Charlie asked.

"Don't care," I smirked.

"Got it. The Bouncer for the Bride has spoken," she grinned before ordering the security guards to assist in closing all the blinds.

I walked back to the former Menswear section which was set up for the groom and his party. I knocked on the door before quickly sneaking inside.

"Hey, Kelsey," Donovan grinned.

"Hey, Handsome. Just a warning that the girls are starting their pictures, so you are officially grounded to this room until they are done. I'm just doing a walk through."

"The front windows," Grady sighed, looking up at me.

"Security risk," I nodded. "The blinds are being closed now, with instructions to keep them closed."

"Thanks," Donovan sighed.

"It's all good," I said, lightly punching him in the shoulder. "And, I might have left something in that big box over there to help you guys pass the time," I said pointing to the box in the corner.

I hadn't walked far when I heard loud cheers. I had hidden a cooler with a case of beer, three decks of cards and a small TV inside the large box. The boys still had two hours to kill so it would make the time go by faster.

Next, I went up to Tech's loft office to check on the security feeds. Sara was arguing with Tech about something when I stepped into the room.

"Whoa, what's this all about? You two never argue," I said.

"I'm working on a program that would act as a heat sensor for the security cameras overlooking the woods," Sara said, turning back to the computer.

"But she's supposed to be downstairs for pictures," Tech sighed.

"This is more important," Sara insisted.

"Little-bug, Tech and I agree with you on its importance, but Lisa is only going to get married once, and we have to focus on what she needs from us today. And, right now, she needs her flower girl."

"Fine," Sara said, stepping away from the laptop. "Get Carl. He will understand what I'm doing," she said as she stomped out of the room and ran down the stairs.

"Why is she so stressed?" I laughed.

"Because she kept trying to explain the program coding to me, and I couldn't keep up," Tech laughed. "She thinks I wasn't concentrating hard enough."

"Ah well, you'll get used to it. I feel that way every time Katie upgrades my cell phone to a newer model," I grinned.

As I descended the stairs, I called Jackson, and he assured me that he could have someone escort Carl to the store. He also admitted that they would be cutting it close to get the cake decorated in time, but there was still hope. I rolled my eyes. There was an abundance of worrying being wasted on dessert.

I walked a quick circuit in the back room where security was detailing every move that the caterers made as they set up for their service. Donovan's partner, the other bouncer, assured me that he had it handled.

I stepped into my assigned place, just as the photographer started snapping pictures.

Lisa, Anne, Hattie and Katie all sighed at my timely return.

"What? You all thought some catastrophe was going to happen before pictures, and I would ruin my dress, didn't you?" I grinned.

"I ordered a spare dress for just such emergencies," Lisa admitted.

"Bitch," I laughed.

"Slut," Lisa called back in good humor.

"Ok, ladies," the photographer called out. "How about we stick to the traditional 'cheese'?"

We all properly behaved for all of about thirty seconds before Lisa started singing: 'It's my party, and I can swear if I want to, swear if I want to, swear if I want to.'

'You would swear too if it's happening to you!' the chorus/bridal party sang along.

From there, it got a little crazy, but the photographer just kept taking pictures as we cussed at each other and danced to the music that the band started to play. An hour later, I called it quits and ushered the girls back to their room in the old Bridal and Gowns department to await the designated hour.

As the Bouncer, I was free to roam about.

I inspected all the wedding presents, checking the cards and ensuring I recognized the names. I looked under the table to verify there was nothing hidden under the tablecloth. Turning toward the back, the security guard in the corner grinned.

"Your cousin has searched under each table, twice, and inspected all the presents," he grinned.

"And, did you search under the tables?" I asked.

"No. Why?"

"Because if Donovan comes out and asks you if this room is secure, you better damn well be able to answer knowing that you personally checked every detail," I said before walking into the backroom.

"I think you scared him," Grady chuckled walking up behind me.

I looked back to see the guard rapidly searching under each table.

"Why aren't you tucked away with the groom?"

"I couldn't stay cooped up any longer. Getting that caged feeling," Grady complained, loosening up his bow tie.

"Stop that," I laughed, fixing his tie.

Grady grinned down at me.

• • •

"You can let the boys out of the room. The girls are tucked away and won't be out until the wedding starts. I would appreciate the extra eyes on the store anyway."

Grady continued to grin down at me.

"Enough," I laughed and walked away.

I had no idea what was going through Grady's mind, but whatever it was, it involved naughty thoughts. I could see it in his eyes as they danced with humor. I shook the school-girl feeling off and refocused on security.

The caterers were unloading their supplies, one box or crate at a time, while patiently waiting for it to pass inspection before they could move it forward. I was glad to see that security was being so diligent, but we needed more guards to clear the items, or there wasn't going to be a dinner.

I stepped back in the main room and flagged the boys for assistance. Between the backroom security, all the groomsmen and myself, we were able to inspect everything as it was unloaded and help the caterers move the items to be set up.

I walked over to talk to the Chef.

"Thanks for the extra help," he grinned.

"No problem. Sorry about the hassle but it's necessary. What about your staff? Do you know everyone?"

"I gave Tech a list of names and he cleared everyone—whatever that means. I have sixteen people other than myself working today. The entire staff is wearing purple bow ties with baby blue polka dots," he grinned, pulling his bow tie out from under his chef's coat, so it was visible.

"I special ordered the bow ties and handed them out personally to each employee when they got here. If someone is in uniform but not wearing this ugly tie, then they don't work for me."

"Brilliant," I grinned. "I appreciate it. I'll make sure security knows. Holler if you need anything,"

As the news spread that anyone wearing the designated ugly bowtie had already been vetted, everyone relaxed a bit. I grabbed a heavy wool coat from my locker and walked out the back door.

Chapter Seven

Tyler and two other guards were spaced apart, watching their assigned areas. I expected three more were up front and one guard, most likely Charlie, was on foot patrol.

I meandered up to Tyler with my best pouty face.

"You're going to get me in trouble with your cousin," he grinned as he pulled his cigarettes out, handing them to me without taking his eyes of his territory.

"It's okay," I grinned, lighting up. "I can kick her ass even if you can't."

"Rub it in," Tyler grinned.

"Slacking again, Tyler?" Charlie bellowed from behind him.

Tyler jumped a foot in the air as he spun around to face Charlie.

The groomsmen, having just stepped out of the back of the building, witnessed it and laughed as they approached. Tyler turned bright red.

"Permission to patrol the area, Ma'am?" Tyler saluted Charlie.

"At ease soldier," Charlie grinned. "Yes, grab the other two and walk a bit while the groomsmen are outside. Let me know if you see anything."

"You got it," Tyler grinned.

Grady went to steal my cigarette, but I jumped out of the way in time to save it.

"No way, I had to steal this one," I grinned.

Whiskey passed his pack over to Grady and Donovan stole one as well.

"If Lisa smells cigarette smoke on you, *on your wedding day*, she's going to rip you a new one," I warned.

"Fine," Donovan grumbled handing the cigarette back to Whiskey. "I'm going to help monitor the early guests that are arriving."

"Kelsey!" Tyler called out to me.

Tyler had stopped a black SUV from entering the back parking lot. Agent Kierson leaned his head out the window, and I waved to let him through. Tyler stepped aside so Kierson could pull forward.

"He's young but good. Doesn't hesitate to step in," Charlie commented.

"He's got good instincts. Be on alert if he warns you of anything," I said.

"Will do," Charlie nodded. "We have time for another quick sweep of the woods closest to the store if the groomsmen are willing to break up and cover the perimeter until we're done."

We all separated in different directions covering all the corners and the doors as Charlie gathered those not wearing ironed and starched clothes and assigned them sections of woods to search.

I scanned the backs of the houses and the field, slowly moving my eyes from right to left over every spare inch until my vision blurred trying to focus on too far off distances. Other than the ruckus of pre-wedding set up behind me, the perimeter I was assigned seemed placid.

Thirty minutes later the guards returned to take over their post. I grinned at Charlie before leading Maggie and Agent Kierson inside. Charlie really was good at this shit. She nodded thanks as if reading my mind.

We shrugged out of our coats, hanging them on the nearby rack inside the door.

"We need to talk," Agent Kierson said.

"Not here," I warned, leading them to the far corner of the room.

Entering the back hallway that connected the stock room and Menswear, I checked the far end door to ensure it was closed and stopped in the middle of the hall's length.

"We should have privacy here," I said a little too quickly.

Grady walked in, and before he was within ten feet of us, Tech jogged through the doorway as well.

"I can let you guys know if I need you," I said.

"I'm staying. You already know what they're going to tell you. I'm here for moral support," Grady said wrapping an arm around my waist.

"What's up?" Tech questioned with his hands on his hips.

"I told you I checked out that house in Louisiana and that Nicholas had been kept there. I didn't tell you that the living room was coated in blood," I admitted.

"Shit."

"Yeah. And, I'm expecting that Agent Kierson is going to tell me that the blood matched Nicholas's, but I know he's not dead. I know it," I said facing Kierson.

"Kelsey, it was a lot of blood for a small boy," Kierson said.

"Nola may have hurt him, but she wouldn't kill him. I've been studying this woman for years. This isn't about me refusing to accept him being dead. This is about Nola. She's playing with me. She's playing with the FBI."

"She's right. Shit, we need to go to the War Room," Tech said before he started to jog back down the hallway.

I checked my watch as we all jogged after him. We had time if we hurried.

We piled into Kierson's SUV, and he drove us to the house. Jackson, Tammy, and Bridget were just moving layers of cake out of the house when we pulled up. After helping them with the last of the layers, we moved to the basement and into the War Room.

"Why are we here, Tech?" I asked.

"The pictures of Nicholas in the security feeds from Pasco's mansion," he said, booting up one of the laptops. "In each picture Nicholas had one of his arms turned so the inside of his arm faced the camera."

Tech pulled up the footage to one of the still-shots of Nicholas being escorted out of Pasco's house.

"See. He's trying to show us something. I noticed the bandage but figured they were drugging him."

"But you don't need a vein to give a sedative!" I squealed catching on. "Damn, Nola's been taking blood.

Look, you can see a bruise like it's been done several times."

"Do you have a picture showing the other arm?" Maggie asked, moving closer.

"Yeah, look," Tech said pulling up the next shot.

"It's the same thing," Maggie said.

"Wait a minute, wait a minute," Agent Kierson interrupted. "Are you guys saying that Nola stockpiled Nicholas's blood just to stage his death a second time?"

"Yes," we all said in unison.

"Why?"

"It's part of her sick game. That's why she got so antsy trying to get me to Florida. She wanted to set the stage. And once again, no one would believe me."

"If you look at Nola's past actions, it makes sense," Maggie agreed. "She likes a big show. She dramatically slits her victim's throats when she has a kill order. She burned her sister and the other prostitutes to fake her own death. Everything she does is over the top."

"Look, Kierson," I said moving the laptop closer to him. "If you don't believe us, believe Nicholas. He's showing us his arm for a reason. He wants us to know."

"Smart kid," Kierson nodded.

"So you believe me?" I asked, completely surprised.

"Yes. I would be stupid not to," he sighed.

I let out a huge breath that I didn't know I was even holding. I turned to Grady who was leaning back against the wall grinning.

"I never doubted you," he smiled.

"Good decision," Charlie snapped, glaring at me from the doorway. "You should have told me!"

"Kid, I'm sorry. I was a mess when Grady got me back here, and I just couldn't repeat what happened in Miami — everyone trying to convince me that he was dead."

"*I would have believed you!*" Charlie yelled. "I wouldn't have had to look at the pictures or wait for the evidence, I would've believed you because I trust that there's no one in this world that knows how Nola's brain works better than you. Just like there's no one in this world that knows YOU better than ME!"

Charlie fled down the hallway, and I ran after her.

"Wait, Charlie, let me explain," I said as I chased her down and grabbed her arm to stop her.

"You're going to be late for the wedding," she said, pulling her arm out of my grasp. "Everyone's getting nervous with the Best Man and Bouncer missing. That's why I came up to the house, to send you both back."

She turned and walked away. She didn't look back.

"Charlie, please…," I cried.

"I'll talk to her," Kierson said moving past me and jogging to catch up with Charlie.

"Shh," Grady coaxed me as he wrapped his arms around me. "She doesn't understand how bad it was. She doesn't know what it did to you to see all that blood."

"The house in New Orleans—how bad was it?" Tech asked.

"I threw up," Maggie admitted to Tech.

"Damn," Tech sighed.

Chapter Eight

I stepped away from Grady to grab some tissues and wipe my face. Today is Lisa and Donovan's wedding. I need to pull it together for their sake.

Tech's phone rang, and after a moment, he handed it to me.

"It's Lisa," he said.

"Hey," I said answering, trying to clear the tears from my throat. "I'll be back in a blink of an eye."

"That's why I called. I heard several of you ran up to the house in a hurry. If you guys need to go, then go. Don't wait because of us. We agree that your son comes first."

"It's fine, really," I assured her. "Charlie and Kierson are already on their way back, and the rest of us were just leaving. So, quit fretting. I'll see you in a minute."

"Only if you're sure," Lisa said.

We disconnected, and I turned to the mirror behind the bar. "Shit."

"I got this," Reggie said, walking down the stairs with a makeup kit. "You three head back and let me straighten her up a bit. We'll be right behind you."

Maggie, Tech, and Grady left out the back slider, and Reggie dumped the makeup bag on the bar-top and started working his magic. I slowed down my breathing and mentally prepared to smile and pretend I was okay.

"You can do this," Reggie said as kissed my forehead and propelled us both up the stairs and to the SUV.

"Thanks," I said as I hopped out of the SUV thirty seconds later, plastering on my fraudulent smile.

"Anytime, Sis," Reggie said, blowing me a kiss before driving off to park.

One of the Players opened the store's front door to let me inside.

I noted everyone was in position and quietly talking as I raced to the back of the main room and snuck behind the heavy curtain hiding my friends.

"Alright Lisa, last chance," I smiled.

"I am so ready to marry Donovan it's ridiculous."

"Then let's get on with it," I grinned and stepped back out to motion the band to start playing.

The curtains partially opened with Sara leading the party out and down the makeshift aisle. I walked further off to the side so I could have a better view of my friends getting married while keeping an eye on the room at the same time. When it was finally Lisa's turn, the curtain was opened wider, and Lisa stepped out and joined her father to walk down the aisle.

The rest of the ceremony was a bit blurry. I was having trouble accessing the room for security threats as my eyes pooled with tears. James stepped out of the seating area and came over, wrapping an arm around me and handing me a tissue.

"It's all good. I'll keep watch why you have your girly moment," he chuckled.

I giggled and wiped my eyes as I watched the rest of the ceremony.

James stayed by my side to help keep an eye on things for the next few hours. Everyone was having a fabulous evening, but none more than Lisa and Donovan. Every time I spotted them, they were laughing, dancing, or kissing.

The dinner was excellent, and the cake was absolutely sinful. We even told Lisa that Tammy had made it, and Lisa was over the top pleased with how it turned out. Of course, we didn't tell her that Tammy made it only because Hattie forgot to order it.

The slide show was a hit with the unexpected pictures of Reggie and Donovan sleeping together. Katie had to pass a tissue to Lisa because she had fat tears streaming her cheeks as she ducked her head in Donovan's shoulder laughing. Donovan was pointing a finger at me and threatening revenge. I just rolled my eyes.

The Bianchi family seemed to be enjoying themselves too. They all drank a bit too much, laughed a bit too loud, and even Papa Antonio, despite his prior statements, was fast dancing on the dance floor with Katie.

I had settled myself on the stairs to Tech's loft office, so I had an elevated view of the entire room. I noticed Anne setting a package on the gift table before walking over to talk to Whiskey near the bar. I looked back at the package. It was wrapped in brown shipping paper. I looked at my watch and confirmed it was 9:00. A little late for packages, I thought as I took off running, pushing people out of my way to get to the table.

"What is it?" Grady yelled from across the room.

"Unknown Package!" I yelled, wrapping my arms around it and racing for the back doors. "CLEAR OUT OF THE WAY!"

Guests and caterers jumped out of the way as I ran. The Chef saw me coming and threw himself into the door in time for me to run through it and down the stairs. I ran straight into the field as fast as my legs would move.

When I was about forty feet into the dead grass, I set the package down and started back toward the building. My heart seized when I looked up and saw Grady was running toward me.

"NO! RUN!" I screamed at him. "IT'S FROM NOLA!!"

The ground shook as the field behind me exploded, and the air blast threw me forward and into Grady. He caught me mid-air and rolled on top of me as chunks of dirt and grass rained down around us.

I was trying to catch my breath when Grady suddenly picked me up and ran, carrying me, toward the cars in the East parking lot. Once we were deep into the lot, he ducked behind a car and started pulling me along as he hid us from sight.

"Grady—,"

"Shh," he said covering my mouth tightly. "They'll hear you. Stay down."

"Kel," Donovan's voice called to me in a low whisper, not far away.

Even if my mouth wasn't covered by Grady's hand, I wasn't sure I would have been able to answer Donovan. Fear froze me as I realized what was happening.

Grady was having a flashback brought on by the bomb.

Grady was a lot stronger, a lot bigger and was a better fighter than me. And, worst of all, we were both heavily armed.

Chapter Nine

I slowly turned in Grady's embrace to face him. He didn't resist as he was restlessly searching our surroundings. He also didn't notice Bones and Donovan moving in closer. In his mind, we weren't in the store parking lot. We were somewhere else, somewhere far from here, somewhere in his nightmares.

I motioned for Bones and Donovan to halt. Grady could pull his gun at any time and kill them if I couldn't bring him out of this.

"Grady," I whispered not two inches from his face. "Grady, it's Kelsey."

Grady looked at me for a split second before he scrambled to move us further into the parking lot.

"Grady, I need you to concentrate. Hear my voice. Do you know me?"

He ducked down, covering both of us from some invisible evil that I couldn't see. He was deeply wrapped in his flashback. I felt him shift and knew he was about to move again. I unstrapped my gun from my thigh and dropped it to the ground just before he dragged me to a space a few vehicles down.

We were getting closer to the woods, and I wasn't sure what would happen if he tried to drag me through them.

I faced him again, this time climbing onto his lap and wrapping my arms around his waist.

"Grady, where are we?" I asked, trying to keep him distracted as I carefully unsnapped his holster.

"They have us surrounded. We have to clear out before they move in. There's too many of them," he growled, looking around in a panic.

I slid his gun slowly from the holster, just as he bolted between another set of cars.

The gun dropped loudly to the asphalt, further spooking him, as he moved four more car lengths closer to the woods.

Knowing that neither of us had guns unless he was wearing an ankle holster, it was now or never.

"Grady! Listen to my voice!"

He tried to muffle my mouth, but I bit him.

"It's Kelsey, Grady! You're back home! There're no enemies!" I yelled three inches from his face. "LOOK AT ME!"

For a split second, I saw a look of confusion before his eyes clouded with the flashback again. Only now—*I was the enemy.*

Grady turned me, my back to his chest and carried me by my throat two more cars lengths away. I fought back. I pivoted and threw an elbow to his rib cage, breaking away enough to turn and throw a punch to his throat. But it wasn't enough. He threw me to the ground with his body weight pinning me down.

I reached for my boot and pulled a knife, but he read my movements and broke my grip, stealing the knife away from me.

The cold steel blade glinted an orange hue from the parking lot lights as he held the knife tight to my throat.

"Fuck," I whispered.

"Kelsey, you have only one move left," Donovan whispered.

I didn't know where Donovan was at but knew he was close enough to see me if he was calling out my next move.

"I won't do it," I whispered back, tears slipping from the corners of my eyes.

"If he could, he'd tell you to save yourself. It's your only choice," Donovan whispered in the darkness.

"No. I won't do it. Tell my family that I'm sorry. Tell him, I'm sorry. And, that I know it's not his fault. Make sure he knows that Donovan."

"Please, Kelsey," Bones whispered. "Don't quit. He wouldn't want that."

I looked up at Grady and into the eyes of a man I didn't know. A man that killed for a living. A man that killed to survive.

"Grady," I called to him one last time. "Grady—"

Grady's eyes focused for the briefest moment again.

"Grady, kiss me," I said, leaning up as the knife pressed into my neck.

Grady released the pressure on the knife and kissed me.

I pulled him closer and continued to kiss him. I wrapped my arms around him and stroked my fingers through his hair as he pulled me up from the asphalt and wrapped his arms around me.

• • •

I wasn't sure where the knife was, so I kept kissing him, losing myself in the moment. He sat me on the hood of a car as both of his hands roamed my body. I heard the clatter of the knife hit the ground, and Donovan and Bones tackled Grady, throwing his body away from me.

Dave and Steve rushed past me and helped to hold Grady down. Steve passed Donovan a set of cuffs to secure Grady.

"What the fuck?" Grady asked.

"Grady?" I yelled. "Is that you?"

"Kelsey, what the fuck is going on?" Grady yelled back.

"Let him up," I yelled, moving Dave and Steve out of the way. "I mean it, move off."

"Kelsey, let's make sure he's settled down," Donovan warned.

"Fine, keep the cuffs on him and make sure he doesn't have an ankle holster but then, back off," I ordered.

Donovan checked his ankles and then helped shift Grady into a sitting position.

"Grady, are you really back?" I asked squatting down in front of him, holding his face in my hands.

"Shit," Grady said bowing his head. "Flashback?"

"It's alright," I assured him.

"Donovan, did I hurt anyone?" Grady asked, closing his eyes.

"No permanent damage that I can see," Donovan answered.

"But I hurt someone?" Grady asked again.

"Grady, look at me. It was me, okay?" I pulled his face up to mine. "You almost hurt me. But I'm right here. I'm just fine. I'm one tough bitch, remember?" I kissed him on the cheek before I stood up and looked around. "We don't have time for a pity party. We have a store full of guests, a field blown to hell, and I need your help to track down a psycho. Now, are you with me? Or do we need to have you strapped in a padded room for a day or two?"

Grady huffed several breaths and nodded his head.

"Fuck," Grady growled. "Get me up. Get the damn cuffs off. Where's our exposure?"

I stared at Grady for a moment as he focused on me. It was him. The real him. I nodded to Donovan to un-cuff him.

"The store would've been locked down as soon as I ran outside. I need to search the woods, though, and I can't take you with me so soon after a flashback. Can you set up the perimeter for the store?"

"Got it, go," Grady answered as Steve helped him off the ground.

I was just about to turn to leave when Grady reached out to me, pulling me to him and kissed me. "Be safe."

I looked up at him and grinned before running back to where I dropped my Glock. Tyler met up with me and handed me a flashlight and an ear piece. He passed out earpieces to Grady, Bones, and Donovan.

Everyone but Grady followed my lead as I ran halfway down the field and started into the woods.

"Tech, anything on the heat sensors for the woods," I asked, as I scrambled through the brush.

* * *

63

"Negative," Tech said into my earpiece. "The bomb messed with the heat readings. The whole area spiked and then went black. Sara's trying to re-boot the program to see if she can get it working again."

"Nola was here. Let's hope we can catch up," I said as we fanned out, moving East.

"How do you know it was Nola?" Bones asked over the earpiece.

"Because I'm her favorite toy, and you don't get rid of your favorite toy when you enjoy playing with it so much," I answered picking up the pace.

"Remote detonator," Grady said over the earpiece. "She waited until you were far enough away to blow it up. Was that her intention all along?"

"No," I answered as I veered quickly to avoid colliding with a tree.

"She was going to wait until you stepped outside," Donovan said, realizing Nola's intent.

He charged through the woods like a mad man.

"You fucking bitch!" he yelled into the blackness.

We all ran as fast as we could, but we pulled up when we came out the other side of the woods into the clearing. The neighboring business sat straight ahead of us. No lights were on in the parking lot. Everything around us was deadly silent.

"NO!!!" I yelled running toward the building.

Bones and Donovan passed by me halfway around the building. Bones stopped short when he cleared the side and reached back to stop me. Donovan slowed to a walk and approached the car.

"No, please, no," I whispered as Bones held me back.

Donovan turned and shook his head letting me know that the cop inside the car was dead.

"Somebody needs to tell me what the fuck is going on," Grady growled over the mike.

"Tech, call 911. We have an officer down," I answered, buckling to my knees.

"I can't do this. I can't keep fucking doing this."

"Kelsey, talk to me," Grady said over the earpiece.

My body trembled, my breathing was ragged, and I choked on my tears. Bones reached out in comfort, but I pulled away roughly.

"Kelsey, you need to talk to me," Grady said again.

"No," I whispered back.

"Walk me through it. Pin the rest back and stay in the game," Grady's smooth voice coaxed. "Walk me through what happened tonight."

I nodded silently, inhaling several deep breaths to calm myself.

"She was watching. She planned the whole thing," I answered.

"Details. Start at the beginning," Grady said.

"I saw Anne set a package on the table and walk away. Question Anne. I don't know how she got the package."

"Okay, I am sending someone to talk to Anne. What happened next?"

"The brown shipping paper. It stood out. It was too late at night for a package delivery."

"So you knew it was a threat. You grabbed it and ran out to the field with it. Did you look down at the package? Was there anything written on it?"

"Yes, I read it. I read it as I ran out to the field. I didn't process what it said until I saw you running toward me."

"What did the package say, Kel?"

"Best wishes to the bride and groom. May your wedding start with a blast. Love Nola."

"Don't go there, keep focusing, what's next?"

"I was almost to you. I needed you to turn and run the other way. What were you thinking?"

"We can deal with my stupidity later. What happened next?"

"You were carrying me off into the parking lot. I wasn't sure what was going on because I was still thinking about the bomb. The timing, the distance I was away from it when it was discharged, it was too perfect. It was her. I knew it."

"I agree. Anything else. Did you see anything in the woods?"

"No. She would have taken off as soon as I hit the ground. She would have expected me to give chase. She was gone before we started in the woods. I already knew that but needed to make sure."

"How did you know about the cop?"

"The police were stationed on the outskirts of both properties, but after the bomb, the only cop cars that came to the store arrived from the West."

"You're sure?"

"Yes. You need to check with Dave and Steve and see if they had more patrolman out here. There could be more bodies."

"They already told dispatch to have all patrolmen call in."

"Grady—," I started to say, but my voice cut out.

"I know, Kel," Grady whispered. "But you can't let her win."

"But how do I make her stop? I could've lost everyone tonight. A police officer was killed because of me."

I stood and paced back and forth, tears swimming in my vision as my mind raced with all the what-ifs.

"This is not on you. We'll figure this out. We'll increase security for your family. Then, you and I will hunt the bitch down. Deal?"

I paced, nodding silently to his words.

"Kelsey- Deal? We find her?"

"Deal," I agreed, squatting to the ground as four police cars pulled into the lot. "We find her. We find my son. And, then I'm going to rip her fucking cold heart out."

Chapter Ten

Since Nola was wanted by the FBI, Kierson was able to get us released from the scene pretty quickly. Watching the other officer's faces as they struggled to accept that one of their own was gone, was too much for me to bear.

Tyler held the front door of the store open for Donovan, Bones, Grady and I to walk through. I waited and watched Tyler lock it behind us before I walked past them over to a chair and stood on top of it. The room was already quiet as we entered, so there was no need to gather anyone's attention.

"I need to speak to my family in private. If you can give us a few minutes please," I said before stepping back off the chair and walking into the menswear department.

Katie, Alex, Hattie, Sara, Anne, Charlie, and Lisa were the first to enter. Strolling in after them was Pops, Reggie, Wild Card, and Jackson.

"Lisa? Where's your husband?" I asked, rolling my eyes.

Lisa looked around and stomped out of the room.

"You married me, so get your ass in here!" she yelled across the room.

Everyone laughed.

"This is so strange," Donovan grinned walking in with Lisa. "I'm always being kicked out for the family meetings."

"Well, get used to it," I said. "Okay, so everyone's going to be pissed, but here goes—You need to leave. Pack your bags tonight and be ready to move out first thing in the morning. Pick your location—New Jersey or Texas."

"You're sending us away?" Lisa asked.

"Hell yes," I answered firmly.

"She doesn't have a choice," Donovan sighed. "That bomb wasn't meant for her. It was meant for all of us."

"Holy shit," Anne gasped, grabbing for Sara and lifting her into her arms.

"Nola knows she can hurt me by hurting all of you. I can't risk any of you staying here. We're too exposed. Lisa's family and my Texas family have the means and property setups to protect everyone. I need everyone to pick their locations."

"You tell us," Lisa answered. "We go where you tell us to go."

Everyone nodded in agreement.

"Fine. Lisa, Donovan and Alex, the three of you go to New Jersey. Hattie, Anne, and Sara, the three of you go to Texas. Katie, if you're willing, I'd like you, Tech, and Carl to follow me. I'm going hunting. I'll try to keep the three of you away from any danger but could use your help to find Nola."

"Game on," Katie grinned.

"And me?" Charlie asked.

"By my side, Kid. Where you belong," I said, tearing up.

Charlie threw her arms around me, crushing me in a hug.

"I'm sorry about earlier. Kierson showed me the pictures. I didn't understand," she cried.

"I know. But I do need you for this. We fight together, just like we fought the monsters growing up. Agreed?"

"Agreed. We do it together."

We both wiped our tears away, and I turned to Pops.

"Pops, you good with teaching some more northerners the Texan way?"

"I think I can handle it just fine. Don't you worry about them none. They'll be safe. You just go do what you have to do."

I nodded and walked out.

I went directly to Antonio who was waiting with his arms crossed, glaring at me. Phillip stood tense next to him.

"I need your help," I said.

"What kind of help?" Antonio barked.

"I am sending part of my family with you in the morning. I need your word that you will keep them safe until I finish this."

"Is Lisa one of them?"

"Yes. Lisa, Donovan and Alex will be going to New Jersey."

"I promise they will be protected."

"And, I need you to reach out to anyone and everyone you know. I want information on Nola Mason. I want every contact name and location that you can root out."

"Phillip, start making calls," Antonio barked at Phillip.

Phillip nodded. I pointed for him to go up and see Tech, and he nodded again.

Antonio turned his attention back to me.

"If you find her and need help, you call me. I'll personally show up to take care of her."

And, then he spat on the floor.

"Well, okay then," I grinned.

I looked around at the crowded quiet room.

"Can someone get me a damn drink?" I called out.

"Right here, Sunshine," Hattie said, walking up with a tall glass.

"Thank you, Hattie," I smiled, taking the glass.

"You're most welcome, Sunshine," Hattie grinned.

Antonio snorted.

I walked over to Alex and whispered in his ear. He nodded, handed me a set of keys and walked away as I stepped outside. Around the corner, I unlocked the door to the new building being constructed for Bridal & Gowns. Walking to the center of the room, I sat on the cold cement floor.

"How bad are you hurt?" Grady asked as Charlie ran past him to sit next to me.

"Where's the med kit?" Charlie asked.

"I sent for Doc. I'll be okay," I assured her taking a drink of my cocktail.

"Still protecting me from the bad stuff?" Charlie grinned.

"I'd tell you if I was dying," I grinned.

"I don't believe you, Luv," Alex grinned, leading Doc into the room and turning on some of the lights.

"Well, Kelsey, how bad is it this time?" Doc asked setting his bag down. "I see you have a cut on your neck and bruises."

"That's just a scratch. It's my back. I burned it in the blast," I admitted, taking another large gulp of my drink.

"Shit," Charlie said.

"I need some supplies," Doc ordered as he looked at the damage. "Get Haley. I can send her to my clinic to pick up what I need. Actually, we should take Kelsey there, it will be quicker."

"Can't do that Doc. I don't know where my nemesis is at right now, and everyone's safer if I'm here," I said.

"Kelsey, this is going to hurt," Doc warned.

"Why do you think I am chugging this cocktail?"

While Haley and Alex retrieved all the needed medical supplies, Doc pulled the stitches from all my prior week's injuries. I had four on my upper arm and a few on the side of my head. He just gave me the 'shame on you' glare and snipped and tugged them out.

When Haley returned, she assisted Doc as they separated each small strip of melted material from my back, one piece at a time. The burn itself wasn't that bad, but the melted material being removed was taking a few layers of skin off with it in the peeling process. It was like getting a rug burn every ten seconds on a new spot on my back.

Charlie got me a bottle of vodka when my cocktail was empty.

"You ready for a sedative yet?" Doc asked.

"Nope. Need to stay awake. Somebody needs to distract me," I said, gripping Charlie's hand tighter.

"You're going to break her hand," Grady grumbled, taking Charlie's place.

"Okay, you crush Grady's hand while I think of a good story," Charlie grinned.

"Sounds like a plan," Pops said as he walked in with Reggie and Jackson. "Seems my baby girl got herself hurt and is hiding out again. Was she like that as a kid too?"

"Not at first. When she was seven, she broke her arm trying to defend me from my abusive father. Her mother told her that if she didn't say that she fell off her bike that neither one of us would be allowed to visit Nana over the summer. Visiting Nana was my only escape, so we kept quiet. She's kept quiet every time she's been hurt since then."

"How long did that shit go on?" Pops asked.

"Until I was twelve," Charlie said. "Best damn day of my life. My best friend stole a car, loaded it up with everything she could think to pack, drove over to my house and picked me up. When she turned sixteen, she graduated early from high school, filed for emancipation and had custody papers signed, so she became my legal guardian."

"What prevented your parents from dragging you back?" Reggie asked.

"I may have threatened to kill them," I shrugged.

"You're lying," Grady chuckled.

I stuck my tongue out at him.

"She's never given me a straight answer as to how she kept them away," Charlie laughed. "I don't know how she did it. I don't know how she got the Chief of Police to rent a house to her either, but she did it."

"She blackmailed them," Alex grinned. "That's the girl I know and love."

I grinned, but I didn't say anything. I wasn't sure if I would ever admit to anyone what all I had done to get Charlie out of her house and somewhere safe. But, I knew that it was worth it, and I didn't regret it.

I cinched up as another layer of skin was removed along with the melted fabric.

"Sorry," Haley whined from behind me.

"It's fine, Haley. You just concentrate on getting the job done," I said.

"So do you guys have any happy stories?" Grady asked.

"Lots of them," Charlie grinned. "But they're not your typical girls growing up stories."

"Imagine that," Jackson said rolling his eyes and joining us on the floor.

Pops and Reggie settled beside him.

"Tell them the preacher story," I grinned.

Charlie's eyes lit up. "I was fourteen and on an accelerated program to finish high school, while we both took college courses. We studied like all the damn time. But Sunday's during the daylight hours we always went out to do something fun. One Sunday afternoon at the park, we ran into the local preacher. He started bellowing a sermon and directing his nasty comments at us. Called us out as being white trash heathens, if I recall correctly," Charlie grinned over at me.

I grinned back before taking another healthy swig of vodka as another large layer of material was separated from my back.

"Kelsey was so mad," Charlie giggled. "And, we are talking her silent-mad, where she's too angry to even speak."

"Ah, shit," Reggie laughed.

"She marched us home, but instead of going inside, she marched up to the neighbor's door and asked if we could borrow a bible for the week," Charlie grinned and looked at everybody.

"Oh, yeah," Alex grinned.

"Yup, Kelsey has always prepared for war," Charlie laughed. "So all week long we studied the bible and wrote down passages. And, come Sunday morning, we dressed in our best and walked to church, hand in hand."

"Amen," I grinned, pretending that was the end of the story.

"Keep going," Pops chuckled.

"Preacher started his sermon and about two minutes in, he recognized us as we sat in the center of the front row.

He stopped his planned sermon and started spewing his filth at us again. Kelsey and I both stood and started volleying verses back at him about forgiveness, self-sacrifice, generosity of the soul and charity to his fellow man. Preacher got so frustrated that he misquoted a verse and Kelsey corrected him on it and continued the verse which was actually about protecting children when you kept the verse going."

"I can just imagine my spitfire tearing him up," Pops laughed.

"Oh, it wasn't just him. The whole church erupted. Half the church was on our side, and half the church was on the preacher's side. A fight broke out, and we ran," Charlie grinned.

"Our neighbor brought us a lasagna that afternoon," I said.

"Why was she always so nice to us?" Charlie asked.

"She was a friend of Grandma Harrison's. Her name was Helen Swareck. I remember her hugging me at their funeral and whispering in my ear, *always be brave little one*. It was creepy but sweet."

"Do you suppose she knows something about our grandparents' deaths?" Charlie asked.

"I don't know, Kid. I'm not even sure if she's still alive."

"So when did you move to Miami?" Grady asked, switching which hand I gripped and shaking the previous one.

"When Charlie turned sixteen, her emancipation application was approved, and we loaded up and drove out of town. A month went by, and we found ourselves in Miami and claimed it as our new home."

I smiled as I thought about those first couple years in Miami. We were happy. We were finally free from our past, and we grew in ways that we could never have imagined.

"It's good that you two had each other," Pops said.

Charlie nodded at Pops before she turned back to me and grinned. "I wouldn't want it any other way."

Charlie continued to spin stories from our childhood until Doc declared that the worst was over, and they rubbed a cold cream on my back and upper arms. It felt wonderful.

"I'm never wearing satin again," Haley grumbled. "That shit melted. You would've been fine if you were wearing a good old cotton t-shirt."

"I don't think Lisa would've approved of me wearing a cotton t-shirt," I grinned.

Alex dug me out some clothes from the stacks of nearby totes, and I changed behind some boxes. We were just getting ready to pack up when Wild Card and Bones came in.

"What are you guys doing over here?" Wild Card asked.

"Always coming up a little short on the draw, aren't you, big brother?" Reggie laughed, clapping Wild Card on the shoulder and walking out.

Charlie grinned and walked out with Doc and Haley. Pops and Jackson stayed back, waiting for me. Grady gathered the supplies that Doc left for me.

Bones walked up to me and glared down. Pops and Jackson stiffened, and Grady set the supplies back on the floor, before stepping beside me.

"We need to talk," Bones growled.

"Not until you fix your attitude, Bones. I have more important things to do," I said, turning to walk away.

Bones reached out and roughly grabbed my upper arm. Shooting pain ran up my shoulder, and as I was dropping to my knees, Pops caught me.

Grady went after Bones.

Grady punched Bones twice before Bones was able to defend himself and they squared off. Both of them had been trained to fight to the death, and I was grateful when Wild Card and Jackson stepped between them, creating a barrier.

"What the fuck?" Bones yelled.

"She's hurt, you self-centered prick!" Grady yelled back, leaning over Jackson's shoulder but not struggling to overpower him.

"What do you mean she's hurt?"

"The bomb! She just spent the last hour with Doc and Haley stripping melted fabric off her back and arms!"

Bones turned to me and started to calm.

"How bad is it?" he asked.

"Get your shit together before you seriously hurt someone Bones," I said before exiting the building.

Chapter Eleven

"I thought you boys told me that Bones was good enough for my baby-girl?" Pops said storming out with Jackson and Wild Card. Grady followed behind them.

"That's not the same man," I sighed, turning to Pops. "It's complicated. I knew his wife was dead and ordered for her body to be left abandoned in a warehouse. Add to that his unwillingness to accept he'd married a woman with such low morals that she was invested in the human trafficking business — He has a lot of shit going on in his head right now."

"Everything you just described is childish compared to the shit you've been dealing with your whole life. But I don't see you treating people cruelly. You need a man that is willing to step up to the plate and help you fight your battles rather than add to them," Pops yelled before walking away.

"Why do I feel like I should be grounded and sent to my room?" I sighed.

"I know that feeling," Wild Card grinned. "And, he's never wrong which just adds more fuel to the fire."

I stopped and glared at Wild Card.

"Sorry, forgot about your burns. You really should've said something," Wild Card cringed.

"And, ruined Donovan and Lisa's night even more than I already have?" I said as we walked around the building and met up with the others at my truck. "Where is everybody, anyway?"

"Locals went home. All the out-of-towners, except Lisa's family, were taken to the airport and put on flights to Chicago. Katie booked them rooms next to the airport and helped them set up transfer flights. Everyone else is at the house. We downsized to your house and Donovan's, so security is tighter."

"Thanks," I nodded, getting into the passenger side of my truck as Grady took the wheel.

"Why don't you ever drive your own vehicle?" Grady asked, starting up the SUV.

"It's cheaper if she lets other people drive," Wild Card chuckled.

We had to park in front of Alex's house and walk to my house. As we approached the driveway, I heard motorcycles in the distance. Tyler moved from the shadows and stepped in front of me.

I looked at the gun that Tyler was holding and laughed.

"Tyler, have you ever fired an M16 before?" I asked.

"No, but I was told it was pretty easy to manage," he grinned.

I shook my head and held out my hand. He reluctantly gave me the gun, and I passed it to Grady. I looked at Wild Card and Reggie.

"We'll see who else got into your private stash," Reggie grinned, and they jogged away.

"This is yours?" Grady grinned.

"I have a few M16's and AK's lying around," I shrugged.

"A few?" Charlie rolled her eyes.

Four motorcycles turned onto our dead-end road and slowly approached, pulling into the driveway. I raised my arm and gave the hold signal to all the guards.

Maggie and James walked out of the house and joined us.

When they killed their bike engines, I stepped up to greet Renato.

"You're back from Mississippi already?"

"Got back this morning. My phone just rang about twenty minutes ago, though. Nola was spotted in Indiana, heading south. I alerted some of the other chapters along the path, and hopefully, we'll get lucky and spot her again."

"Thanks. That means we can sleep a little easier tonight. I'm sending my family away tomorrow for their safety. Not sure when any of us will be back, but the Players will be around. Come on in for a drink," I offered, leading the way to the house, knowing they wouldn't turn down a cold beer.

"I'll alert the local police that Nola was already spotted out of State," Maggie said stepping off into the side yard.

"What happened to your hair?" Renato asked.

I stopped cold.

I started to reach up, but Grady firmly grabbed my wrists to stop me.

He looked down at me and shook his head.

"No…."

"Sorry. No one had the heart to tell you," he grinned.

"No..."

"I can fix it, I swear," Reggie said jogging up to me carrying three M16's. Wild Card grinned, carrying two AK's.

I stepped into the house and yelled as loud as I could yell—like a five-year-old having a complete meltdown, "*DALLAS!!!*"

Dallas came running up the basement stairs, pulling her top back into place and stopped dead in her tracks when she saw me.

"Your Hair!" she screeched, slowly circling around me.

When she stopped to face me again, she still looked unsure.

"I'll have to cut it to your shoulders, but I can spice up the colors to distract the rest," she nodded trying to convince herself. "Dave, run out to my car and get my Gucci tote bag out of the back."

Hattie handed me a cocktail as Dave slipped past me.

I could feel my lower lip trembled.

"Don't even think about crying," Dallas warned. "You know I don't do tears. Buckle that shit up and be the badass bitch that I love so much."

I chugged a large portion of my cocktail as Dallas had me sit in a chair in the kitchen. She started cutting out huge chunks of hair, and I continued to drink. It was like a game. Every time I saw an oversize section of hair fall to the floor, I drank. My glass never got past the half-empty mark before someone was exchanging it with a fresh one.

By the time she got done cutting and started coloring, I was pretty tipsy.

Alex leaned down and looked at me. "You do know it's Dallas that you're letting work on your hair, right? Not Reggie?"

"Have you ever seen me go to a hair salon for a cut or color?"

"No."

"That's because I go to Dallas's house and we drink. She colors and cuts my hair, and then we go to the bar and celebrate my new hairdo."

"No Shit?" Alex grinned.

"No shit," I grinned back. "If anyone can salvage it, it's her."

Dallas shoved my head under the kitchen faucet, washing the dyes out, followed by blow-drying and styling my hair. When she stepped back, the whole room looked at once.

When everyone cheered and clapped, I finally exhaled.

"Unbelievable," Reggie smirked.

Whiskey removed the decorative mirror from the living room wall and brought it out to hold in front of me. Dallas had managed to make the cut look like I had my longer hair tucked under and the rest of my hair layered out to frame my face. It was also heavier on the colored streaks of gold, red and brown, to distract even myself from the fact that it was about a foot and a half shorter than I normally wore it.

"Bravo, my friend," I smiled. "You saved me!"

• • •

I stood and hugged Dallas.

"Glad you like it, Darling. Consider us even for the Miami situation. Now, I need to get back downstairs," Dallas said, hurriedly. "I sort of left Goat, *tied up* if you know what I mean."

Dallas ran down the stairs, and I turned back to everyone else.

"Isn't Goat the club member that oversees the remodeling at the store?" Renato asked.

"Yup," James grinned.

"Is he really tied up in the basement?" Renato asked.

"With Dallas, I'm sure of it," Whiskey grinned.

"What did my mom mean when she said to consider you both even for the Miami situation?" Dave asked.

"Dave, you're my friend, and for that reason, I am so not going to tell you what your mother did in Miami," I grinned.

"You don't want to know," Grady chuckled.

Charlie and Reggie laughed and walked out of the room.

* * *

Chapter Twelve

I was getting tired, but there were plenty of people still around, so I made my way into the living room to visit with everyone. I was surprised to see Bones' sister Rebecca sitting next to her grandfather on the couch.

"Rebecca, I thought you both would've caught a flight out. Is everything okay?"

"We were hoping we could have a moment to talk business before we left," she said looking nervously over at her grandfather.

"Sure," I nodded and led them back to my rooms. I was pleased to see that someone had cleaned up all the excess bedding and the room had been straightened. "So, what is so dire that you held off fleeing the State?" I asked, taking a seat behind the small desk.

"What are your intentions with my company?" Teddy Barrister barked.

Bones obviously got his brass balls from his grandfather.

"To make money, of course. Is there a problem?" I asked, gesturing toward the two small guest chairs.

Obviously, this wasn't a social visit, and Teddy opted to pace while Rebecca chose to sit.

"I wasn't aware that you and my brother had a history when you invested," Rebecca said. "It's obvious that something happened between the two of you and of course, now we're concerned about how this impacts the company."

"I wasn't at odds with your brother when I invested. I might've felt a bit guilty for your company's situation, though. I was the one that alerted the FBI to the criminals in Texas, resulting in your father's arrest. But, that's not why I chose to invest either. I invested because, you, Rebecca, have what it takes to take the company to the next level. But if there's a concern, I'll consider selling my investment, with stipulations of course."

"Ah, here we go, blackmail. I told you she's bad news, Rebecca," Teddy grumbled, still pacing.

"Blackmail? What the hell is going on in here?" Bones asked from the doorway as he walked further into the room. "Grandfather, what do you mean Kelsey is blackmailing you? For what?"

"She owns twenty percent of the company!" Teddy yelled. "She bought out the investors that wanted to leave after your father was arrested. We vetted her, but it never came up that she knew you or that she even lived in Michigan!"

"Impossible. Kelsey doesn't have that kind of money," Bones insisted, shaking his head.

The door slammed shut, and Grady walked over and leaned against the wall behind me. Bones glared at him before turning to his sister.

"Rebecca, what's going on?"

Rebecca sighed and looked back at me. "This would be so much simpler if the men just stayed out of our business," she smiled.

I grinned back. "I'm not blackmailing you, Teddy. But you and your grandson are clueless when it comes to what is best for Barrister Industries."

"I started that company from scratch. No one knows that company better than I do!"

"Thirty years ago, yes. Today, that's not true," I said standing and walking over to face him. "Now, it's your granddaughter that knows it best. She knows every employee, every competitor, every move that's made in the industry. She's worked from the ground up like you asked her to do, proving to everyone along the way that she has what it takes to sit in that CEO chair."

"Bones has a better handle on business and has already agreed to step in. We vote him in next week," Teddy glared.

"Then I don't sell. Not yet at least," I said, walking into my atrium.

"What do you mean you won't sell?" Bones asked following me in. "What do you want?"

"To give Rebecca the option of making her own choice. She won't have that if I sell."

"What choice?" Rebecca asked following us in.

Grady moved into the atrium, but leaned on the outside wall, ever the bodyguard. Teddy stomped in and sat on one of the couches, folding his arms across his chest, being petulant.

"What choice do I have?" Rebecca said. "My grandfather will never think I'm good enough and just like always, my brother is ready to swoop in and save the day," she said rolling her eyes.

Rebecca was the one pacing now. I looked over at Grady, and we shared a grin.

"Rebecca?" Bones asked, stepping in her path. "You want the job as CEO? I don't understand."

"I don't just want it, Bones, *I earned it!*" she yelled, stepping into his personal space. "I have worked my ass off for years to get where I am. I was there Bones. I was at Barristers the entire time. Father might be an ass, but he stayed out of my way. I had the favor of the board. I was the one that was turning the profit, trimming the expenses, pushing new marketing programs. But when father was sent to prison, I was put on the damn shelf and told the men will handle everything — not to worry my pretty little head about it. But, it's my time. I earned this!"

"You can't possibly run a company as large as Barrister Industries," Teddy insisted. "It's just not right. I know you think you don't want to settle down, but once you do, you'll see, a family will be your focus." Teddy stepped away from Rebecca and approached me. "Ms. Harrison, what are your intentions with your investment in my company?"

"As long as Rebecca has a seat on the board, she'll hold my proxy vote. If she were to ever leave, I'd sell my investment."

"How can you possibly own twenty percent of the company? That's ludicrous," Bones said shaking his head.

"And, how can you assume that you are better qualified to run Barrister's when you don't even know who owns it?" I asked.

Rebecca laughed and quickly threw a hand over her mouth to stifle her giggles.

"Sell your investment, Kelsey. I will find someone to buy it," Bones growled.

"I will sell when Rebecca advises me it's time to do so. But I'm not so sure she's ready to throw in the towel just yet."

"What does that mean?" Bones glared.

"It means, big brother, that over the years, while you've been content with the ten percent of the company that we each were given, I've been increasing my investment. I own twenty percent. And, with Kelsey's proxy vote, I'd carry forty percent of the vote. The remaining board members will decide who sits in the CEO chair. *And, they know me.*"

"They won't vote for you if I tell them to vote for Bones," Teddy argued.

"I think you're wrong," she challenged back. "Especially when I tell them that either I get the CEO chair, or I quit to work for the competition."

Bones watched his grandfather storm out of the suite and down the hall. He turned back to his sister, grinning, truly seeing her for the first time.

"Damn. You're not my baby sister anymore."

He stepped over to the atrium window and rubbed the back of his neck.

"Kelsey, is she really ready?"

"The company will fall without her. She *is* Barrister Industries. I will certainly pull my money if she leaves. And, I know I'll have to take a loss to do it because other investors will be backing out too. You'd be looking at potential bankruptcy."

"Listen to her, Bones," Grady warned. "I know you don't know this side of Kelsey, but she's been in the big leagues for a long time now. She's in way deeper with much bigger fish than Barristers. It wouldn't even dent her pocketbook if the company goes belly up, but it'd destroy your family."

"You made that much money selling books?" Bones asked me, eyebrow askew.

"No. I made that much money gambling on people and horses," I grinned.

"I don't know you at all, do I?" Bones said as much to himself as to me. He looked out the window again before turning and walking back to his sister. "I'll talk to grandfather and the other board members. The CEO chair is yours."

He kissed her on the forehead and walked out of the suite, closing the bedroom door behind him.

"Holy shit," Rebecca said, falling onto the atrium couch. "I can't believe all that just happened."

"And, it will probably happen again if you continue to let your grandfather bully you. You can love him as your grandfather, respect him as the founder of the company, but don't let him undervalue you as CEO, or it will reflect poorly on the company."

Rebecca nodded and looked around.

Grady grinned and went over to the small cabinet along the wall and poured us each a glass of fine brandy.

• • •

"You read my mind," Rebecca grinned.

"It wasn't hard," Grady chuckled. "Kelsey gets that same look on her face after she goes toe to toe with people who underestimate her."

"Have you two known each other long?" Rebecca asked, taking the offered glass.

"About two weeks," I grinned.

Grady chuckled and sipped his brandy.

"Seriously? I would have guessed you grew up together," Rebecca grinned. "What about Bones? I don't get it. He seems to hate you one minute and then the next he's asking your advice on our family business."

"We were close until last week. I knew Penny was dead, and I chose to wait to report it. Innocent people could've been hurt," I admitted taking a seat on the other couch and motioning for Grady to join us.

"Crap, it's you!" Rebecca said, leaning forward. "You're not only rich, but you're *that* Kelsey Harrison? You were a cop in Miami?"

"It's hard to believe, isn't it?" Grady grinned. "Hanging out with her is like hanging out with ten different people."

"I wear a few different hats, but let's not make it sound like I have multiple personalities."

Rebecca smiled, standing and setting her glass on an end table.

"Well, as fun as this is, my grandfather will intentionally fly off without me if I don't get to the airport. It's going to be an interesting flight home," Rebecca grinned. "Thanks for the support. I promise that I will get that CEO chair with or without my grandfather's help."

"Go make us some money," I grinned and stood to shake her hand.

Grady rose too and offered to give her a ride to the airport. When they were gone, I sat back on the couch and looked up at the beach paintings on the atrium wall.

They called to me as they always did, wishing me back to a time when Charlie, Nicholas and I ran and played on similar beaches from sunrise to sunset.

A knock on the bedroom door pulled me back to the here and now.

"Come in," I called out.

Reggie and Wild Card entered carrying stacks of assault weapons.

"Damn, what stash did they raid?"

"Wasn't it your bedroom collection?" Reggie asked.

"I don't think so," I answered, going to my closet and opening the hidden gun safe. All the guns I kept there were accounted for. "They must have found the one I kept at the old house."

"You kept assault weapons at your old house after you moved out?" Reggie asked.

"I wasn't ready to go back after everything that happened there. By the time I finally did, I had forgotten about them," I shrugged. "Can one of you let Bridget know that I want all the Glocks and the tear gas canisters back too?"

Reggie laughed and went to track down Bridget.

"Is there anywhere else that you may have left enough weapons to start a war?" Wild Card asked.

"A few safe houses I have scattered around. And, your house of course."

"What?"

"I have a collection in my old bedroom. You didn't know?"

"No. How many guns do you have hidden in my house?"

"I think I was up to twenty-two by the time I left. Reggie might have confiscated a few of them, though."

"Assault rifles?"

He was getting pissed. He glared at me while his face turned deep red.

"Jackson's the one that taught me how to shoot them!" I said, completely throwing Jackson under the bus.

"Jackson!!" Wild Card bellowed on his way out of my bedroom.

I laughed and followed after him.

"What?" Jackson asked at the end of the hall.

He was wearing one of Hattie's aprons and had a stack of dirty glasses in his hands.

"Did you teach Kelsey how to shoot assault rifles?" Wild Card steamed.

"Well, I figured if she owned them, she should at least know how to use them," Jackson shrugged and walked away.

"Don't worry so much," Pops chuckled. "I made sure she got a good price on them."

"And, I helped her build her hidden gun case to keep them in," Reggie said walking in with an arm full of tear gas canisters.

I took the canisters on the top of the pile, and Pops grabbed some as well.

"You're all nuts," Wild Card yelled. "And, half of you are blood-related!"

"Are we talking about the hidden guns in the spare bedroom at your ranch?" Grady grinned at Wild Card.

"I thought you took Rebecca to the airport?" I asked.

"James wanted to take her," Grady winked.

Oh, boy. Bones was not going to like it if James and Rebecca hooked up. James was tempting a bull with that move.

"Stay on topic," Wild Card yelled. "So you also knew there were guns hidden in my house?"

"I figured they were yours," Grady chuckled. "I didn't know at the time that you had a devious ex-wife that was into all that shit. I was pretty damn jealous about a few of them too. She has a Smith and Wesson Frontier revolver in there that is impressive."

"Ah, that one might have been relocated since your last visit," Reggie grinned, rubbing the back of his head. "I got a bit nervous about someone getting their hands on that little collectible."

"So that's where the gun came from? The one you had cased and framed and hung on your living room wall?" Wild Card glared.

"What? I wouldn't want the finish to go dull," Reggie grinned as Jackson threw an arm over his shoulder and kissed his cheek.

"Are you done bitching yet?" I grinned. "It's getting late, and we all need to get some sleep. Does anybody need anything before I crash?"

"Jackson and I are bunking with you tonight," Reggie grinned.

"Fine," I said rolling my eyes. "I'm glad I have a king size bed."

"I've got dibs on one of the atrium couches," Grady called.

"I get the other one," Wild Card called.

"Fine, I don't care. I just want to sleep."

Chapter Thirteen

It was two in the morning by the time everyone found a spot and called it a night. And, unfortunately, I woke the next morning, after only three hours of sleep.

Thoroughly annoyed but knowing I wouldn't be able to fall back asleep, I crawled over Reggie, gathered some clean clothes and escaped to my bathroom. I took a long hot shower hoping to relieve the stress that was already building.

After showering, I threw my hair up in a clip, applied minimal makeup and dressed in my favorite bitch gear, consisting of hip hugger jeans, my favorite black heeled boots and a tight v-neck form fitting top with long sleeves. I finished the look with the bracelet that held a locket picture of Nicholas. I rubbed the locket before sneaking out of the bathroom and down the hall to the kitchen.

"Good Morning, Hattie," I grinned, accepting the coffee she already had waiting for me at the breakfast bar.

"Good Morning, Sunshine," she smiled back. "You didn't get much sleep last night."

"No, but hopefully I will be able to sleep later when we drive south," I said after taking my first sip of coffee.

"You're not flying?"

"No. I have too many supplies to take. And, I'd prefer to have a few of my own vehicles with me. They have a few hidden compartments," I grinned.

"Yes, I know," she said rolling her eyes. "I accidentally hit a switch in the backseat one day, and one of those hidden compartments popped open, housing several guns. I dropped the groceries I was carrying. The milk jug exploded when it hit the parking lot — soaking me, the rest of the groceries, and a woman that was walking by."

"Shit. Sorry," I giggled.

I looked off toward the living room, hearing someone stirring. A minute later, Pops walked in to join us. Hattie went to stand, but Pops held a hand up to stop her.

"I'm a grown man, Hattie," Pops grinned. "You don't need to wait on me. I can pour a cup of coffee without messing up your fine kitchen."

Pops poured his coffee and leaned on the other side of the breakfast bar.

"Good Morning, Pops," I grinned.

"Good Morning, Baby Girl," he grinned back.

Reggie stumbled in, eyes half closed and walked directly to the coffee pot. He poured himself a cup, got out a coffee carafe and poured the rest in the carafe, before making a fresh pot of coffee. He then walked over and stood next to Pops and used the carafe to top off Hattie's and my cups.

"I think I'm going to like Texas," Hattie giggled.

"I think you're going to like it too," I grinned. "Which reminds me—Pops, I had to send Hattie's gun in for restoration. She hadn't shot or cleaned it in a couple decades. I gave her one of my Glocks, but she needs some lessons on it."

"We'll get the cans set up and make sure she's well practiced," Pops grinned.

"And, I don't know how to ride a horse," Sara said, coming down the stairs.

She walked over and climbed the side of my barstool as I pulled her and her pink-slipper-self up onto my lap.

"We can handle that. You'll be ready for the competitions before you know it," Pops winked at her.

Sara giggled and tucked her head under my chin. I wrapped my arms around her.

"Aunt Kelsey?" Sara whispered.

"Hmmm?"

"I'm going to miss you."

"I'm going to miss you too, little bug," I said as I kissed the top of her head. "But Pops, Reggie, Jackson, and Wild Card have so much to teach you, the time is going to fly right by. I'll be there to see you before you know it."

"This is where my bunkmate slipped off to!" Charlie teased Sara as she came down the stairs. "I woke up and realized I was left all alone!"

Sara giggled as Charlie pulled her from my lap and hugged her.

"Thanks for sharing your bed with me, little bug," Charlie kissed her on the cheek before setting her back on my lap.

"You're welcome, Aunt Charlie," Sara giggled.

I saw Charlie tense up, and I reached out, grabbing her hand. She hadn't been called Aunt Charlie since Nicholas was taken. She squeezed my hand back before accepting the cup of coffee that Reggie offered her.

The front door opened, and Bones entered, carrying several boxes of donuts. I passed Sara to Charlie, so I could help clear the top of the credenza to set the boxes on.

I pushed a pile of mail off to the side and opened the first box, selecting a glazed donut. Holding it with my mouth, I moved the large pile of mail over to the dining room table. Hattie retrieved napkins. Pops brought my coffee cup. And Reggie filled another carafe of coffee as we all settled around the large table.

"What time are you leaving today?" Bones asked me as Sara climbed onto his lap to 'share' part of his lemon custard donut.

"Everyone flying is leaving before nine. Those of us driving are leaving late morning. I have a few things I need to prepare before we can head out."

"I'm coming with you," Bones announced.

"I don't recall inviting you," I said, leaning back in my chair and looking at him.

"I noticed," he grinned.

"Look, Bones, I don't have the time to focus on the bullshit between you, me, and the crap that happened with Penny. I need to focus on finding my son."

"I'm aware," Bones nodded.

"And, I won't tolerate any pissing matches between you and Grady either."

"Understood," Bones nodded. "I've been an ass. My sister chewed me out at the airport last night and reminded me of all the shit that Penny used to pull. I don't know why I reacted the way I did. But, I can help you in New Orleans. I know some guys from the service that live around there that will help us."

"Good," Grady said walking in, followed by Wild Card. "We could use all the help we can get."

The basement door opened, and Donovan and Lisa appeared.

"Did you come through the tunnels?" I laughed.

"They're so cool!" Lisa grinned. "I'm never walking through the snow to come over here again."

Donovan grinned and rolled his eyes, but I knew he was secretly just as impressed with the tunnels that connected the houses.

"I'm glad you're up," Donovan said, taking a seat and pulling his giddy wife onto his lap. "As willing as my wife was last night to go wherever you chose to send us, she's changed her mind."

"Lisa, you can't stay here," I started to argue.

"I know. If Pops has enough room, Alex, Donovan, and I would rather be with everyone else in Texas. We want to stay together, as a family. I would feel safer if I was with them."

"Between the three ranches, there's plenty of room," Pops said.

"What the hell are we going to tell your father?" I asked Lisa.

"I talked to him last night," Donovan said. "I made it clear that my wife's safety came first and her happiness next, and if she wanted to go to Texas instead of New Jersey, that's where we were going."

"And, how did that go?"

"He glared at me for ten minutes straight while I stood there and stared back. Then he laughed and said that it was fine as long as she was safe," Donovan said. "Then I drank a shot of Jack Daniels and went back to bed."

"Bravo," Reggie cheered with his coffee cup.

"You've got balls, dude," Grady chuckled. "That's almost as insane as Reggie getting a haircut from Benny the Barber."

"The hitman?" Donovan asked, looking at Reggie in shock.

"I didn't know he was a hitman! I thought he was just some old guy Kelsey wanted to talk to!"

Bones spit up his coffee, laughing.

I was only half listening as I took another bite of my donut and continued to sort the large pile of mail. Most of it was solicitations and ended up in a pile I had started on the floor to be burned. I was about to throw another envelope onto the floor when I stopped and took a closer look at the address label. *To: KNC Enterprises.*

"What the hell?" I said to myself, leaning over to pick up the mail in the throwaway pile.

I sorted back through the stack, finding most of it was for KNC Enterprises.

"What is it?" Charlie asked.

"These were sent to KNC Enterprises," I said looking up at Charlie.

She jumped up from her seat and started flipping through the stack of mail. More than half the pile was credit card and business loan solicitations.

"Hattie, how old is this mail?" I asked.

"That's all from the last few days. Katie usually picks it up, but with Lisa's wedding, she hasn't sorted it out yet."

"I need Katie. And, Tech. I need both of them, right now," I said as I clutched a pile of the mail to my chest and ran down the stairs, down the hall, and into the War Room.

Chapter Fourteen

I dumped the mail on the center workstation and started pacing back and forth.

"Kelsey, what—," Bones started to say.

"Shh!" Charlie whispered. "She's thinking."

I could hear everyone gathering in the room, but they stayed quiet as I paced back and forth. I occasionally glanced at the mail, but most of the time I watched the floor.

Grabbing a permanent marker in one hand, I ripped the corkboards off the far wall with the other. I drew a thick dark line horizontally across the wall.

"Grady, pull the file that Baker gave us of Nola's visit to the Other Layer to extort money. Charlie, get my lawyer on the phone."

"It's only six a.m.," Charlie said.

"I don't care. I pay him well. He can lose a little sleep," I said as I stared at the black horizontal line on the wall.

"Katie, you here?" I asked without turning around.

"Ready and waiting," she answered from behind me.

"When did the junk mail for KNC Enterprise start coming?"

"About three weeks ago," she answered. "Why?"

I drew a mark toward the end of the timeline on the wall and wrote 'Mail' under it.

"Because that company name has intentionally never been associated with this address," I answered.

"Shit," Grady said, starting to understand what was happening.

He grabbed the marker from my hand and made a mark on the horizontal line with a date on top and the Other Layer under it.

"Molly's disappearance," I called out. "What was the date that she disappeared?"

"A week later," Tech answered.

Grady wrote the 'Molly' on the timeline and marked the date.

"I've got Grover on speaker," Charlie called out.

"How many times do I have to tell you, Charlie—it's *Goveir*. Hell, just call me Ethan. But stop calling me Grover!" he grumbled over the speaker.

"Sure thing, Grover," Charlie grinned.

"Stop it, both of you," I snapped. "Ethan—is there any chance you messed up and used my current home address for KNC Enterprises?"

"No. I use the PO Box for everything, and on the rare occasion if I need a physical address, I use my law office address," Ethan answered over the speaker phone.

"Any unusual business activity for the KNC accounts? Strange mail coming through?"

"I recently started getting late notices. I began calling on them, but they're for accounts I've never heard of. I'm handling it, though."

"Do you still have the notices?"

"They're at the office. I can fax them to you later today."

"Later, won't work, Grover. Get off your ass and fly like an eagle. We need those notices now," Charlie hollered over the speaker phone before disconnecting the call.

"You know, he's a hell of a lawyer. You should be nicer to him," I fake glared at her.

"He's also not bad in the sack, but let's stay focused, shall we?" she grinned. "What is all this? Why are we worried about our company bullshit right now?"

"Nola knew about Kelsey owning the Outer Layer which is owned under the KNC Enterprises name," Grady answered. "Nola may have used the company name to open some fake accounts."

"Shit, I think this is more of Genie's expertise than mine," Tech said, pulling the phone over and using it to call Genie on speaker.

I heard Anne in the hallway calling Maggie and telling her to get her ass over to the house.

"My wish is your command," Genie answered half asleep.

"Wake up, Genie," I yelled. "We have a lead and need your magical skills."

"Kelsey? Shit, okay, okay, let me throw on a robe and move to my office. Is this about Nicholas? Did you find him?"

"I think Nola opened some fraudulent accounts under the company name: KNC Enterprises. I need you to see what you can track down. Start with the business's credit history in the last six months. See what new accounts show up and what the credit inquiries show."

"I need a warrant to track this past the credit history. And, a Tax id number would be helpful."

"The sole owners of KNC Enterprises are in this room, and Charlie and I give you full permission to dig as deep as you need," I said.

Charlie called out the tax id, knowing it by heart. In the early days, she did all our personal and business tax filing for us.

"Okay, I got it. Holy shit, you two are rich," Genie exclaimed.

"Move past the dollar signs. The only financial transaction I have made recently under that company name was an investment in Pittsburgh for Barristers Industries. Is anything else showing?"

"While ignoring the millions invested in Barristers," she mumbled, "Yes — hit the mother-load of credit checks and new accounts being opened. They started five months ago and spiked last month with several new credit cards being opened. I see four new accounts in the last 30 days."

"Genie, I need statements on anything charged to those cards. I have never had a charge account set up under KNC Enterprises. I run everything direct through each subsidiary."

"I'm on this, but it will be faster if I hang up. Where do you want the data?"

"Send everything to Tech as you get it. We'll run with it from there," I said before Genie disconnected the line on us.

"What the hell is KNC Enterprises?" Katie shouted.

"It's a company that Charlie and I started. K- for Kelsey, N-for Nicholas, and C- for Charlie. KNC Enterprises. It was originally just KC Enterprises, but when I adopted Nicholas, we had the name changed to include him," I answered as I started pacing again.

I looked back at the timeline as Katie continued asking questions and Charlie filled everyone in on the fact that we were much wealthier than anyone in Michigan knew.

"So, six months ago, Nola strolled into the Outer Layer and demanded extortion payments. A week later, she kidnapped Molly and sold her to Pasco," I said aloud. "I'm missing something. How did Nola connect me to the Outer Layer and to Molly?"

Baker? Before I left Miami, I sent a message to Baker, one of my business partners, telling him to make sure that Molly was taken care of. With her father's criminal background, I figured that Molly would be more comfortable with Baker than an uptight lawyer.

"Charlie, get Baker on the phone," I ordered.

"Who the fuck is calling me this early in the morning?" Baker snapped over the phone line minutes later.

"Good Morning, Goldilocks. It's Charlie. Consider me the nice one for this phone call. Kelsey looks pissed."

"Baker, when I left Florida, I told you to reach out to Molly McNabe and make sure she was taken care of. What did you set up?" I asked turning toward the phone to concentrate on the call.

• • •
108

"I did what you said, met her in the park. Told her that her expenses would be covered and that if she ever needed anything to let me know."

"What contact did you have with her after that?"

"Is Molly okay? I've been trying to get in touch with her for months but haven't heard back from her. I called the University, but they wouldn't tell me anything."

"Molly's dead. Nola killed her months ago," I snapped, my blood pressure rising by the second.

Grady placed a calming hand on my shoulder, and I nodded and took a deep breath.

"Dead? Nola killed her?" Baker said, sounding stunned. "God, she was such a sweet kid."

I could hear the sincerity in his voice.

"Baker, I need you to tell me exactly how and when you and Molly communicated. It's important."

"Yeah," Baker sighed. "She'd mail her bills to me. I made sure they were paid. Other than our initial meeting, I'd only seen her in person on her 21st birthday. She showed up at the club. I chewed her out and had my driver take her and her friends somewhere more respectable. I even sent some of my security guards to keep an eye on them and get them home safely."

"When are you supposed to make the next extortion payment to Nola?"

"Today, the first of every month."

"Send it. I can't have Nola knowing that I found out anything about the money transfers," I said turning to look back at the timeline drawn on the wall. "I'm still missing something. How did Nola find out about KNC?"

• • •

"Molly?" Maggie asked, walking further into the room. "Young girl, missing her mentor, no family. Nola could have worked a con on Molly to get the information. She could have met Molly weeks before she kidnapped her."

"Who's that?" Baker asked.

"Got to go, Baker. Make sure you wire the money," Charlie said, hanging up on him.

"Carl," Sara called out as she climbed up onto a stool and opened a laptop. "I need help digging into the University's database."

"I can do that," Carl agreed, stepping forward.

"Stop," I sighed, looking at my intelligent as hell, and just as absent-minded friend. "Carl, you need to put on some pants before you can help Sara."

Everyone except Sara and Tech turned toward Carl and was surprised to see that he had a shirt and tie on but no pants.

"Sorry," Carl pouted as he ran out the door.

Sara giggled, and Hattie sighed.

"Are you sure you're going to be able to keep up with him if you take him with you?" Hattie asked.

"It will be fine. Sara won't be there so he can run around naked as much as he wants as far as I'm concerned," I shrugged.

"I already know better than to look up from the computer monitor when Carl's around so it will be mostly Katie that gets flashes of his winky," Tech laughed.

I looked back at the timeline, but nothing else jumped out at me.

• • •

"Alright. Check out Molly's social background, but I don't think that's the connection. We need to get moving though. Everyone relocating to Texas, go finish packing. Katie, cancel their flights and book two private jets. The first one is going to Texas. Have the second jet fueled and ready to fly the rest of us out when we get a destination," I instructed. "Bones, call the club for me and see if we can get some guys to drive the SUV's down. I'll want the vehicles close. They can start driving south, and we'll call them later with more details."

Everyone scattered, following orders.

"You better go pack while we run some background checks on Molly and wait for Genie to get back to us. I already have my bags ready to go," Tech said.

"I'll help them," Charlie said pulling out the stool next to Sara. "I'm already packed as well."

"Yell for me if you find anything," I said, before walking out of the War Room.

Chapter Fifteen

"New Orleans," Tech said from his workstation in the War Room.

I had been going over the new shipping reports from Mayfair Shipping to see what contraband was being moved from which locations.

"What about it?"

"Genie is sending me a pile of information. New Orleans is stamped all over it."

"That makes sense. With most criminals, after discovery, they'd move to a new city. But Nola likes familiarity. And, there are too many eyes looking for her in Miami right now."

"Should I call the airport?" Katie asked.

"Yes, but give them Biloxi as our destination. It's a little over an hour drive from New Orleans, and we can access it by water too. We'll set up base camp there for you guys. The Demon Slayer will be close if we need them for extra protection too."

I picked up my phone and called a number I knew by heart.

"Sheriff," Eric answered after the first ring.

"Hey, Eric, it's Kelsey. How's Lenny doing?"

"Good, but not good enough to get messed up in whatever you're up to," Eric laughed.

"You know me so well," I laughed.

"I should. We dated for two years, remember," he chuckled. "So what kind of crazy scheme do you need help with now?"

"I need a boat in Biloxi," I admitted, biting my lower lip.

"The speed boat is still in storage, which we need to discuss, but I can bring the cabin cruiser over. It's small enough to still get you from point A to point B quickly."

"That will work. I'm jumping on a jet and will be there in a couple hours. I left some cash hidden at the restaurant. Grab what you need for expenses."

"I'll take care of it. Call me when you get settled," he said before hanging up.

"Would that be Sheriff Eric that you just called?" Charlie grinned.

"I'm surprised that he was so agreeable. He's hiding evidence for me right now, and usually, that's enough to twist his panties for a good year," I smirked.

"What evidence?" Charlie asked.

"Max sort of died while we were on a boat trip. I asked Eric to secure the boat until I can track down Nicholas, then I'll go in and report it," I admitted.

"I still say you need to destroy it all," Grady said, looking up from the file he was reading on one of the laptops.

"What happened?" Charlie asked.

"Don't answer that," Maggie said coming back into the War Room. "I don't want to know. The Players are back and have loaded the luggage. It's time to leave."

We all gathered the laptops and our phones and moved upstairs. I laughed as we bundled up in down-filled coats and leather gloves for the trip to the airport. In a few hours, we would be changing into t-shirts due to a sixty-degree temperature difference.

We landed in Biloxi around six o'clock, and I was surprised to see Nightcrawler waiting curbside with several vehicles and club members.

"Heard you might need a ride," Nightcrawler grinned.

"You heard right," I grinned back. "I booked rooms at the Holiday Inn for all of us."

"Not necessary. We set up a house next to the clubhouse. It's nothing fancy, but the old ladies are stocking the cupboards, and the club will be nearby for protection."

"You sure? I can't promise that the people I'm going after won't retaliate. Nola already tried to blow up everyone once this week."

"I heard. We voted, and the club is in," Nightcrawler said, taking my suitcase and loading it into a truck. "Whatever you need. Your enemies are our enemies."

"Appreciate it. I need to run an errand while everyone gets settled. I'll be there in about an hour."

"Here then," Nightcrawler said, handing me a set of keys. "I believe you left something in New Orleans on your last visit." He nodded his head to the first vehicle in line, which was one of my SUV's with its hidden compartments.

"I'm driving," Charlie grinned as she took the keys out of my hand and passed her suitcase off to Nightcrawler.

Before anyone had time to argue with us, we were pulling out of the airport and turning into traffic.

"Marina?" Charlie asked.

"Yup," I smirked. "Eric rented a slip and had the boat dropped in the water an hour ago. I need to check the stock and talk to Eric."

"I'll check the boat out while you talk to Eric. Which marina?"

"The one to the West, Small Craft Harbor. It will be easier to get in and out from there without drawing as much attention. It's closer to the clubhouse too."

"You need me to book a slip in New Orleans to use when we're there?"

"Not necessary, Katie has it handled," I grinned.

"Wow. It's weird having people helping. I'm used to us handling all the details."

"Yeah, if it weren't for the fact that we could easily get ourselves killed, it might even be called fun," I smiled.

"You're so warped," Charlie chuckled.

"Probably," I grinned. "So I've meant to ask you, are you investigating Grandma and Grandpa's Harrison's car accident?"

"Shit," Charlie winced. "I was going to tell you. I got my hands on the official police report, but it's pretty light. Nothing points a finger at our twisted parents."

"You need to leave it alone, Charlie," I sighed.

"What are you hiding, Kelsey? Why are you protecting them?"

"Who says I'm protecting them, Kid?" I said looking over at her. "Maybe I'm protecting myself."

She nervously glanced over at me, trying to understand my meaning, but didn't ask any more questions.

We pulled up to the marina and looked around. A pleasant mix of locals and tourists roamed up and down the docks and along the boardwalk. The sun was shining, and it was warm enough that I was already regretting my long sleeve shirt.

"Eric is at the marina bar. He said the boat was in slip 115," I said as we got out of the truck.

"I'll meet you at the bar when I'm finished. I'm assuming this is Lenny's boat with all the contraband storage units?"

"That's the one. It should still be stocked from when we used it for the raid on Pasco, but the FBI was involved, so I'm not positive."

We split off, and a few minutes later, I was pulling out the barstool next to Eric at a high table overlooking the water.

The waitress came over to take my drink order and Eric ordered for me.

"She'll take a tall lemonade, grilled ham and cheese on rye, a side of fruit, and a cup of coleslaw. Her cousin will be here in a few minutes, and she'll want a bud light, bacon cheeseburger medium-well, with a side of fries and a shit load of ketchup."

Eric grinned before taking a long drink of his beer.

"I'm not that hungry," I said after the waitress left.

"Nope, but my guess is you haven't eaten yet either," he said, looking back at me with a challenging eyebrow raised.

"Fine, I'll eat," I smirked.

"Good, now before Charlie gets here, explain what happened on the boat that I am hiding for you."

"I took Max by gunpoint out to Caveman's Bay to have a private discussion about Nola," I admitted, looking around to make sure no one was listening. "I didn't search him well enough, though, and he used a pair of nail clippers to cut his flex cuffs off. Before I knew what was happening, he jumped into the water and started to swim for shore."

"In Caveman's Bay? That's a shark nest!" Eric said a little too loud.

He was leaned back, a look of shock on his face.

"I know, right?! I tried to save him, but he was a goner soon after hitting the water."

Eric leaned forward and rubbed the palms of his hands down his face.

"A jury is never going to believe that story," Eric whispered.

"You're right—But, I was wearing a video recorder. The whole night was recorded on a laptop that I also have secured."

"Okay, so you can prove that you didn't kill him, but the video will show that you kidnapped him."

"Yes, but a good lawyer can get that down to illegally detaining or some shit. I might have to do a short stint in county, but I won't have to worry about spending thirty years in prison for murder."

"Do you hear yourself? You're okay with going to jail as long as they don't send you to prison for a few decades?"

"Pretty much," I nodded. "But we have to stall. As soon as I come forward, they'll ground me to one location until everything is settled. So, I can't confess until I find Nicholas."

"Shit. What a mess," Eric grumbled, downing the rest of his beer.

He held up the glass bottle to the waitress as she set my lemonade down.

"I know I'm putting you in a bad spot holding onto evidence, but it was the only thing I could think of to maintain some semblance of chain-of-custody."

"No, I get it. It's smart actually. The worst they can do to me is bad mouth me publicly. I'm an elected official, so they can't take away my badge. And, half my county is in love with you so it would actually help in the next election," he grinned.

"When we turn in all the evidence, just play dumb. You thought I was still carrying a badge, and you were assisting another police department. You didn't know anything other than that."

"Play dumb. Yeah, I think I can handle that," Eric said rolling his eyes and taking a drink from the fresh beer that the waitress handed him.

Charlie joined us just as our food was delivered. Despite saying that I wasn't hungry, the food was delicious. I dove in while Charlie and Eric exchanged barbed greetings.

"Boat have everything we need?" I asked Charlie.

"For the most part. I can fit everything else we need in a duffle bag and move it over either later tonight or in the morning. It also has a suitcase filled with men's clothes," she tattled.

"You're staying?" I asked Eric.

"Sounded like this was an all hands on deck type of gig," Eric shrugged. "I took some vacation time. I figure at the very least I can run the boat. We both know Charlie can't drive a boat worth a shit, and I doubt the northerners you hang out with these days can man it either. And you have more important things to concentrate on," he said leaning back on his barstool with his beer.

"Thanks," I grinned before taking another big bite of my sandwich.

Chapter Sixteen

Charlie and I arrived at the clubhouse, and a biker pointed out the house that was set up for us next door. We parked in the long gravel drive in front of the detached garage. A large grassy area with patio tables led up to a big country-blue deck that led into the main entrance of the house.

Charlie and I carried the takeout bags through a long, narrow L-shaped foyer that ended with the bathroom on one side and the kitchen on the other. Off the kitchen, a small dining room table sat to the left and a large living room to the right.

"I don't know what you bought, but the smell is making my mouth water," Tech said taking a load of bags out of my hands and carrying them back to the kitchen counter.

"Dinner time," I hollered loud enough to draw everyone into the small kitchen.

"Main course offerings are charbroiled cheeseburgers, grilled ham and cheese sandwiches, or blackened grouper sandwiches," Charlie said as Tech helped her open up the bags. "For side dishes, we have, well, everything that was on the menu."

Charlie and I stepped back as everyone started to dive into the food. Carl took a pile of fries and ran off with the ketchup. Maggie went chasing after Carl to retrieve the ketchup. I looked back as Nightcrawler stepped into the kitchen.

"You better get in there before it's too late," I grinned.

"Don't mind if I do," Nightcrawler smirked and grabbed a burger. "The Marina Grill. I love their food."

"We ate while I caught up with a friend. The owner's nephew agreed to make deliveries for us this week. They serve breakfast, lunch, and dinner," I grinned.

Katie took the menus from me and noted the name and phone number scribbled on the top. She nodded her approval as she continued to shovel her sandwich in her mouth.

"I think she's happy," Charlie said.

I reached into the refrigerator and pulled out a beer. Walking back through the foyer and out to the patio tables, everyone followed, carrying their food. As they sat at one of the two tables, I walked a few steps away and lit up a cigarette.

"We had a memorial service for my niece," Nightcrawler said, walking up to stand next to me. "I think it helped my sister to at least know that she was gone."

"It's hard not knowing," I nodded. "You lay awake at night wondering where they are, if they're hurt, scared, hungry. Then you wonder if they're even out there anymore," I whispered back.

I looked across the small yard.

"This awful feeling keeps pushing at me that I'm running out of time. Tick-tock, Tick-tock. It just keeps getting louder and louder. Nola's taking way too many chances lately. If she's losing control, I don't know what she'll do to Nicholas."

My hand shook as I held it up to take another long drag of my cigarette.

"So, put that cancer stick out and let's get back to work," Tech said.

I turned around, and everyone was quietly listening to our conversation. Charlie turned away with tears in her eyes, and Bones reached over and wrapped an arm around her. I threw the cigarette into the gravel-covered driveway and led everyone back into the house.

"What do we have?" I asked as we gathered in the living room.

The furniture had been moved out of the center of the room to the outside walls. Two eight foot tables were placed side by side with folding chairs surrounding them, creating several workstations. It wasn't fancy, but it would serve our purpose.

"First, internet service here sucks. Second, we can't find any mention of Nola or anything that looks suspect in Molly's social media or university records. Third, Genie has a list of expenses and cash draws from the new credit card accounts. There are four cards that were opened. The authorized signers are Nadina Mason, Tina Scappella, Thomas Cartwright and Phyllis Cartwright. All the names, of course, are aliases, but Genie is running the names to see if Nola ever used them before."

"Thomas Cartwright," I said pulling open the laptop that I had been using this morning. "That name was on the shipping logs for Mayfair Shipping. He has a cargo container that leaves Bay St. Louis every week."

"If it's on Tuesdays, it's the same boat that's used to make deliveries to us," Nightcrawler said, stepping closer to look over my shoulder.

"He meant, 'allegedly' used to make deliveries," I grinned at Maggie.

"Sure, he did," Maggie smirked.

"Shit. It's really weird having a Fed around," Nightcrawler grinned.

"Get used to it. We need her and her team," I said. "I need you to take Grady and Charlie to the shipping docks and show them around, discreetly. We need to know the layout."

"Got it," Nightcrawler said, leading Charlie and Grady out.

"Tech, copy the credit card list onto a drive for Carl. Carl, I need you to put all these charges in a spreadsheet with the name they were charged under, locations and what type of charge it was. Then lay it all on top of a map in date order, so I can make sense of it."

"I can do that," he said, while Maggie reached over with a napkin and wiped the ketchup off his chin.

I shook my head and turned to Bones.

"We'll move over to New Orleans in the morning. I don't know what the game plan will be yet, but if you have help available, they should meet us at the marina."

"I'll make some calls," Bones nodded.

"Maggie, I don't want to put you in a position where you feel obligated to report a crime and arrest someone, especially if the person you arrest is me, but I can't make out these shipping records. I don't know what I'm looking for."

"We can work out an immunity deal for you later. I can claim I was verifying the facts until we write it up," she said taking my laptop and moving it to an open area. She grabbed a pad of paper and a pen and started taking notes. "He sent you all this from his personal email address?" she said referring to Ronald Mayfair.

"Yeah, he's a dumbass," Tech grinned. "He even used his home computer according to the IP address. You won't have a problem locking his ass up when this is all over."

Maggie grinned as she scrolled through the documents.

"Katie, where is the club at with the other SUV's?" I asked.

She pulled up an app on her phone before answering, "Tennessee."

"Have them re-route to New Orleans, in the marina district. Eric can pick them up and bring them over here by boat. Then we'll have two of the SUV's already in New Orleans."

"Got it. Give me your phone, and I'll call this Eric guy, too."

I gave her my phone, and she walked out to join Bones on the small back porch off the living room.

I was about to review the shipping records with Maggie when several Demon Slayers carried bags and large boxes into the living room. Tech directed them where to install the touchscreen televisions. Katie walked by, passed me my phone, and dragged the air mattresses and some of the bedding into the downstairs bedrooms.

"What's all this?" I grinned.

"Now that I know you're filthy rich, I figured we'd do this right," Tech said.

"Okay then," I nodded, turning my attention back to the shipping logs.

My phone rang, and when I answered it, I was greeted by an operator asking if I would accept a collect call from an inmate at the prison in Miami. There was only one inmate that would have access to this number. Mickey McNabe.

I accepted the charges and jogged up the stairs to the second floor as I waited for Mickey's call to be connected.

The Cape Cod style house had two bedrooms downstairs and one long bedroom upstairs that provided four twin beds. With the gable roof the guys would have to duck to get in and out of bed, so most likely the girls would be occupying the second floor. I turned and looked at the overnight bags and confirmed that both Charlie's and my bags were there.

"You got a minute?" Mickey asked when the call was finally connected.

"Do you have a lead for me?"

"No, Nothing solid on Nola. I have everyone out looking, and they have your hotline number."

"Thanks. But, that doesn't explain the phone call, Mickey."

"I heard you have old Ronald's nuts in a vice. Nice job on that by-the-way. When he sent you the shipping files, did he included his vacations near Cuba?"

"I can't say I noticed anything along those lines, no," I grinned.

"Squeeze away, Harrison. Make it hurt," Mickey chuckled. "And, if you need help deciphering the records, his son Carter hates his guts."

Mickey hung up, and I laughed as I descended the stairs.

"Was that Mickey McNabe?" Maggie asked.

"Yup," I smirked. "I didn't notice any foreign shipping logs or ports listed in the files. Did you?"

"No. Everything appears to be Southern or Eastern US coastlines," Maggie answered leaning back in her chair. "What did Mickey say?"

"He wanted to be sure I was aware that Mayfair Shipping makes runs to Cuba," I grinned.

"Shit," Maggie said. "We'll need to get those immunity papers typed up."

I nodded as I called my lawyer.

"I hope this is Kelsey and not Charlie," Ethan answered.

"It's all good, Ethan. Charlie's out running an errand," I said. "I need a couple favors. I need you to send everything you have on Ronald Mayfair's son to Tech. And, then I need you to shut down all credit cards and lines of credit for Mayfair Shipping. Put a hold or a cancellation on everything."

"Do you want the bank accounts locked down too?"

"No, not yet. I don't want to shut down the business, I just want Mayfair's attention."

"Being he uses the company card for everything he does, I would say you'll have his attention pretty quick," Ethan chuckled. "I just emailed the information on the son, Carter Mayfair. I should have the charge cards turned off within the next hour."

We disconnected, and I turned back to Maggie. "Where's Kierson today?"

"He was driving here. He's probably only a couple hours away by now."

"Tech has an address for Carter Mayfair. See if Kierson is willing to swing by and bring him along for a little chat. Word on the street is that Carter would gladly assist us in taking down his father."

"I'm sure Kierson would be glad to arrange a visit," Maggie grinned.

Tech handed her a piece of paper with the address, and she stepped out on the back porch as Bones stepped back inside.

"I have a dozen guys meeting us at the marina in the morning," Bones said.

I nodded and turned to Carl. "Carl, how are you coming on the list of credit card charges?"

"I was done with that a while ago. I'm playing solitaire now. But I just won again. Online chess is a lot more fun, but Tech disabled the wifi on this laptop," Carl pouted. "I can fix it. I just need to wait until Tech goes to bed."

"Good to know," I winked at Tech. "Can I see what you have on the touchscreen?" I asked nodding to the wall mounted screens.

"Not without wifi," Carl glared at Tech.

Tech chuckled, put a flash drive in Carl's laptop and transferred the file to his laptop. A moment later, four lines appeared over a map. Each line was a different color that indicated which alias was used for the charges. Each dot on the line had a date stamp and the general type of purchase: hotel, food, retail, etc. And, each dot sat on top of the charge location.

A star on the line indicated an online purchase with the shipping address listed below it. I was a little curious how Carl managed to get the shipping address if his laptop wasn't online, but decided not to ask.

The purchases on three of the four cards were between Baton Rouge, New Orleans and Bay St. Louis. They moved back and forth routinely. The fourth card was floating around Fort Smith, Arkansas.

Charlie, Nightcrawler, and Grady returned, but everyone talked quietly behind me, as I kept my eyes working each line, one at a time through the charges, dates, and cities. I was surprised to realize when my phone rang that I had been studying the map for an hour. Katie was just leaving to pick up the Devil's Players from the marina.

"Kelsey."

"What the hell do you think you're doing?" Ronald Mayfair threatened over the phone.

"I warned you. Send me the rest of your shipping logs or I will sink you quicker than the titanic," I said before hanging up.

"Was that my father?" a man standing at the entrance to the living room asked.

Kierson stood next to him smirking.

"It was," I grinned. "Do you have a problem with the fact that I'm planning on sending him to prison for the rest of his life?"

"None, whatsoever. Carter Mayfair," he grinned, extending his hand.

"Kelsey Harrison," I said, shaking his hand. "We have the US shipping logs, and I just threatened your father for the rest of the logs. We could use your help to sort through everything."

"Where do you want me?"

I pointed to the chair next to Maggie, and she showed Carter the shipping records and got him started. Then she pulled me by the elbow into the kitchen and asked Kierson if he brought the immunity documents.

He pulled a stack of papers from his bag and handed them to me. The papers basically stated that I bought control of the shipping company so that I could gain access to their records and bring down any illegal activity. It also stated that the US government would not hold me responsible for any illegal activity as part owner of the company. Win-Win. I signed on the dotted line.

Kierson relayed that he had papers for Carter too since Carter had inherited five percent of the company from his grandfather. I nodded to have him sign off, and Carter happily did so.

It was only ten o'clock, but most of us couldn't keep our eyes open any longer. Nightcrawler pulled some club members to watch the house, so we could all go to bed early. Kierson, Maggie, and Carter stayed up and continued working on the shipping records.

Chapter Seventeen

I slept like the dead, for six full hours, and then I was wide awake.

I sat up and looked around the upstairs bedroom. Charlie slept beside me in the next bed. Across the room, Maggie and Carter had the other two beds.

I quietly snuck out of bed and pulled on some sweatpants. I was already wearing a Michigan State t-shirt, and while I wore it sans bra, it was too early to care. I moved down the steps and into the living room. The room was empty. Tiptoeing past the dining room, I pulled the makeshift curtain to hide Tech and Katie cuddled in peaceful sleep on one of the air mattresses.

In the kitchen, I wasn't surprised to see Grady, leaned back in a chair at the small kitchenette table with a cup of coffee for him and another sitting waiting for me. I grinned, grabbed the coffee and nodded to the foyer.

I walked barefoot through the grass to the patio table. At four in the morning, the early fog hovered over the night sky, blocking the moon and the stars, and a warm breeze drifted across my exposed skin. The quiet that surrounded us was the peace that I really needed.

"Kelsey, don't shoot me," a voice called out from the darkness.

"Tyler?" I asked.

"Yup," he chuckled coming around the corner of the house. "I've been patrolling the house all night."

"You want a cup of coffee?" Grady asked.

"No thanks, man," Tyler shook his head. "I only have another hour before James takes over."

"Sit, relax," I gestured to the patio table. "You staying or flying back?"

"James and I decided to stay. We'll help keep an eye on Katie, Tech, and Carl while the rest of you run around the globe doing your military mission shit," Tyler grinned.

"Thanks. I trust the Demon Slayers but," I said, pausing to figure out the words I wanted to say.

"But they don't know how you think. And, they don't know what to watch for. You need someone that will be suspicious of everything," Tyler grinned.

"Exactly," I grinned back.

Bones, Charlie and Katie all stepped out of the house and joined us, coffee cups in hand.

"What time do we have to be at the marina?" Bones asked.

"Not for a couple hours," I answered, looking away.

"What's wrong?" Grady asked.

"I'm not sure yet," I answered truthfully.

"Drink your coffee. Whatever is working its way around in that crazy brain of yours will be able to work faster once your caffeine level is back up to normal," Charlie grinned.

"Brat," I chuckled.

Tech came stumbling out the door, pouting. "There's no hot cocoa."

"Shit," I said as my thoughts finally clicked together.

I jumped up and ran into the house.

"It's not that big of a deal, Kelsey," Tech said scrambling after me.

"I don't care about your hot cocoa. Get Carl," I ordered.

I started frantically turning on the laptops as Tech threw open one of the bedroom doors and yelled for Carl to put on some pants. Maggie came running down the stairs, hair sticking out in multiple directions, but moving at high speed.

"Maggie, wake up Genie. I need her help if you don't want me to have Carl hack illegally."

Maggie called Genie, directed her to wake up, get dressed and call us back when she was set up in her home office. Grady walked over and sat on the couch along the far wall, leaned back, relaxed and grinning.

Bones sat next to him and asked. "What's happening?"

"Kelsey just figured something out. You're about to see her do her thing," Grady chuckled.

"Do my thing?" I smirked.

"Yeah, that about sums it up," Charlie grinned.

"Well, do *your* thing and get the touchscreens on. I need to see the displays," I told Charlie.

She turned on the screens as Tech and Carl signed into their laptops. Maggie's phone rang, and she answered on speaker.

"Okay, Kelsey, let's hear it," Maggie grinned.

"I need that map with the charges back up on the screen," I said, turning and waiting for it to appear. When it did, I scrolled quickly through each line and started bouncing up and down in excitement. "SHIT!"

I turned back and looked around, but so far, I was on my own mental roller coaster.

"Carl, this one," I pointed to the Arkansas line.

Carl grabbed Tech's laptop and zoomed in on the Arkansas line.

"Yes, the grocery store charge. I need the receipt for that purchase. Send whatever information we have for that purchase to Genie. Genie, when you get it, I need to know each item bought. And, I need it now. If you can't get it, then I'm going to green light Carl to do some really illegal stuff to get it."

Tech took his laptop back and sent the information to Genie. Carl grinned looking excited but Genie said that she could have it to me within two minutes, and his smile turned into a pout.

"I've got milk, bread, butter, cereal, eggs, fruit," Genie started to rattle off.

"Stop. What type of cereal?" I asked.

"Raisin Bran and Apple Jacks," she answered sounding confused.

"Holy shit, you did it," Charlie squealed and started dancing up and down with me.

"What is happening?" Bones asked.

"She just found her son," Grady grinned. "Nola would be buying takeout food, not stocking up on groceries. And, she certainly isn't the cold cereal type."

"It's his favorite cereal, Apple Jacks," Charlie grinned, happy tears rolling down her cheeks.

"Expand the map again, Tech," I said.

Tech put the map back to the original setting for all four charge accounts to show.

"These three lines are all restaurants, room service, and takeout. This is Nola and her guards. She's retail shopping. She's jumping around to different hotels. But the Arkansas line is survival food, basic necessities, and remote lodging. She moved Nicholas further away."

"But Nola's still in the area?" Bones asked.

"Yes, and we need to find her. But if I can track down my son while you keep Nola off her game in New Orleans, I have a chance to get to him before she can move him again."

"Consider it done then," Bones grinned. "Tech, can you print a list of those charge locations? We'll concentrate on those areas and try to flush her out."

"I need you to delay your morning trip. Give me a couple of hours to get to Arkansas and start searching."

"I'll call Eric and ask him pick up Bones' friends and bring them here. They know the area better so they can get their game plan mapped out," Katie said as she walked away to call Eric.

"Genie, I need every bit of information for the Arkansas purchases," I called out.

* * *

"I'm already running them, pulling one receipt at a time. I'll put copies in your cloud drive so you and Tech can both access them," she said before she abruptly hung up.

Carl was still pouting when I leaned forward, placing my hands under my chin, grinning at him.

"Carl, you did a great job on that map. You helped me find where they're keeping Nick," I grinned.

"I did?" he smiled.

"Yes, you did. And, since I know that you somehow managed to get your laptop online, can you pull up the online purchase receipts that were delivered to Arkansas?"

"Sure," Carl happily complied.

"What do you mean he went online? I disabled his internet access," Tech said looking up confused.

"I don't know how he did it. But in order to get the shipping addresses, he would've had to have been online," I grinned.

"Carl, you're killing me," Tech chuckled.

I quickly scanned the online purchases: books, games, fishing poles, clothes, etc. All the things you would need for a little boy.

"I need to change. Katie, can you book a flight?"

"Already being fueled and waiting to call in a flight plan. I held yesterday's jet and reserved it for another day. I figured if you were rich, it didn't matter," she grinned.

"Charlie, Grady, I need you both in Arkansas. Bones, work with Katie on tearing up New Orleans. Maggie, keep working the shipping logs. If we can't root out Nola, at least we can shut down another one of her income sources and lock up a few more of her men. Make sure you're set to roll in on Tuesday's shipment either way."

I didn't wait for anyone to respond as I ran up the stairs to dress and pack an overnight bag. Charlie was beside me doing the same. It was time to go get our boy.

Chapter Eighteen

Juggling our coats and overnight bags as we walked down the stairs, I stopped before I reached the bottom. I could hear Bones and Grady arguing in the living room.

"You just don't get it, do you? Kelsey doesn't need me to protect her any more than you would need me to protect you. She's a hell of a soldier. I've never met anyone that has her skill at strategizing," Grady said.

"I think your judgment is clouded by the fact that you're trying to get in her pants, my friend. You're overestimating her abilities and seeing what you want to see," Bones argued.

"Seriously?" Maggie intervened. "You really think that everyone, including three FBI Agents, would sit around unconcerned if we thought she wasn't that good?"

"Those girls are in over their heads," Bones snapped.

"What girls?" another male voice asked.

I grinned, recognizing the voice.

"Hey, Mitch," Grady sighed. "Bones here, thinks I need to protect Kelsey and Charlie. He says they aren't trained to go to Arkansas and hunt down the guy that has Nicholas."

"Shit, those two can spin circles around most of the men that were in my unit," Mitch chuckled. "Hell, Kelsey saved my ass from getting shot in Miami."

"See?" Grady said.

I decided enough was enough and finished walking down the steps. Kierson was leaning against the far wall grinning. He must have known we were on the stairs.

"Hi, Mitch," I greeted him, kissing him on the cheek as I walked by.

"Hi, Mitch," Charlie giggled mimicking me.

"Bye, Mitch," Grady chuckled, following us out. "Check in with Katie."

"Who's Katie?" Mitch hollered after us.

We spent our time on the plane studying the receipts and a map of the Fort Smith area. Based on the gas receipts, I was guessing they were somewhere within an hour's drive to the Northeast, closer to the Ozark Mountains. The location would offer several nearby interstates to leave by if needed and plenty of cabin rentals to choose from in remote locations. We decided our best option was to go to the Sheriff's office in White Rock and hope they had some suggestions as to where to start searching.

An SUV rental awaited us as we stepped off the plane and a man handed me a set of keys as I passed him a tip. We quickly loaded up, and I drove as Charlie programmed the GPS.

"I thought Kelsey didn't drive," Grady grinned from the back seat.

"It's not that simple," Charlie said. "Kelsey's a great driver unless she needs to drive in reverse. Then it's a

50/50 shot that she'll smash out the taillights or drive into a pond."

"I only drove into a pond once. You need to get over that," I grinned.

"Uh-huh," Charlie giggled. "You forget that while you climbed out the window, jumped on the hood and escaped, without a drop of pond water on you, I was in the backseat. By the time I got out, I had to swim out. And, there were leeches!"

"Yeah, sorry about the leeches," I laughed.

"You seriously drove into a pond?" Grady asked.

"No, I reversed into it. There's a difference," I corrected.

"Only when you're driving," Charlie grinned.

The GPS indicated for me to turn left into a plaza parking lot. I was a little confused until I saw that the small building at the end had a Sheriff's sign posted in front of it.

"Okay, the story is we are looking for someone in the area – no mention of Nicholas or kidnapping or anything else. We can't take a chance that the locals won't bungle it if they get involved, so we are following a guy and heard he was hiding out this way. Got it?"

Charlie and Grady both grinned and got out of the truck. I took a deep breath and followed them inside.

I watched the Sheriff saunter toward us in a slow manner.

"Grady, take the lead," I whispered before the Sheriff was within hearing distance.

"Hi there," Grady greeted the Sheriff offering out a hand to shake. "I was hoping you could help me out. My cousins and I are trying to track down my brother. He skipped out on his bail bond, and my mom put her house up as collateral. We heard he came out this way, and we want to drag his ass back up north. Any idea where he might hide? He would be paying with cash."

"And, what exactly did your brother do to get arrested?" the Sheriff asked.

"Bar fight," Charlie answered shaking her head. "No one was seriously injured, but there was a table, and a couple chairs broke. I still can't believe the dumbass ran."

Since they appeared to have the Sheriff handled, I moved over to an oversized map along the wall. It showed all the foot trails, nearby restaurants, campsites, and cabin rentals. I concentrated to attempt to memorize everywhere my eyes traveled.

Catching movement in my peripheral vision, I glanced over to the side of the room. A young deputy shook his head at the BS story that his boss was soaking up. The sheriff was recommending we check the campsites within the Ozark National Forest. The deputy looked at me with a raised eyebrow. I nodded toward the door, taking one last look at the map before I walked out.

A few minute later, the deputy walked around the building and met me on the other side of the SUV.

"So what the hell is really going on?" the deputy asked.

"If I tell you, are you going to be stupid enough to tell him?" I asked nodding back at the building.

"Hell no. He wouldn't believe me anyways. He still calls me City Slick," the deputy grumbled. "I grew up on a reservation."

"Well alright then. I used to be a cop in Miami. The other woman traveling with me is still a cop in Miami, but obviously out of her jurisdiction. The man with us is ex-military. We are tracking a man that fled the New Orleans area about two weeks ago. He'd want to stay somewhere remote. He'd also want plenty of exit routes to escape."

"Is he the type to hike and pull up a tent?"

"He can't. He has my eight-year-old son with him," I fully admitted. If this backfired, I might have to kidnap the deputy and cuff him somewhere.

"Holy shit. You're Kelsey Harrison." He turned back to look at the Sheriff's office building. "And, the other woman is the 'Other' Officer Harrison."

He was referring to the news story that ran when we took down Darrien Pasco's trafficking business. It aired on every major network for a whole three hours before other stories took its place in the ratings.

"Nice to meet you," I said offering my hand.

"It's a pleasure, ma'am. And, I'll be glad to help you as long as you don't tell the Sheriff."

"Deal. Can you meet us somewhere?"

"Head back East about ten minutes and meet me at the Canteen Bar and Grille," he said tucking his head and strolling back around the building as the Sheriff escorted Grady and Charlie out the front doors of the office.

Grady did the good-old-boy routine with the sheriff one final time, slapping him on the back and laughing a bit too loud, before turning to me and rolling his eyes. Charlie was hurrying beside him.

"What a waste of time," Grady complained getting in the backseat.

"Agreed," Charlie added, putting on her seatbelt.

I pulled out of the plaza parking lot, grinning. A few minutes later, I found the bar and parked in the mostly deserted parking lot.

"We're not desperate yet. No need to start drinking at noon," Charlie laughed.

"She must be hungry," Grady shrugged, getting out of the car.

Charlie got out and walked beside me toward the bar.

"No, she's not hungry. She's up to something," Charlie grinned.

I walked into the bar and selected a table near the back. The young deputy entered through the back door and unrolled a map.

"Okay, so the way I see it, your guy is most likely hiding in one of these three areas," he said, sitting down to point out the locations and explain his logic. He had good instincts and everything he was saying made sense. We followed closely along as he described the nearby roads and terrain.

The waitress came over, and I ordered four cokes. I handed her a fifty and told her if she forgot we were here then she could keep the change. She tucked the bill in her bra, and after she dropped off our drinks, I never saw her again.

"Fishing poles," I said looking at the deputy, but my mind was on the online purchases.

"Sorry, ma'am?" the deputy said.

"The man ordered fishing poles online. Do any of these locations have a nearby small lake, something private?"

The deputy rubbed his chin and looked back at his map.

"Well, this one has two ponds nearby that I know would have at least some decent crappie and bream fishing," he said pointing to the middle location on the map. "But, a lot a fisherman come and go, so I wouldn't think a kidnapper would use them." He continued to study the map, and I saw his eyes light up before he pointed to another location. "But this could be it. Old man Harker died a year or so ago. I heard his kid rents out the old cabin. That would be worth checking out. The property has a good size pond that is considered private because they own the property surrounding it."

"Show me how to get there," Charlie said, standing up and leaning over the deputy's shoulder.

The deputy blushed and took a deep breath before he explained the best route to take. Grady asked a few questions about coming in from the backside of the property by foot, and the deputy offered to drive him to the backside if we wanted to take the front. We all agreed it was a good strategy.

After using the little girl's room, I was crossing the parking lot to catch up with them, when my hands started to tremble. I briskly rubbed them together as I looked across the lot. My nerves were a jangled mess. All my sensors were running haywire from being so close to finding my son.

Thirty feet ahead of me, I saw Grady's body being flung backward. My brain slowly processed the familiar cracking noise of a far-off rifle. I ran straight ahead, ducking behind the SUV for cover. Pulling the keys from my pocket, I yelled for Grady to play dead. I didn't know where he was hit, but I sensed that he was alive.

I opened the back hatch of the SUV, pulling out flak jackets. Charlie helped the deputy secure his before securing her own and grabbing the binoculars to search the hillside across the highway. When my own jacket was secure, I pulled a rifle from the back.

Before I could stop him, the deputy darted out into the open space and attempted to drag Grady back.

Rifle loaded and ready, I peered around the SUV just as Charlie called out. "Thirty feet below the ridgeline, to your 2:00."

I found the mark just as the shooter's gun recoiled, sending off another round. I settled my sight, and fired.

The deputy, twenty feet away and still in the open, spun and fell to the asphalt.

"The shooter's down," Charlie confirmed.

I passed her the rifle and grabbed our med kit. I checked the deputy first, who was unconscious, but breathing. He had taken a hit to the arm. It wasn't a serious injury, so I wasn't sure why he was unconscious.

"I think he fainted," Grady chuckled.

I rolled my eyes and turned my attention to Grady. He was hit in the chest, bleeding heavily, but still alert.

"We need to move," he said as he tried to get up.

"Charlie will keep watch," I said, pushing him back and stripping his shirt open to see the injury.

I applied a pressure bandage to the front of the wound and reached behind him to feel for an exit wound. I sighed with relief, feeling the second bloody hole on his back. I opened another pressure bandage and secured it to the exit wound. It was the best I could do with the supplies that we had.

Grady reached up and cupped the side of my face. I looked at him for the first time and tears started to sting my eyes. He pulled me forward and briefly kissed me. It was sweet and comforting. He rubbed his thumb across my cheek before dropping his hand away.

I turned toward the sound of someone running toward us.

"I called the cops," the bartender yelled, as he stopped in front of us. "Sheriff should be here in ten minutes."

"We can't wait," Charlie answered him. "Which way to the hospital?"

"Take the highway East then South," the bartender answered.

Charlie retrieved the police cruiser from behind the bar and with the bartender's help, we quickly loaded Grady and the deputy into the car.

"I'll call the hospital and tell them you're coming," the bartender said before running back to the bar.

"Charlie—,"

"You don't have to convince me to split up," she said grabbing me in a quick hug. "Go get our boy. I'll get them to the hospital."

I ran to the SUV, gunning it out of the lot to the right as Charlie flew down the highway to the left.

Nola knew we were here. And, she would be going after Nicholas.

Chapter Nineteen

My pulse drummed so loudly in my head that I almost missed the turnoff to the South. I calmed my rapid thoughts, focusing on the road and the mental map of the area.

Two miles South, I turned left on a small road that was barely wider than a driveway. I remembered that only three houses resided on this long winding stretch. As I maneuvered around the tight curves that rose to higher elevations, I sped past the first two houses.

The third house was only another mile down the road, and it was the one that I was looking for. I looked up the hillside, hoping to catch a glance of the cabin, and for a moment my heart stopped beating. *Smoke.*

I took the last curve on two wheels, nearly careening over the side of the ridge before straightening out my approach and pulling into the driveway. I pulled my Glock and ran for the cabin that was already spitting flames from several windows.

The door was open. When I entered, I spotted a man's body on the floor near the kitchen, but he wasn't moving. I kicked away the gun in his hand and moved through the smoke-filled house, holding my breath.

The flames kicked up higher as I searched. The heat was intense as the dry wood around me flared to life. I quickly searched the bedrooms but found nothing. The backdoor of the house was open, and I stepped out to take a clean breath of air, before turning back into the inferno and finishing my search.

Other than the dead man, no one else was there. I dragged the man out of the house as a small fire truck pulled in with horns blaring and lights flashing. Two firefighters ran over and helped me drag the body further away from the flames before they ran back to fight the fire.

I searched the man's pockets and emptied them of their contents. Grabbing everything I found, I ran back to my car and tossed it in a heap on the passenger seat. I pulled out, kicking up gravel as I left, and drove away.

I remembered a secondary road led straight from the cabin to the highway. If I could catch up to Nola before she got to the interstate, I had a chance of stopping her.

Following the wider, more modern road, I drove like a maniac back to the main highway. Other than another fire truck heading to the fire, no one else was anywhere around. If Nola left with Nicholas this direction, I was already too late.

I pulled into a carpool lot beside the highway and got out of the car. I looked toward the East and then to the West. They could be anywhere. I didn't know where to go. Instinct told me that Nola would move West, toward the safety of city traffic, before she would turn South. But I had no way of finding her.

My cell phone rang, and I reached inside the SUV and retrieved it from the cup holder.

"Charlie called," Maggie said as soon as I answered. "I have agents from a satellite office on their way to the hospital to offer protection. Did you find Nicholas?"

"No. She executed a man and fled. I was too late."

I leaned over and grabbed the wallet from the passenger seat. Flipping it open, I closed my eyes as tears broke.

Larry.

The man's name was Larry.

According to the messages that Nicholas had left me in the book we found, Larry was the guard that had been hired to watch Nicholas over the years.

"Genie has a lead on a possible vehicle that Nola may have purchased. What do you want us to do?" Maggie asked.

"Sound the alarms. We have to find her. She killed Nicholas's guard. She's going to kill Nicholas," I gasped before dropping to my knees in the gravel parking area.

I leaned forward on my hands, barely having the strength to hold myself up as I threw up. The nauseous feeling only increased as the tears came and fear for my son's safety consumed me. *I did this. I put him in harm's way. I'm responsible.*

Eventually, I forced myself to roll to my backside and sit. I felt numb. I leaned against the SUV and wiped away the tears. They weren't going to do my son any good. It wasn't time to grieve yet.

Genie and Maggie would alert the entire State. The bikers would alert other clubs. Tech would alert Mickey's contacts.

I needed to get to the hospital to check on Grady and pick up Charlie, so we can hit the road and follow any leads that come in. I have to keep moving — for Nicholas's sake.

Plan in place, I forced myself off the ground and got back in the SUV.

Driving East, I was surprised at how quickly I reached the hospital. It was actually not that far from the cabin that Nicholas was being held in if you didn't have to drive all the way around the rocky and forested terrain. I could see the hint of smoke in the far-off distance against the clear blue skies. I parked and walked into the emergency waiting room.

My path was immediately cut off by the sheriff who proceeded to pull his gun on me and order me to get on the floor.

I don't have time for this shit.

Pulling his wrist downward, I spun under his arm, dragging his wrist with me until his arm was pinned behind his back. Before he could fight back, I snatched his gun, stuffing it into the back waistline of my jeans, and using his own cuffs, secured him to the metal support rail that ran along the hallway.

"Just remember that this is your own fault," I said as I pulled his keys from his utility belt.

Walking over to the nearby trashcan, I removed the clip from his gun and tossed both, along with his keys into the trash. I walked down the hall to the trauma area as everyone around me, including the sheriff, stood silently watching me walk away.

Charlie paced the hall ahead of me, biting her thumbnail.

"Stop biting your nails, Kid," I said.

She looked up at me, then past me, looking to see if anyone else was with me. I shook my head, no, and she closed her eyes, dropping her chin.

"I thought for sure he was there," she said.

"He had been. Someone must have tipped off Nola. Most likely that sniper I shot was one of her bodyguards, and he was ordered to kill us while she retrieved Nicholas," I said as I sat in a hallway chair. "Nicholas's guard was killed. Execution style."

"She's going to kill Nicholas now, isn't she?" Charlie whimpered.

I pulled her trembling body into the chair next to me and forced her head to my shoulder, wrapping my arms around her.

"I won't give up, Charlie. And, neither can you. Let's check on Grady, and then we'll go after her. We'll find her. But we have to hurry," I said, kissing the top of her head like I did when she was fourteen, and the boy down the block broke her heart.

She nodded and pulled away, trying to stop the tears. "I just—" she started to say as she stared past me down the hall.

I turned to look, and for the second time, my heart momentarily stopped.

I stood on shaky legs and walked toward the image that was approaching.

My hands shook. Tears resurfaced, clouding my vision.

I walked faster until I was running down the hall toward the main lobby.

"NICHOLAS!!!"

"Mom?" he answered while looking around to see where the voice had come from.

Spotting me, he froze for a moment.

"Mom!!" he yelled and ran into my arms.

I held him tight as I checked his face, his growing hands, and long legs to ensure he wasn't injured. I wiped his tears as I left mine unchecked and flowing at a steady pace. I couldn't speak as I listened to him rattle on questions: How did I find him? Was Larry dead? Did we get Nola?

Charlie sat on the hallway floor with her arms draped around both of us crying and kissing Nicholas's cheeks non-stop.

"Nicholas," I said, placing my hands gently on both sides of his face. "I am so sorry. I never meant for you to get hurt."

"I just want to go home. Can we? Am I safe?" Nicholas asked, leaning into my chest, clutching his arms tightly around me.

"You'll be safe. I promise," I vowed, kissing the top of his head. "Nicholas, how did you get here?"

"Nola showed up. She was really mad. She and Larry started fighting. Larry yelled for me to run. He hadn't locked the back door, and I ran into the woods. I followed a hiking trail down the side of the mountain. I heard a gunshot and just kept running. When I got to the bottom, I saw the hospital and ran here."

"Do you know what Nola was driving? If anyone was with her?"

Nicholas shook his head.

"Nola's still out there?" he asked as he gripped me tighter.

"Yes, but you're safe now," I assured him, rocking his small body back and forth in my arms.

"You have to go get her, mom. I'm not safe until you catch her," Nicholas cried as his body shook in my arms.

"I know," I cried, kissing the top of his head. "Your Aunt Charlie is going to take you to Texas where you'll be protected."

"Aren't you coming?" he asked, his lower lip trembling as he looked up at me.

"Not yet. But soon. I'll be there soon."

He stared up at me as I wiped his tears.

"You're going after Nola?"

"Yes," I nodded, kissing his hair.

"Mom, you have to kill her," Nicholas said, pulling away to face me.

The look in his eyes was years past his age. Haunted. Scared. Damaged.

I leaned over, so his face was inches away from mine. "I will do whatever I have to do, to make sure that Nola will never threaten you again. You have my word," I said, before kissing him on the cheek and pulling him in for another hug.

"Kelsey Harrison?" a young man in a dark suit asked.

A similarly dressed man stood next to him.

"Feds?" I asked from my place on the hallway floor.

They both nodded and showed me their badges.

"Any reason that you cuffed the sheriff to the support bar in the entrance?" the Agent smirked.

"He tried to arrest me for something I didn't do, and I didn't have the time to waste explaining it to him," I shrugged.

Nicholas giggled, and Charlie grinned.

The Agent nodded at his partner, who walked back to the entrance.

"I'm supposed to ensure everyone's safety. That would be easier if we move out of the hallway," he said as he offered a hand to help Charlie up.

I lifted Nicholas up in my arms as I stood.

"How's Grady?" I asked Charlie.

"I don't know yet. They haven't told me anything."

"Well, let's hunt him down."

I walked into several curtained areas, startling several patients before I found the one that held a pale Grady hooked to several machines that monitored his heart rate and oxygen levels. I set Nicholas down on the bed beside Grady, and while keeping one hand grounded to my son, I reached out and squeezed Grady's forearm.

He laid there staring at my son, who stared back at him.

"He was able to run away and found us here," I nodded, trying to blink back the tears that threatened again.

Grady pulled his arm up and reached for my hand, squeezing it tight.

"Nick, I am very glad to meet you," Grady grinned. "Your mom and Aunt have been looking everywhere for you."

"I know. I always knew they'd find me," Nicholas grinned back. "Who're you?"

"Hired muscle," Grady grinned.

I laughed and turned to Nicholas. "Grady is a really good friend that has been helping me fight the bad guys to find you. You can trust him."

"Are you sure?" Nicholas asked.

I couldn't blame him for doubting me. I trusted the wrong people in the past, and it had cost us his freedom.

"I'm sure," I nodded.

"Mitch and Maggie are boarding a plane, heading this way," Charlie said, walking into the curtained area, followed by the two agents. "There's a possible sighting of Nola about an hour Southwest of here. They have BOLO's out in all the surrounding States."

"What did the doctor say?" I asked Grady, looking up at his monitors to see that his pulse and oxygen levels were steady.

"That I got lucky," Grady grinned. "They're monitoring me for infection and internal bleeding, but so far, everything looks good."

I could tell he was in pain, but glad to see that he didn't appear to have any life-threatening injuries. I nodded, before turning back to Charlie.

"Call Wild Card. I want you and Nicholas to have a full escort into Texas. You're not to leave this hospital until he's escorting you both out."

Charlie nodded and stepped back out with the two agents in tow.

"You should go to Texas too," Grady said.

"I can't," I whispered looking back to face him. "I have to finish this."

He raised his hand and gently stroked my cheek.

"Nola's out of her league, babe. Go get her."

I leaned my face into his hand, placing my hand over his.

"Grady –," I started to say.

"Don't," Grady stopped me. "Tell me when it's over."

I wasn't sure what I intended to say, so I was more than willing to put it off. I cared for Grady. But, I also cared for Bones. Thankfully, Grady understood that it wasn't the time to figure it all out. I leaned over, kissing him briefly, before picking up my son and walking out of the trauma area.

Chapter Twenty

Leaving Nicholas nearly broke my heart, but I didn't have a choice. He needed to be safe, and the only way for that to happen was if I tracked down Nola. She was already an hour ahead of me. I couldn't wait any longer.

We said our goodbyes in a quiet waiting room. Nicholas held me so tight I wasn't sure if I was going to be able to leave him. But then he pulled back, and with wisdom beyond his years he moved away from me and clung to Charlie.

"Go find Nola, Mom," he said, as he buried his head in her shoulder.

I watched my hand tremor as I reached out and stroked his hair back one last time.

"Charlie," I started to say.

"I know. I won't leave his side until it's over," she nodded, tears streaming down her cheeks.

I walked out of the small room, past the Feds, past the doctors and nurses, past the angry Sheriff and out the hospital doors. I never looked back.

More sightings of Nola were called in, but no one was able to corner or confirm the leads as I traveled South back toward Louisiana.

I turned off the highway just inside the Louisiana border in the city of Shreveport and drove around for a few hours scouting for any visible signs of her. If she was alone, she would pick a city like Shreveport to hide for a few days, knowing that I would call out a BOLO alert.

Unfortunately, the reason she liked to pick large cities, was the same reason that driving around looking for her wasn't going to lead anywhere. There were just too many places for her to hide.

I picked an average quality hotel and booked a room. The long, emotional day and the lack of sleep that had accompanied my life for almost three years were catching up to me. I felt drained.

I threw my overnight bag on top of the dresser and walked out onto the balcony that overlooked a portion of the city. Nola was out there somewhere. I could feel it. But what could I do about it?

Stepping back inside the room, I retrieved my phone to call Genie.

"And, how is my favorite copper doing?" Genie answered.

"Ecstatic that my son is safe and thoroughly disgusted that I can't be with him," I sighed. "Anything new on the credit cards?"

"No. The last charge was late yesterday afternoon."

"Yesterday? That's too convenient to be coincidence," I said, walking back out onto the balcony. "And, when you add in that Nola knew we were close to finding Nicholas, red flags are flying."

"You think she has someone spying on us?"

"Yes. Let Tech know to check out everyone that's been within earshot. It could be someone with the Demon Slayers. It wouldn't be the first time that Nola planted a mole in a biker club. She could've been using them for one of her other businesses, and it just worked in her favor."

"I'll help run through the backgrounds. Anything else?"

"Send word for Bones to keep hitting New Orleans for information. I think Nola will turn up there eventually, and we need to know her hiding spots. It might be a few days before I get there, but I'll check in."

"Where are you?"

"Shreveport. She knows the roadways are being watched. If she came this way, then this would be the perfect place to hide."

"Those Spidey senses everyone tells me about are tingling, aren't they?" Genie giggled.

"More like humming," I smirked. "I don't know—I just think she's here. I just don't know where to start looking for her."

"Then start with hotels. According to the credit card charges, Nola's not going to stay in anything less than a 4-star. She has to sleep somewhere. I'll send a list to your phone."

"Thanks, Genie. It beats driving around blindly for the next few hours."

I showered and put on clothes that didn't smell like burnt-house. With most of the hotels within walking distance, I chose comfortable shoes, pulled my shoulder bag over my head and set out down the block.

The fresh air helped to keep me going for several hours as I stopped at every hotel, casino, and bar along the way and flashed Nola's picture. By two in the morning, I called it quits and walked back to my own hotel.

The bar inside my hotel was already closed. I asked the man at the front desk if he recognized Nola's picture. He didn't, but he had just started his shift an hour ago. I was kicking myself that I hadn't asked the day clerk before going to all the other hotels.

Back in my room, I slipped out of my jeans and bra and slept in my shirt and underwear. I was too tired to change into anything else.

I woke with a start, as the sun beamed in through the balcony window. I looked at the clock and was shocked to find that it was almost noon. I couldn't remember the last time I slept more than six hours, and I had somehow managed to sleep ten hours.

I started the oh-so-mini coffee pot and pushed myself through the shower. Twenty minutes later, wearing my last set of clean clothes, I stepped inside the small hotel restaurant. I ordered a coffee, breakfast, and a to-go coffee. Hopefully, the caffeine and food would spark a few brain cells to start firing.

I could stay and look for Nola another day in Shreveport, or I could drive south to New Orleans. I was still trying to decide when my phone rang.

"Hey, Tech," I answered.

"I got nothing," Tech sighed. "Genie and I ran backgrounds on anyone and everyone. We couldn't find any link to Nola."

"Shit. Well, we know someone's talking. We'll have to keep information close to our vests until we figure out where the leak is."

"Will do. Genie said you were searching Shreveport. James should be at your hotel any minute. Don't be mad. No man left behind and all…"

"I'm not mad," I sighed. "Thanks. It might be a waste of time though. I can't decide if I'm staying or going yet."

"Well, no matter which direction you go, you'll have someone with you that can drive in reverse," Tech chuckled.

"Ass," I laughed.

I saw James walk through the front door of the hotel. I stood, waving him over.

"James is here. I'll call you later."

I disconnected as James settled into the booth seat across from me, tossing an overnight bag next to him.

"What? No bitching about me driving up here?" James grinned.

"No, I could use the help."

"Bones wanted to come, but I told him his orders were clear to keep banging down doors in New Orleans. I didn't have any orders, so I was free to do as I pleased."

"They find anything yet?"

"Lots of people recognize Nola's photo, but they haven't found any leads to follow."

I nodded looking around the room again.

"You waiting for someone?"

"No," I shook my head.

I drank more of my coffee and finished my breakfast as the waitress brought James' breakfast over.

"What's the plan?"

"Eat your breakfast. I'll be right back," I said getting up and walking back out to the lobby.

The young girl that checked me in the evening before was already back on shift manning the front desk.

"Good Afternoon, Ms. Harrison," she greeted me.

"Hi. I was wondering if you recognize this woman?" I asked showing her a picture of Nola.

"Sorry. She doesn't look familiar," she shook her head.

"That's fine. If you see her, can you call me?" I wrote my number and slid it across the counter to her. "And, I have an email that I need printed."

She helped me figure out how to forward the email from my phone and then she printed and handed me the pages.

"Thanks," I grinned and passed her a healthy tip for assisting me.

"The printout," — she looked around to make sure no one else was watching — "it's a list of hotels. Are you checking them for that woman?"

"Yes. She's wanted by the FBI. I believe she's hiding in Shreveport."

"I know a lot of hotel employees. Let me scan the picture and send it to some of my friends. I can give them your number, and if anyone spots her, they can call you."

I handed her the photo, and she scanned it from the copier before handing it back to me. I passed her a hundred-dollar bill.

"No, that's not necessary," she insisted.

"When you send that message to your friends, let them know I'm willing to pay cash to anyone that can give me information to track her down," I said while folding her hand closed around the hundred-dollar bill.

"I'll get the information out within the next ten minutes. Every hotel in Shreveport will have staff watching for her by dinner time," she grinned.

I went back to the table and tossed down money to cover the bill, grabbed my bag and to-go coffee and started walking out. James downed more of his coffee before jogging past me to open the hotel door.

"I guess it's time to go then," he grinned.

"I just tapped into a golden network of spies. If Nola's in Shreveport, she's about to be flushed out."

My phone rang, and I passed my overnight bag off to James as I juggled to answer it and pull my keys out of my shoulder bag.

"Kelsey," I said while opening the back of my SUV.

"This is Kenny from the Casino. I just got a message with a photo of a woman you're looking for. She was at the Casino grill on the riverbank last night around nine. She ordered steak and wine, paid in cash, and stiffed me on the tip."

"Thanks, Kenny. Do you know if she had a room at the hotel?"

"I don't think so. She left out the restaurant's main doors instead of through the casino lobby. I didn't see where she went from there," he answered.

"You at work right now?"

"No. And don't worry about the reward money. I just wanted to stick it to the bitch for skipping the tip," he chuckled and hung up.

James threw my bag in the back of the SUV and closed it. I handed him the keys.

"Drive East over to the riverbank area. We need to go to the casino-hotel over there. Park in a low-key area," I said.

I dialed Maggie.

"I stayed in White Rock," she said answering the phone. "Grady left against doctor's orders and went to Texas with Mitch, Wild Card, Nicholas, and Charlie."

"He wasn't well enough to leave, but Pops will make sure he gets the care he needs. Why did you stay behind?"

"Damage control," Maggie chuckled. "You left behind a shot cop, a pissed off sheriff, a fire investigation and a state-wide manhunt."

"Oops. Sorry," I laughed. "You going to get me the proper documents typed up so I can just sign on the dotted line?"

"I've already handled it. What do you need now?"

"Access. I need to see the security footage at the Riverside Casino and Hotel in Shreveport. An eyewitness says Nola was at the restaurant last night. But being a casino, security isn't going to be too helpful to an everyday tourist."

"When will you be there?"

"About two minutes," I grinned, seeing the casino up ahead.

"Thanks for giving a girl some advance notice," Maggie sighed.

I could hear her eyes roll through the phone.

"I'll call right now. I'll have security meet you at the main lobby doors."

"No, can do. I don't want to spook Nola if she's around. I'll find the security office myself. Thanks, Maggie."

I hung up as James was parking the truck. Grabbing my shoulder bag, I climbed out of the SUV, and James followed beside me.

"You ever going to tell me what the plan is?"

"You kidding? I'm making this shit up as I go."

James laughed, opening the door to the casino for me.

Chapter Twenty-One

The casino was packed. I kept my eye out for Nola as I followed the outside wall around until I found an executive hallway. Halfway down the hall, a security keypad was mounted next to an unmarked door. I entered 1598 into the keypad, and the light turned green. I laughed and walked through the door and down the hall. I opened the next door, and three men stood staring at me with hands on hips.

"How did you get a security code to get back here?" the man in charge asked.

"I didn't. Whoever uses that code needs their ass kicked," I answered, removing my shoulder bag and tossing it in a nearby empty chair. "Did Agent O'Donnell call?"

He still looked pissed but turned to one of the techs and tapped him on the shoulder. "Yeah. We have the security footage of the restaurant from last night pulled up. Do you know what time she was in?"

"Around nine," I said walking up to watch the footage on the TV screen as it was fast forwarded. "Stop, that's her."

"She entered the restaurant through the casino," James commented.

"Can you follow her backward? I already know she left through the main exit of the restaurant after dinner," I asked.

The computer guy nodded and backtracked her through the casino to the casino bar. Prior to that, she wandered the casino floor for a while, and prior to that, she had entered from the main West entrance.

"Hang on, let me switch to the parking lot footage," the computer guy said, pulling up another video on the next TV screen.

"What's this woman wanted for, anyway? And, why would the FBI be working with a civilian?" the head security guy asked.

"She's wanted for murder, human trafficking, and kidnapping. And, up until yesterday, she had possession of my son. The FBI is working with me because I'm the best chance of finding the bitch and bringing her down," I answered, distracted as the video kept switching to different feeds to follow her.

"That's as good as it gets," the computer guy sighed. "She crossed the street from the West."

"Can you see if she left the same direction after she ate dinner?"

"Sure."

A few minutes later saw in the other video that she left in the same direction that she had arrived from.

"Okay, then. If you guys spot her in here again, give me a call," I said, grabbing my shoulder bag.

"The passcode," the head security guy sighed. "Why should I have my ass kicked?"

I laughed as I turned to face him.

"Most people that have to use code numbers all the time, use numbers that follow some type of pattern on the keypad. 1598 is the most common as it goes diagonally downward and then back one digit. I recommend you switch to a swipe card system."

"Let me guess," James chuckled beside me as we walked down the hall. "You use that code number a lot."

"For just about everything," I grinned.

We both stayed alert as we followed Nola's path from the surveillance video. Looking down the street, a line of hotels and motels filled the next three blocks. She could be anywhere.

"We need to split up. You take every other hotel until we get to the end," I instructed James, handing him an extra photo of Nola. "Either one of us spots her, and we call the other before we do anything."

"Sounds good, just don't get too far ahead of me."

"Then be thorough, but efficient. I recommend you ask in the bars and cafes first, and end at the service counter. The wait staff is usually more talkative."

James nodded and left for the next hotel.

We worked the hotels in tandem down three blocks before I stopped to have a cigarette and James joined me ten minutes later.

"Most of the people I talked to already had a text picture of Nola and your number," James said, lighting up.

"Same here. The girl at our hotel deserved more than a hundred dollars for getting the word out."

James nodded and rubbed his neck as he looked back toward the casino, scrunching his forehead up in concentration.

"What?"

"Huh?" he said, turning back to me.

"What are you looking at?"

"Well, isn't this Nola woman kind of a snobby type? Thinks highly of herself?" James asked.

"Sure. She grew up blue collar, but got into crime for the money and power."

"So why would she walk this far? The snobby bitches I know would never walk three city blocks from one hotel to another."

I looked back the way we came and thought about it. He was right. Nola wouldn't walk that far unless she thought someone was following her. I put out my cigarette and started backtracking.

"I got something right, didn't I?" James grinned beside me as we hurried down the block.

"Yup, you're right. She wouldn't have walked this far. She would, however, have known there was a chance that she was spotted at the casino and would know that they're heavy on security. I'm betting she walked this way before going the other direction to a hotel on the other side of the casino."

"Damn. That's smart."

We returned to the first hotel closest to the casino. We walked inside, went to the back of the lobby and followed several hallways until we came to a private exit into the back parking lot.

Following the walkway, we walked another forty feet — And then I saw it.

An elegant three story hotel with a private entrance and private parking. It had Nola's name written all over it, and it was less than a block to the East.

My phone beeped indicating I had a text, and I handed the phone off to James as I scanned the area for the best approach.

"Some kid from the hotel up ahead—says Nola just left the pool area and is heading back up to her room."

"Can he get us in through a side door, so we don't have to use the main entrance?"

I waited while James texted back and forth with the kid.

"Come on. He's going to get us in through the service area. He had to tell a security guard, but the guard agreed to help."

James and I skirted the block, out of view from the hotel, and met the security guard and poolside waiter at a side entrance where they let us in.

"I'm not going to get in any legal trouble for this, am I?" the guard asked.

"No. My friends from the FBI will handle it if anything happens," I said slipping inside. "Do you know what room she's in?"

"She charged her lunch to room 302," the kid answered.

I pulled out three envelopes from my bag. "One for each of you. The third goes to a kid named Kenny who's a waiter at the casino restaurant. Make sure he gets his share."

James and I made our way to the closest elevators, and I pressed the three button. I checked my gun and turned the safety off. James did the same.

"You need to set aside your badass President-of-a-biker-club shit and stay behind me on this one. Nola's armed, and she'll shoot without warning."

"Unlike Bones, I believed Grady and Mitch when they said they'd follow your lead on any mission. I've no problem setting my male ego aside," James grinned.

The elevator doors opened, and I glanced down the hall before stepping out into the hallway. The numbers on the doors were in the 320's, and I followed the hallway as the numbers decreased.

As I turned to the left to move down the next hall, I spotted Nola stepping into the elevator at the end of the corridor. When she turned to push the interior button, she saw us and pulled her gun, jumping to the side. Neither of us had time to fire before the doors closed.

Running down the hall, I propelled myself through the stairway entrance.

"Shit," James yelled from behind me.

"That didn't go as I had it planned in my head," I yelled back as I danced down the stairs, two at a time.

I reached the bottom and threw open the door, startling several guests and a bellboy. I still had my gun in hand, and James, the oversized dangerous looking biker, blew in the lobby behind me.

I checked the elevator and the halls but didn't see Nola anywhere. The startled bellboy pointed down the hall.

"I got da'da'da' tex-t-t-t-t," he stuttered.

I didn't wait for more information but followed the direction he pointed down a side hall and out the exit door. Nola pulled out of the lot like a bat of hell, into the busy street.

"FUCK!" I yelled holstering my gun.

"We need to get out of here," James said, pulling me along after him across the parking lot. "We can call Maggie and give her an update, but I'm sure someone called the cops, and unless you want to be delayed for several hours, we better book ass and move."

We circled around the block but didn't spot Nola. My guess was that Nola would leave Shreveport. From here, she could go anywhere

I drove us back to the first hotel. Swinging inside, I was pleased to see the young woman that had started the network of scouts throughout the city was still working.

"Did you find her?" she asked looking hopeful.

"We just missed her," I said shaking my head. "There's still a chance she'll stay another night, but I doubt it. Either way," — I pulled an envelope from my shoulder bag — "thanks for all the help. I really appreciate all the leads."

I handed her the envelope and left before she could protest. Each of the envelopes in my bag held a thousand dollars. I had spent a lot more than that over the years on professional investigators with far fewer results. It wasn't her fault that I wasn't prepared and let Nola get away. I should have called for backup.

Chapter Twenty-Two

Because of James' insistence that it was safer, we relocated to a different hotel. We met up in the hotel bar to eat, drink a beer, and think. I barely tasted my beer or dinner as my brain ran through the various directions that Nola could have moved. I really hoped I could track her down before she returned to New Orleans. She would have the home-turf advantage there.

"Damn it," I growled, dragging my hands through my hair and resting my forehead on the bar table.

"Sorry. I'm not so good at the take charge and lead the way part like Bones. Nor the 'you'll figure it out' like Grady," James admitted taking a drink of his beer.

"So if you can admit that you're not the take-charge type, how did you end up as the President of the Devil's Players?" I laughed, appreciating the distraction.

"Please. Everyone knows Bones is in charge. We just pretend," James grinned.

I ordered a cocktail and James another beer as we laughed.

"So what do you need right now? A verbal kick in the ass from Bones or reassurance from Grady?" James asked holding up my cell phone.

"Both?" I shrugged. "There's no winning by answering that question."

"We aren't talking about the happily-ever-after shit. It's not about them right now. It's about you finding Nola. Who can help you figure that out and put that in perspective, right here, right now?"

I grabbed my phone out of his hand and called Grady.

"So, you're alive," Grady answered.

I could hear his smile across the phone.

"I am. Unfortunately, I spooked Nola," I sighed. "How are you feeling?"

"Good enough to talk on the phone and help you figure out your next move. Just feeling guilty that I'm not out there with you."

"You've nothing to feel guilty about. Besides, James is making a pretty good sidekick. It was his ideas that got us close to Nola. Unfortunately, we arrived just as she was leaving."

"You think she'll make a move to New Orleans now?"

"No, not yet. She'll know that the roads are being watched. She'll wait until everyone gets discouraged and leaves their posts."

"So where is she going?"

"I have no clue. I'm missing something," I admitted, taking a drink of my cocktail.

"Are you safe tonight?"

"Yeah. We still have a network of scouts watching Shreveport, but I'd put money on Nola having already split town."

"Then relax, have a few drinks, get some sleep, and when you're least expecting it, the missing piece will fall into place."

"I already started working on that plan," I laughed. "We're in the bar at our hotel."

"Good girl. Nicholas is a great kid by the way. Charlie, Nicholas and I are staying with Reggie and Jackson. Wild Card and Pops set up extra security. He's protected."

"Thanks. We have a mole somewhere. Since I don't know who it is, I don't know how much they know. Warn the others for me."

"That's not good," Grady sighed.

"No, but I'll figure it out. Until I do, I need everyone to be extra careful."

"You're riding her heels, babe. You'll get her. Just stay objective and keep your eyes open."

"Yes, Sir," I grinned.

"Call me anytime, I mean it," he said before hanging up.

I smiled, looking at my phone.

"And what did Grady have to say about this mess?" James grinned.

"My instructions are to eat, sleep, drink, and worry about the rest tomorrow," I grinned back at James, holding up my empty glass to the waitress.

"Sounds like my favorite plan yet," James chuckled holding up his beer bottle.

"Excuse me, sorry, but my shift is almost over. Is it okay if I cash you out? You can start a new tab with the next waitress," the waitress asked.

"Sure," I said pulling a card out. "This is going to sound weird, but are you available to run out and do some shopping for me? I'm a really good tipper," I said pulling a pile of cash out of my purse.

"I don't have any plans," she grinned.

I wrote a list of clothes and sizes that I needed and included swimsuits for both James and I. I handed her the list, and she returned an hour later with everything I asked for and was pleased with the generous tip I gave her.

"You up for a swim?" I asked James.

"No," James chuckled. "But I'm all for sitting in the hot tub while you do stress-laps in the pool."

I threw some money on the table to cover our second tab. James grabbed the shopping bags, and we went back to our adjoining rooms and changed into the new swimwear. My suit was a bit more revealing than what I would normally wear, but since I never planned on returning to Shreveport, I decided not to worry about it.

Fifty laps in the pool later, my muscles finally relaxed, and I felt a bit more like myself. I heard the click of a camera and turned to see James take a picture with his phone of me wringing the water out of my hair.

"And, what exactly are you going to do with that picture?" I laughed.

"Haven't decided yet. Maybe I'll keep it for myself. Maybe I'll share it with either Bones or Grady," James grinned. "It's a good thing you established the friend boundary shortly after we met. Otherwise, I'd be all over you in that swimsuit."

I stepped into the hot tub and took a seat on the other side.

"It's a bit much, isn't it," I laughed. "I'm kind of scared to see what the rest of the clothes look like."

"I'm looking forward to seeing what she bought," James laughed.

"Behave," I said reaching over and smacking him on the shoulder.

"So? Who should I send the picture to?"

"No one. Everyone has more important things to concentrate on."

"And, we all need our mental breaks," James chuckled, pushing buttons on his phone.

I heard a beep and rolled my eyes.

"So who did you send it too?"

"I'm not telling," he laughed getting out of the hot tub. "Time for bed. It's getting late, and I know you'll be up with the birds, demanding coffee."

We both toweled off, and when his phone chirped, I tried to grab it before him, but I was too far away. He laughed at whatever he read on the screen and turned the phone off.

Chapter Twenty-Three

As predicted, I woke at sunrise and started up the customary one-cup coffee pot before jumping in the shower. Still wrapped in a towel, I walked out of the bathroom and dumped the bags of new clothes onto the bed.

I was pleasantly surprised by the selection. I picked out a black bra and panty set, followed by tight boot cut jeans and a New Orleans VooDoo t-shirt that was long in length, form-fitted in the torso, and offered a low v-neck. I grinned at my reflection as I pulled on my boots and checked my knives.

I wouldn't be able to wear my gun with the t-shirt, but it would be in my shoulder bag, so I was content.

James walked through the adjoining door after one quick knock.

"Glad I was dressed."

"Not me."

I finished off my one-cup of coffee and turned to gather my bags. James being a gentleman, took them for me.

"What the hell is New Orleans VooDoo?" he asked.

"Arena football. Like most of the teams, they don't exist anymore. The sport didn't get the coverage it deserved."

"You like sports?" James laughed as we entered the elevator.

"Just Hockey and Arena Football—Full contact sports with temperature-controlled stadiums," I grinned.

"Learn something new every day," James said shaking his head and pressing the first-floor button.

James took our bags out to the SUV as I commandeered us a table in the restaurant and ordered us coffee. I was on my second cup when he walked back in, ending a phone call and joining me.

"Everything alright?" I asked, nodding to his phone.

"Yes," James grinned. "Someone wanted to make sure I behaved last night."

"Which someone?"

"The same someone that got the picture of you in that skimpy swimsuit."

Knowing that James wasn't going to tell me, I ignored him and got the waiter's attention. We ordered breakfast, and the waiter topped off my coffee again.

"You better slow down on the coffee. Even for you that's a lot of caffeine."

"Worry about your own addictions."

"So, your mind is spinning this morning, aye?"

"A bit."

"Talk it out with me."

"The damn mole. Tech and Genie couldn't figure out anyone connected to this mess. I was guessing it was one of the Demon Slayers that overheard something, but Tech said they all checked out."

"I doubt it was them, anyway. Other than Nightcrawler, we've been pretty tight lipped. Their club has provided the house and some security, but they don't know who's doing what and where. We kept them out of it intentionally after Tyler reminded us how easy it was for Sam to spy on you."

"I knew I liked Tyler," I grinned.

"He's learning from the master," James grinned.

"I'm going to assume you meant me," I laughed as the waiter set our food down.

"I actually did," James chuckled. "Bones might be teaching him to fight, but you're the role model that Tyler looks up to. You've kept us alive way too many times for him not to respect you."

"He just needed to learn to trust his gut. Soon, Donovan will be poaching him for security jobs left and right."

We were almost done eating when my phone rang. I wiped my mouth and pulled it from the side pocket of my shoulder bag. It was Dave, my friend and local cop back in Michigan.

"Dave, what's wrong?" I asked.

Dave wouldn't be calling me on the burner phone unless it was something serious. Both him and Steve had the number for emergencies only.

"I have bad news. There was a fire last night," Dave said.

"Was anyone hurt?"

"No, everyone's safe. The Fire Marshall just did an official walk through."

"What's the loss?"

"The store. The main store will need a complete rebuild, and the new additions have a lot of damage. I'm sorry Kelsey."

"It's not your fault," I assured him. "Nola must've left someone in the area to watch us. Work with both clubs to see if you can track down any leads."

"We're on it," Dave said. "We all split up last night and started rooting out the cheap motel guests and running alibis. Not everything going on was completely legal, but Steve and I disappeared when the clubs got a bit vigilante."

"James is with me. I'll see if he can get the clubs a little more organized. Keep me informed if you find anything."

Dave apologized again, and we disconnected.

"What happened?"

"Everybody's okay," I said, nodding to myself.

"Then what happened? Why do you look like you want to cry but are trying to convince yourself not to?"

"The store was set on fire last night."

"Shit. Kelsey—,"

"Don't," I said stopping him. "Everyone is safe. It's just buildings. Drywall, cement, and lumber. Everything is replaceable." I got up and walked out of the restaurant.

James followed me out a few minute later carrying two to-go coffees. He handed me one of the coffees as I smoked a cigarette.

"I called home. Goat and Renato are running down every lead they can find. They'll call me if they find out anything."

I nodded but didn't say anything.

"Why would Nola do this?"

"Punishment. I saved Nicholas. I moved my family somewhere safe. I'm chasing her and have been close to catching her. She wants me to think that she still holds the power to control my life."

"And, is it working?"

"Hell no. She could've easily left some scumbag behind when she was in Michigan and called in the order to torch the buildings. What I can't piece together is how she knew we were on to her and had enough warning to get to Arkansas before me. She even quit using the charge cards soon after I found out about them."

"So that's your lead. Who knew about the charge cards?"

"Everyone in our circle."

"I didn't. I knew you had a lead that took you South to Louisiana and then North to Arkansas, but I didn't know why. I don't think Tyler did either."

"Alright, well, I figured it out when we were still in Michigan. Pops, Wild Card, Bones, Charlie, Tech, Sara, Katie—they were all there."

"Well, we know it's not them. Who else?"

"I kept Maggie in the loop, and Genie did a lot of the research to track the charges down. Carl helped with researching some of the online purchases."

"I feel good it's not them," James said shaking his head. "What about this Eric guy?"

"No way. He would protect Charlie or me without question. And, he didn't know about the credit card charges. He only knew that I expected that Nola was in New Orleans."

"If he's such a good friend, why didn't you tell him about the credit cards?"

"That's not how it works with Eric," I shrugged. "He doesn't ask any of the details unless it affects him directly. Otherwise, he just goes along with whatever my most current scheme is."

"So, he's Reggie the second," James grinned. "Okay, who else did you talk to?"

"I don't know!"

I lit another cigarette, pacing back and forth.

"Slow it down, when did you first realize that something was going on with the credit cards?"

"I was sorting the mail. There were solicitations to a company I own that should've never been associated with my home address. I called," — I turned to James, dropping my cigarette — "I called my corporate attorney!"

"Now we're getting somewhere," James grinned and called Tech on speaker phone.

"Yo, Prez. What's up?" Tech answered.

"You're on speaker," James said. "We need some research done."

"Hang on," Tech said, and a beep followed. "You're on speaker here too. Genie relocated to join us in Biloxi, so she's here with us."

"My lawyer, Ethan Goveir. He lives in Atlanta, Georgia. He's been my lawyer for almost a decade."

"The guy that Charlie slept with that she calls Grover?" Tech asked.

"That's the one," I sighed. "I actually don't know him that well. I've only been in the same room with him a half dozen times in the last ten years."

"Bank accounts are skeleton thin," Genie called out. "No prior criminal history, and his license is up to date."

"Divorced three years ago, pays child support and alimony according to his social media bitching," Tech sighed.

"Phone calls to an unlisted number started back in August," Carl spoke up.

"Carl, how in the hell did you get online again?" Tech grumbled.

"Carl—what phone calls?" I interrupted.

"Don't know," Carl said.

"Hang on, Kelsey," Genie called out.

We could hear what sounded like a room full of clacking going on over the speaker phone before they all stopped at once.

"It's him," Tech said.

"How do you know?"

"The phone calls are from New Orleans and started a week before the extortion of your club," Genie said. "And, Ethan's teenage daughter disappeared a few days later. She was reported found two weeks after that, but the family wouldn't say where she had been."

"The mother and both daughters moved to California right after the incident. Ethan didn't contest the move even though it violated their custody agreement," Tech added.

"Ethan wouldn't trust that Nola couldn't get to his daughters again. He'd keep cooperating with Nola to keep them safe," I said.

"How do you know this guy isn't intentionally working against you?" James asked.

"I don't know. Maybe it's just wishful thinking that I didn't trust the wrong person with access to half a billion dollars, but I've never even noticed a single penny out of place," I shrugged. "I'm on his side unless someone can convince me otherwise."

"I'm not a profiler, but this guy did community volunteer work and is active in his church. I'm sharing Kelsey's belief that he's only doing what he has to do," Genie added.

"I can't find any other dirt, but I can keep digging," Tech said.

"No, we have bigger problems. He knew about Mayfair Shipping. He didn't have all the details, but he knew that I was using Mayfair for information. We don't know if he shared that intel. Genie, call Kierson and see if he can have Ethan picked up and questioned."

"We'll take care of it," Genie said.

"Kelsey, did you seriously say a half a *billion* dollars?" Tech asked.

"Bye, Tech," I said, disconnecting the call.

I turned to James and grinned. "You make one hell of a partner, James."

"I can't take the credit. I've watched how Grady and Charlie coax out that brain of yours. I'm just mimicking what works for them," he grinned.

"I've known you for almost a year, and I've only known Grady for a couple of weeks," I shook my head. "We barely know each other."

"And yet, he's the one that you chose to call to help you get your head on straight last night," James said. "So, are we driving to Atlanta?"

"No. Let's get to New Orleans," I said as I gathered my shoulder bag and coffee.

Chapter Twenty-Four

We arrived in New Orleans quicker than expected and drove to the marina. I texted Eric, and while we waited, James and I bought some tacos from a nearby vendor for lunch. I was licking my seasoned fingers when Eric arrived.

Reaching over for my napkin, Eric wiped my mouth and chuckled.

"They're really good tacos," I giggled.

"I know," he grinned. "I had them yesterday while I was waiting around for your band of mercenaries."

"Problem?" I asked with a raised eyebrow. I continued to use multiple napkins to finish cleaning the grease off my hands.

"Nope," Eric said sliding his sunglasses on. "I just would have done it a bit different. I don't think threatening the locals is the best approach."

"I kind of gave them free reign. I had planned on leading the search, but then plans changed."

"Where were you anyway?"

"Nobody told you?"

I was shocked that Eric didn't seem to know anything.

"You and Charlie left, that's all I know. I'm an outsider to your new friends, remember?"

"I'll fix that. But, the most important thing to update you on is that we got Nicholas back," I grinned.

"What? Oh, Kelsey, that's amazing," he laughed and picked me up from my stool and twirled me around. "Where is he? Where's Charlie?"

"Safe. He's with Charlie. Until Nola's caught," I said shaking my head.

"We'll find her," Eric grinned and kissed the top of my head. "I'm so proud of you."

"I'm just so happy he's safe," I grinned, tearing up.

"Me too. Now let's go," Eric laughed. "There's someone I want you to meet."

Eric threw an arm around me and led us up into the heart of New Orleans. I introduced James to Eric along the way, and they chatted a bit about Bones and his friends bullying the locals. From the sounds of it, Eric had been running around behind them and mending a few fences and building sources. James grinned and winked at me.

Eric led us into a small bar near the backside of the French Quarter. Both men had to duck under the short doorway. A handful of locals were scattered throughout the bar, and I selected a table over by the far wall. James ordered a round of beers.

"What are we doing here?" I asked as I sipped my beer.

"Waiting for Layla to start work," Eric said, looking around.

"A waitress?" James asked.

"No, a fortune teller," Eric smiled. "A smoking hot fortune teller."

"This is your big plan? Get our fortunes read?"

"No," Eric sighed. "But Layla agreed to reach out to some other locals and see if she could get a lead on where Nola hides when she's in town. She'll meet me before her shift starts."

The front door opened, and a leggy redhead with brilliant green eyes walked through the door. She looked around, spotted Eric and walked our way. She looked sad as she approached.

"Hey, Layla," Eric greeted her kissing her on the cheek and gently holding one of her hands in both of his.

"Eric," she smiled, but her eyes still held a look of pain as she stared up at him.

He rubbed a hand on her cheek and grinned down at her.

"Layla, this is my friend Kelsey and her friend, James. Kelsey's the friend I told you about. She found her son, but Nola Mason is still on the loose somewhere."

Layla pulled herself up onto a stool.

"I'm happy to hear you have your son. My heart bled when Eric told me what you and your family have been through."

"Thank you. Do you know anything that can help find Nola?"

"No, not yet. I did talk to a witch that said if you can get something personal of Nola's, she can do a tracking spell. But it has to be something that is important to her. Something she would think of often."

"A locator spell?" James chuckled. "Like in the movies?"

I elbowed James, *hard*, in the gut.

"I can't say I believe in magic, but I'd be willing to try anything at this point. But the only thing that is important to Nola is *me*," I said shaking my head.

Layla looked at me as if she was trying to puzzle something together.

"I need to touch you," Layla said.

"No," Eric said abruptly, getting off his stool and pulling Layla with him away from us.

Eric and Layla quietly argued several feet away from us.

"What the hell is going on?" James whispered, leaning toward me.

"I have no idea," I shook my head. "Eric's acting so protective. It's strange."

"Him being protective is not the strange part. Bringing us to a fortune teller who wants to touch you and who knows a witch that can do a locator spell—is the part that's a little too Stephen King for me."

"Eh," I shrugged. "To each their own."

Layla pushed past Eric and started setting up her fortune-telling table at the back of the bar. Several customers started lining up to wait for her services. Eric tossed some money down to cover our beers and walked out. James and I scrambled to catch up.

"What the hell, Eric?"

"It's fine. We can meet the witch tonight. Layla gave me the address. We have a few more places to stop," he said, as he dropped his sunglasses back to cover his eyes and led us through an alley and out into the nicer section of the French Quarter.

Eric introduced me to several other locals that worked in the Quarter and inquired if they had seen Nola. I gave them my number and thanked them for keeping an eye out.

I went inside a few high-end restaurants, peeling off some cash for the maîtres d's to call me if they saw Nola. And, at the end of the block, some kids were hanging out, looking to be up to no good. I gave them each a twenty and told them if they called me with information on Nola, I would pay a lot more. Several of them seemed interested in earning the bigger jackpot. One of them eyed my shoulder bag a bit too closely.

"We need to get back to the marina," Eric announced. "Your buddy and his thugs will be expecting a ride back to Biloxi."

"Wow. You really don't like them, do you?" I grinned.

"No."

Chapter Twenty-Five

Crossing the boardwalk, I spotted three men harassing a young prostitute. The men were backing her up closer to a brick wall near an alley. I veered off in their direction. I could sense James and Eric following behind me. Accessing the men, all three were well built, toned from working out regularly, closely shaved heads and thick necks. And, they had been drinking.

I pulled my shoulder bag and handed it back to James, before I stepped in front of the woman, blocking the men from her.

"You boys need to walk away," I said.

"Oh yeah? Well, I think that's none of your business, Bitch," the middle man laughed.

"I'm making it my business. And, you really don't want to see my bitch side. You're liable to need stitches."

"You threatening me?" the man asked, stepping forward again.

The aroma of stale beer and whiskey was strong enough to make me gag as he leaned into my face. He clicked the lever on a switchblade and the knife extended. He held it up toward me in a threatening manner.

I grinned back at the idiot.

"That was really fucking stupid," Eric laughed behind them.

As they turned toward Eric, I grabbed the man's wrist, wrenched it forward and slammed his forearm with enough force over my leg that I heard the bone crack. He screamed out in pain. Eric threw a punch at the guy closest to him, and I led with a right hook to the third guy.

Before I could continue my assault, a large arm reached past me and picked the third guy up by his neck and tossed him into the brick wall.

Bones stepped in front of me as all three men froze. The one on his knees, holding his arm, leaned away. Bones was furious.

I turned back to the prostitute who had squatted down and held her arms over her head to protect herself. Her body trembled in fear. She couldn't be more than 19 or 20 years old.

"Hey, you're alright," I assured her guiding her over to James. I nodded to him, and he walked off toward the docks with her.

"What the fuck, Bones?" one of the men asked.

"What the hell do you think you're doing?" Bones yelled.

"What you told us to do! Get information," the guy on the ground said. "We were talking to a call girl when this bitch interfered."

Bones picked him up by the neck and slammed him into the brick wall.

"That Bitch, is Kelsey Harrison, the one paying you. And, if she was pissed enough to break your arm, that means you did something that I might likely have killed you for," Bones sneered in his face.

"Chill, Bones," I called him off. "Fire their asses and let's move on. I have a date with a witch tonight and a million phone calls to make."

"What do you mean you have a date tonight?" Bones growled looking back at me while he still held the other guy by the throat.

"As in, she has an appointment, you, jealous control-freak," Eric barked before turning and stalking back to the boat.

James returned and stood there grinning at me. "I gave the hooker one of your envelopes and expressed our apologies. She'll call if she sees Nola."

"Thanks. Help Bones settle up the pay and get rid of anyone else that I'd take issue with. I'm going to help Eric get the boat ready to go," I said before walking toward the docks.

"You're not yourself," I said to Eric as I walked over the ramp and onto the boat.

"Yeah, well, it's been an interesting couple of days," he grumbled.

"What's going on Eric? You've dealt with plenty of assholes before. And, while I'm not happy that they were on my payroll, I'm more worried about whatever is eating at you."

"It's nothing. It doesn't have anything to do with you or those assholes Bones hired."

He pulled the lines from the front of the boat, and I walked back to pull the lines from the back. I kept sliding in my heeled boots. I wasn't quite dressed in sailor garb.

"So, does your unusual mood have anything to do with that Layla girl?" I yelled across the length of the boat. "And, why did you freak when she wanted to touch me? What was that all about?"

"No. And, nothing," he snapped in frustration. He threw the ropes that he was gathering into a pile and turned back to me. "Don't let her touch you, Kelsey."

"Why?"

"I don't believe in all that fortune crap, but some of the things she knew, some of the things she said, well…"

"Eric, what did she see?"

"It doesn't matter. It's just a bunch of BS to draw in the tourists. It's fine. I'm just tired," Eric said before turning to walk up to the captain's chair to man the controls.

James, Bones, and five other men I didn't recognize walked across the ramp and stepped onto the boat. They all moved over and claimed bench seats.

"See?" Eric yelled with his arms out gesturing to the guys.

I grinned and looked at James.

"Alright, let's work together here. James, grab the ramp and load it onto the boat. You two—," I pointed to the two men in question, "—pull the ropes from the sides and help manually guide us out. Bones, grab another guy and move up front to push us out into the main lane."

I took position near the port side and used a guide pole to help maneuver us out. Working together we were perpendicular to the slip and Eric engaged the motor to a forward idle before looking back to me for the all clear signal.

The signal given, he started us down the narrow channels that ran in a maze until we would reach open water. I gathered and tied up the guide ropes. Several of the men watched what I was doing and helped. I asked a few others to check the hull and make sure everything was secure and wouldn't be knocked around when we increased speed.

I looked across the water as Bones walked over to me. A Harbor police boat was pulling around the corner of another passageway, heading toward us.

"You and your boys armed?"

"Yes," Bones answered.

"In the hull, there is a pantry cabinet with a waste basket in the bottom. Pull the waste basket out and find the hidden latch under the shelf. Put the weapons in there," I said, sliding my hand into my shoulder bag and tucking my own gun into Bones' inside cut pocket.

Bones nodded and made the rounds, quickly collecting the guns and heading down to the hull just as the Harbor Police pulled us over.

Eric cut the engine back to an idle, and I walked over to the port side and threw the dock bumpers over the side. I pulled out a pair of sunglasses and slid them on before tossing a rope over to the approaching boat.

"Good Evening, Officers," I greeted them.

"Evening, ma'am," one of the officers greeted back. "Permission to come aboard?"

"Granted," I nodded.

Two of the officers climbed over the rails from their boat into ours before standing with hands on hips looking around.

"We weren't breaking any laws; so, can I ask what you're looking for?" I asked.

"You were going a bit too fast in the channel," one of the officers said.

"Not true. We were well under the wake rules," I said. "I was a cop myself for many years. The captain up there is a Sheriff from Florida. We know when another cop is fishing for something, so tell us what you're looking for, and we'll be glad to help."

"You were a cop?" the younger cop asked.

"In Miami," I nodded.

"What brings you to New Orleans?" the older officer asked.

"Part vacation and part looking for someone," I shrugged.

"Looking for who?" he asked, his eyes narrowing.

"Feel free to call the FBI and ask them that. At this time, I am not at liberty to say," I glared back.

Nothing stunk worse than a dirty cop, and this guy reeked of it. The other officer looked back and forth between him and me in confusion.

"Maybe I'll just do that," the older officer snapped.

"Good. Now if there's nothing else, we need to be going," I said.

"Are there any weapons on board?" he asked, ignoring my encouragement to leave.

"Why, heck no. That would be darn right illegal being we're not licensed to carry in Louisiana," I grinned.

"Place your bag on the deck and turn around," he ordered. "Officer Jenner—search the other passengers."

The older officer rested his hand on the handle of his gun, attempting to intimidate me.

I snorted before setting my bag on the floor and raising my hands as I turned my back to him. His pat-down search turned out to be more of a free grope. Jenner efficiently searched the other men, including going up to search Eric. They seemed to be having a friendly chat before the dirty cop called Jenner back down to watch us.

The dirty cop went down to search the hull. I heard him knocking things around, and I was getting nervous that he would try to plant evidence on us when he finally stormed back up the ladder and said it was time to leave.

After they stepped back onto their own boat, Jenner untied the ropes, tossing them back to me. I pushed us away, using the guide pole. I waved the all clear to Eric.

"What the hell was that all about?" James asked.

"Dirty cop," I glared across the water at the bastard in question.

"Shit," one of Bones' guys cussed beside me.

"James, call Tech. His name was Officer Parsons, badge number 552657. I want to know everything about this guy."

James nodded and stepped away.

"Really glad you had that hideaway built to hide the guns in, Babe," Bones grinned.

"I didn't build it. Lenny, the guy that owns the boat, is a smuggler," I said.

"The guy that was bitten by an alligator?" Bones asked.

"That's him."

"And neither you nor Eric, ever arrested him?"

"Lenny has really good weed," Eric answered for me, grinning.

I looked up and saw that one of Bones' guys was driving the boat. I looked back at Eric, and he nodded that he approved. He probably gave him a verbal test on waterway regulations before he relinquished his chair.

"Did Lenny leave us a present?" I grinned.

"Especially for you," Eric grinned. "I may have made a dent in the stash already, though." Eric looked around at the crowded narrow channels. "What did Harbor Patrol want?"

"I don't know yet. Be sure everyone is prepared from now on to be pulled over at any time."

"Sure thing," Eric nodded and moved down into the hull.

I finished tying the last rope off and looked around again. We were moving out to the open water, but we would be visible by other boats for another mile or so until we were further away from New Orleans. I walked over to the pull lever fire alarm and slid the unit up, opening an air tight compartment behind the alarm. I pulled the stash of weed and moved down into the hull.

"Hell, yes," James laughed following me.

Within minutes, everyone except the temporary captain and two of Bones' men playing lookout, were in the hull, and we had three joints being passed around. I hadn't smoked in years, so I was completely content after one hit.

I opened the small windows to move clouds of smoke out.

"So, how did that Lenny guy get bit by an alligator?" James asked.

"He went to his fishing shack after he drank a bit too much and walked off the path," Eric answered. "A gator bit him to protect its territory. Luckily, Lenny got away, but the scent drew in more gators."

"Yeah, Wild Card said you sent Kelsey up by herself to retrieve him. Mighty brave of you," Bones sneered.

"You're so clueless," Eric laughed.

"Don't start," I sighed. "James, were there any updates when you called in?"

"Sounded like a lot was going on, but they wanted to wait until you were back at the safe house," James said taking one last hit off the joint before stubbing it out.

I stood and gathered the buds and tossed them out the window.

"Hey, we could have still smoked those," James complained.

"Lenny keeps a healthy supply on his boats. Don't worry your pretty little head over the scraps," I said.

I pulled my phone out of my shoulder bag to check my messages. Unfortunately, my cell phone was dead. I wasn't sure how long ago my battery had died, so I borrowed James' phone to call and check my messages.

The first message was from Agent Kierson saying that they hadn't located my lawyer but that his office had been tossed. He wanted me to call him back.

The second message was from a casino dealer in Shreveport letting me know that he had seen Nola two nights ago at the casino. You're a little late, buddy.

The third, fourth, and fifth messages were from Maggie, telling me to call her.

The sixth message was from Dave, telling me that they found the guy that set fire to my store. I checked my watch. The message was left a half an hour ago.

Using James' phone, I called Dave back.

"Hey James, where's Kelsey?" Dave asked, answering the phone.

"Right here," I said. "My phone died. You found the guy?"

"Renato found the guy. He finally agreed to turn him over after he talked to him in private," Dave chuckled. "You were right. Nola hired him before she left town on her last visit. She called yesterday and gave the order to torch the store and houses, but he chickened out on the houses. He's told us everything he knows, but he didn't even have a phone number for Nola."

"I'll make sure Katie gets in touch with the insurance company. We'll figure the rest out later," I said. "On the bright side, I forgot to tell you this morning when you called that we found my son."

"Damn, Kelsey, that's good news. I'll be sure to tell everyone around here. They need some cheering up. Everyone feels bad about the fire," Dave said.

"They're just buildings. I feel worse about getting Grady shot than I do about the fire," I laughed.

"He's going to be alright, I assume," Dave chuckled.

"If he keeps his ass in bed, he should be fine," I grinned. "We'll see how long it takes him to land himself back in the hospital, though. I have to go, but I'll try to call again in a couple of days."

"Sounds good. Stay safe."

"Heard about the store. Sorry about that," Bones said.

"It's all replaceable," I shrugged.

"Grady really going to be okay?" Bones asked.

"He should be dead, but the bullet somehow blew through his chest and missed his lungs. He had a chipped rib," I said. "A fricken chipped rib!"

"Lucky son-of-a-bitch," one of the other guys laughed.

"I still can't believe someone got the drop on him," another guy shook his head.

"We both missed it. We'd just gathered the information about where Nicholas was being held, and we were getting ready to go after the bad guys and rescue Nicholas. I thought my senses were going haywire because we were so close to Nicholas. The next thing I knew, a rifle is cracking in the distance, and Grady was thrown on his back."

"Damn," Eric said shaking his head. "You must have been really keyed up to not pick up on a sniper."

"She can sense it?" one of Bones' guys asked, looking at Bones.

Bones shrugged, and Eric nodded.

"It's damn scary the way she picks up on that shit," Eric nodded. "She saved my ass from getting shot by a smuggler. I never even knew he was there."

"Another weed smuggler?" Bones grinned.

"No. Guns. Heavy artillery. She was working a case that led out into my jurisdiction. We were touring the swamps and landed right in the middle of a gun trade. Shit got real," Eric chuckled.

"They blew up our boat with a rocket launcher," I laughed, remembering the day well. "We had to bail into the water and start swimming. I was freaking out about leeches until Eric yelled that there was a gator behind us. I swam my ass off, blowing right past Eric."

"I'll bet," James laughed.

"It wasn't funny that she left me for gator bait," Eric fake glared at me.

"I shot the gator as soon as I pulled myself up onto the bank," I rolled my eyes.

"And, gave away our location to the smugglers."

"So, you would've rather been eaten by the gator? Besides, I got us out alive. And, we caught the bad guys. So, quit your bitching."

"Wait a minute," one of Bones' guys said. "Was this out by Whitewater bay about six years ago?"

"Sure was," Eric grinned.

"I read about that. That was insane! I didn't think the story was true because it was so farfetched."

"Hey, the medical examiner backed my story on the python killing that one guy. I didn't make that shit up," I laughed.

"You must've been scared out of your mind," Bones said, placing a hand on my knee.

I turned to look at him, thoroughly disappointed. Everyone was right. He really didn't know me at all. I got up and walked topside to get some fresh air.

We would be pulling into Biloxi soon, so I went up to the helm and offered to take over driving.

"You know, you marrying Wild Card, that kind of made sense. I didn't like it, but it made sense," Eric said stepping into the helm. "You and this Bones guy, I just don't get it, Kelsey."

"You don't have to approve," I said, keeping my eyes on the water ahead. "And, until this is all over, I'm not wasting my time and energy on figuring it out either."

"Now that sounds more like you," Eric said kissing my cheek before stepping back out. "Just don't become someone you're not, to make it work with him."

I pushed thoughts of Bones out of my head as I turned past the last reef and cut back the throttle. I turned on the lights as dusk was finally moving in and moved at the required snail's pace, past the lighthouse, and into the long narrow marina.

Chapter Twenty-Six

It was another twenty minutes before we arrived at the house in Biloxi. I looked at the clock and was discouraged to find that I only had an hour before I had to turn around and drive back to New Orleans for my meeting with the witch. *Wow—That sounded crazy even to me.*

"Hi, honey, I'm home," I called out as I led the troops inside.

Katie ran up to me, eyes swollen and nose red, throwing her arms around me.

"What's wrong, Katie?"

Tech came into the kitchen and leaned against the wall. "It's the store," he answered for her. "She's been a wreck all day."

"Katie, they're just buildings. We'll rebuild. I promise."

"What if you change your mind? What if you don't want to live in Michigan anymore?"

"I would still rebuild," I shrugged. "You, Alex, Lisa, and Anne love working at that store. So, I'd rebuild it for you guys."

"You'd do that?"

"Setting aside the fact that you guys make me a shit load of money, yes, I would do it because it makes you all happy. You're my family, silly," I grinned at her.

She wiped her eyes, and Tech slid the box of tissue across the table to her.

"Why do you smell like pot?" she asked.

"Don't answer that," Maggie laughed walking into the room. "I need to talk to you about your lawyer."

I tossed my duffle bag to Tech and turned to follow Maggie. Eric stopped me, reaching into my front pocket of my jeans and pulling out the small bag of weed.

"James, I think you should have this," Eric laughed.

James grinned and walked back outside with my confiscated goods.

I pouted as I ran to catch up with Maggie upstairs. Genie climbed the stairs behind me.

"Kierson hasn't been able to track your lawyer down yet. And, his office has been trashed. At first glance, all the files on your company are missing."

"Genie, see if there are any John Doe's from the last twenty-four hours that were either shot execution style or had their throat slashed. Maggie, call Kierson so I can talk to him."

Maggie called Kierson and handed me the phone.

"You still at Goveir's office?"

"Yeah. I've been here most of the day," Kierson said.

"Go over to the file cabinet and push the fake plant back a few inches. You'll have to force it, it's weighted," I instructed.

A few minutes later, Kierson started cussing. "I've been here all damn day, Kelsey!"

"Sorry—my phone died. And I was busy doing other things. Are my files there?"

"Yeah, he has boxes of files hidden in the wall. And, there's an envelope with your name on it," Kierson said.

"Can you get it all cleared to bring this way?"

"Shouldn't be an issue. But you can't keep any of it until it's been officially released."

"Technically, it's covered under attorney-client privilege," I reminded him. "So, let's keep playing nice in the sandbox, shall we?"

I disconnected and handed the phone back to Maggie. She snorted and tucked it in her pocket.

Genie stomped back up the stairs and glared at me. "Two phone calls, and I found the lawyer's dead body. Do you know how pissed Kierson will be when I call and tell him?"

"Pretty pissed, since I just hung up on him," I grinned.

"Text him," Maggie grinned.

Genie giggled and ran back down the stairs.

"We might not be able to figure out if Ethan told Nola about Mayfair Shipping," I said as I sat on the edge of one of the beds. "But you need to do the sting on Tuesday no matter what and hope for the best."

"Agreed. Any sign of Nola?"

"Not yet. If she has cargo moving on Tuesday, my bet is that she'll be close by."

"It's worth a shot. Carter was moved to another location but helped us sort out all the logs, including the ones going back and forth to Cuba. We have enough to put Ronald Mayfair away for life."

"And, another corrupt King falls," I grinned.

Maggie went back downstairs, but let me borrow her phone to call Texas. It wasn't until the fourth ring that Charlie finally answered.

"Yeah, what's up?" she rattled off, sounding distracted.

I heard Pops bark off orders in the background, something about picking up a chair before Nicholas was yelling back that he didn't have to. Charlie exhaled a huge breath.

"So, he's got some anger issues?" I asked.

"He's back and forth. One minute he's the sweet boy we know, and the next, he's throwing the dining room chair."

"Has he picked the chair up yet?"

"No," Charlie sighed.

"Put me on speaker, Charlie."

I heard a beep, and then Charlie announced I was on speaker phone.

"Nick, I know you're angry, but you will not take it out on everyone else. Please, pick up the chair and apologize."

It was silent on the other end of the phone until I heard a chair scraping across the floor followed by a meek whisper of an apology.

"Thank you. Now, why don't you ask Wild Card if he'll set up the punching bag for you tomorrow, so you can work out some of that anger? I'm sure he'd do it if you ask him nicely."

"Would you?" I heard Nicholas ask.

"No problem, buddy. I'll pick you up in the morning, and you can help me set it up," Wild Card answered.

"Nicholas, do you want to talk to your mom in private?" Charlie asked.

"No. She's supposed to be finding Nola," Nicholas snapped back.

I heard a door slam, followed by surround-sound 'sighing' throughout the room.

"Sorry, everybody. I'm trying to hurry," I said over the speakerphone.

"Don't you worry about it, Baby Girl," Pops called out. "You do what you have to do—we'll do the rest. And, we heard about the fire. I'm sorry."

"We can rebuild. It's fine. Just keep him safe. I have to go. Love to all," I said, hurriedly disconnecting.

I slid off the bed, onto the floor and cradled my head in my arms. In the last day and a half, I rescued my son, Grady was shot, my store was burned to the ground, and my son was going off the rails hundreds of miles away from me.

I needed all of this to be over.

James walked in and handed me my phone.

"As soon as Tech swapped out the battery, someone was calling for you," he grinned before walking back down the stairs.

"Kelsey," I answered, not looking at the display.

"He didn't mean it," Grady's voice soothed over the phone. "It's going to take him time to work through the anger. The punching bag was a good idea. Reggie's also going to teach him how to ride a horse, and Jackson said he would teach him how to rope."

"Jackson sucks at roping," I smiled.

"That's what Wild Card said," Grady chuckled.

"Grady, the videos that Nola said she was making him watch—," I started to ask.

"She lied. He told me he barely ever saw Nola, and she never brought videos to watch. Most of the time it was just him and one of Nola's goons. The guy took good care of him, though, from what we can tell."

"Thank you. I feel guilty enough being away from him right now, but that makes me feel better."

"He's in good hands, Kelsey. He's a great kid."

I took a few deep breaths, refocusing my thoughts. "How are you feeling?"

"Sore and tired. But I'll be fine."

"I'm sorry I got you shot."

Grady snorted. "When all this is over, you can buy me a drink to make up for it."

"Deal," I grinned.

"So catch me up. What have I missed?"

"Well, the mole was my attorney, Ethan Goveir, but he's dead. After losing Nola in Shreveport, I haven't had any tips to find her, but if Ethan didn't give up the Tuesday shipment details, we might get lucky and find her there. Either way, I think she'll move back to New Orleans. Then there's a dirty cop with the Harbor Police, but I'm not sure what that's all about yet. And, I have an appointment with a witch to do a tracking spell, so that should be interesting. I think that's about it. Oh, and I smoked some killer weed on the way home tonight."

"I'm jealous now," Grady chuckled. "And, the witch thing sounds like fun too."

"We shall see."

"What else?"

"My friend Eric is here. He seems upset about something, but won't tell me what. Maybe it's just all the crap he's had to put up with from Bones and the men Bones' hired. Hell, I broke one guy's arm less than a minute after meeting him, so Eric's probably dealt with a lot the last few days."

"Mitch mentioned that some of the guys that Bones hired were assholes. But a couple of the others I know and trust. Especially Wayne and Ryan."

"So, they're not all douche bags?"

"No, not all of them."

"Excuse me, ma'am," one of Bones' guys interrupted from the top of the stairway. "That Tech guy asked me to get you."

"Are you Wayne or Ryan?" I asked him.

"Wayne."

"Well, I have it on good authority that you are not a douche bag," I grinned up at the large man who filled the doorway.

He had sandy brown hair, similar to Grady's, kept longer than normal but far from the hippy stage. His eyes were hazel, though, whereas Grady's were a deep blue.

"That's good to know," he grinned back.

"Grady, I have to go, but I'll pass the phone off to Wayne if you promise that when you get done talking, you'll get some rest."

"Not much else to do around here."

I heard Wayne cheerfully greet Grady over the phone as I descended the stairs.

"What do we have?" I asked, stepping off the last step into the living room.

"We ran that cop's background," Genie updated me. "His bank accounts look dirty, but we don't know who he's working for."

"Stay on it. We might have just spooked another illegal operation in town that doesn't have anything to do with our search."

"I've got all of Ethan's phone records. He made a call the day we flew to Biloxi, but I'm not showing any other calls since then," Tech said. "Unless he talked before he died, I think the shipping sting is still a secret."

"Good. We'll plan on the sting going forward unless we hear something new. It's Sunday, so let's schedule another recon trip to the shipyard tomorrow so that everyone is ready. Maggie's in charge of the sting, though. I need to be on the outside in case Nola shows."

"You can't be alone. You need someone assigned to you," Bones said.

"I'll be with Kelsey," Eric said.

"Oh, so you think that you're man enough to protect her?" Bones snapped.

• • •

"It was my job, long before it was yours, asshole," Eric stood up to face Bones.

"Knock it the fuck off!" I yelled, fists clenched at my sides.

I stood positioned between the two, fuming.

"Damn it. You two really suck sometimes."

I heard Katie snort, but I turned to glare at Bones.

"Bones, don't tell me what I can or can't do."

I spun to face off with Eric next.

"Eric, stop trying to interfere in my personal life. I'm a big girl, I'll handle it."

I paced back and forth several times before I yelled again. "Wayne!"

"Yeah," he chuckled from behind me.

I turned to see he was standing at the bottom of the steps with the cell phone still held up to his ear.

"Hang up on Grady. We have a witch to visit," I said walking over to Eric and tossing a pad of paper at him. "Write down the address."

Eric wrote the address down and passed it to me, looking at the floor, trying not to smirk.

"Talk to you later, brother," Wayne chuckled and hung up.

I led us out to one of the fully loaded SUV's and climbed in the passenger seat. Wayne climbed behind the wheel and started driving, smiling the whole way.

Chapter Twenty-Seven

I wasn't surprised when the directions led us past New Orleans city, and deep into the bayou. I also wasn't surprised to find that our destination was an old turn of the century one story house that had the glass missing from the windows and candles burning brightly inside.

"What kind of witch are we meeting?" Wayne asked nervously.

"Probably voodoo," I shrugged getting out of the car.

"Ah, shit," Wayne grumbled, walking up behind me.

"Do you still have my cell phone?" I asked walking up the steps.

Wayne pulled my phone out of his shirt pocket and handed it to me. I turned on the video recorder and tucked it back in his shirt pocket with the video lens facing out. In case this went sideways, I wanted a recording.

"Are you sure this is a good idea?" Wayne asked.

"No," I laughed and walked inside the house.

Inside stood seven women standing beside a chalked circle on the floor, chanting. Layla stood off to the side looking jumpy. I nodded to Layla and waited for the witches.

"Come forward, Kelsey Harrison," the witch that appeared to be the leader called out. Her fellow witches stepped back away from the circle and turned to look at me.

I walked into the room, only a few feet away from the circle. The lead witch walked up to me and placed her hands on my head.

"Close your eyes and concentrate on the woman you hunt," the witch ordered.

I closed my eyes and thought of Nola. In my mind, I traveled through all the years that I had known her, seen her, knew she was nearby.

"Their lives are linked," the witch called out to the other witches. "But there is another linked line to this woman as well. We must avoid changing the other line."

"What does that mean?" I asked.

"You are linked by fate to Nola Mason. Your futures are intertwined. Her connection to you is black, fed by your anger, pain, and sorrow. She also feeds the line. Her energy is filled with hate, jealousy, rage. You both seek to find each other."

"And the other line? Is that someone else that's coming after me?"

"The other line is blue. It's linked by friendship, compassion, and sacrifice. It's not related to your current search," the witch said staring intently at me, watching for a reaction.

"Sounds good. So, what's the plan?" I asked.

"Once you enter the circle, you will not be able to leave. We will call the spirits to strengthen the black line that binds you both. The black line will aid you to find her, but it will also aid her to find you."

"Strengthen our connection? So, you want to make all the evil thoughts I have about Nola, even eviler? I don't think so," I said, taking a step back. "Look, is there any way to do one of those map spells, where the marble rolls to her current location?"

"It doesn't work like that, but if we had hair, blood, clothing—we could try to track her," the witch shrugged.

"Shit."

"You are right to be cautious. The spell we have prepared will change your perception of Nola Mason, and there is no guarantee that even after death that the line will fade," the witch warned.

"No then," I said shaking my head. "I won't be haunted by this woman for the rest of my life. I'll find another way."

"I was hoping you would say that," one of the other witches chuckled.

"Me too," another laughed.

"Everyone knew this was a bad idea, but would've done it anyway?" I grinned.

"The spirits wanted us to offer you the choice," the lead witch said, studying me too closely. "In another life, you were a strong witch yourself. They felt they owed a debt to you."

"Cool," I said, because what the hell else do you say to someone when she says such a thing to you. "Well, I appreciate the offer." I pulled an envelope out of my shoulder bag and laid it on the rickety side table.

I nodded to the witches and turned to leave out the front door. Halfway down the front steps, Layla called for me to wait and came running after me.

"Wait, I wanted to talk to you about Eric," she said, grabbing my arm to stop my retreat.

Blackness filled my vision, and my body went limp.

Flashes of rapid images replaced the blackness, in bright illumination like a slide show in a dark theater. But it wasn't just the images. Each one was accompanied by smell, sound, and pain.

I heard myself screaming out as a whip was lashed across my back, and I was thrown forward. I felt the blade of a knife slice into my side. I smelled blood, sweat, and urine in the air. I felt my body being kicked and punched as I was too weak to fight back. Hungry. Thirsty.

And, I felt the overwhelming sense of despair. Wishing that it was over. Wishing that I was dead.

As suddenly as the visions started, they ended just as abruptly. I fought to pull air into my lungs. Wayne knelt beside me holding me in one arm and checking my pulse with the other. Finally able to pull a large breath into my lungs, I looked over to see the head witch was holding Layla only a few feet away. Layla also struggled to breathe as sweat drenched her forehead. Her face appeared almost translucent.

"What the fuck was that? What were those images?" I asked.

"You could see them?" the head witch asked in shock.

"She does have the power!" another witch exclaimed.

"I don't want to hear mumbo-jumbo about past lives right now. What was that?" I demanded.

"Fate," Layla cried.

"Shit," I gasped. "*Eric.* He didn't want me to touch you. Did he experience the same thing?"

"Not like that, he didn't. I've never had anyone else be able to see their fate when I touched them," Layla shook her head.

The head witch still held her, propping her up in a sitting position.

"But you saw Eric's fate? What did you see?"

"He needs to go a different direction. Or his path will end abruptly," Layla said as the head witch dragged her up from the porch steps and led Layla inside the house.

Wayne pulled me up and led me to the car. My knees were still shaking, and he lifted me into the seat, securing my seatbelt like I was a small child.

"Find us a bar, will you?" I said after ten minutes of silence.

"Fuck yeah," Wayne said taking the next exit.

"Pass me my phone."

He handed me my phone, and I stopped the video and saved it to a folder. I texted Katie telling her that the witch appointment was a bust and that we were stopping off for a drink. I had a text from Bones telling me he was sorry. Eric texted me that he was going back to the boat to sleep. And Grady texted me asking if I was going to need an exorcism.

❖ ❖ ❖

It didn't take Wayne long to find us a bar. Picking a corner table, I ordered a double round of tequila shots, which we quickly and silently downed, back to back, before ordering beers.

"What the hell happened back there?" Wayne asked.

"What did you see?"

"Layla ran up to you and grabbed your arm to stop you from leaving. Then you both fell onto the steps and started thrashing like you were possessed." Wayne rubbed a hand across his forehead, wiping away the sweat that was building. "Then you both started screaming—," he shook his head remembering. "It was like you were both being tortured."

"Got it," I nodded taking another drink of my beer. "I think I need another round of tequila."

"That shit looked too real, Kelsey."

"Oh, it's worse than that, it felt real," I admitted holding up a shot glass to the waitress to bring another round. I could still feel the remnants of the stings across my back.

After doing another shot, I looked back at Wayne.

"Don't tell anyone what happened tonight. Either they wouldn't believe us, or worse, they would, and they'd freak out."

"What about Grady?"

"Especially not Grady," I said shaking my head. "He's recovering from a gunshot wound, remember?"

"Then you have to tell me what you saw."

"I saw Nola. I was chained to a wall, and she was having men torture me."

Wayne collapsed his head in his hands and was silent for several minutes. When he finally looked up, he motioned for the waitress. He handed her several large bills and asked her to bring us the entire tequila bottle.

Chapter Twenty-Eight

Light burned through my eyelids, and I pulled a sheet up over my head. It was no use, though, the intensity of the sunbeams continued to blind me. I pulled the sheet back and rolled over. The world spun a bit, and my stomach rolled. Diving out of bed, I ran down the stairs and to the bathroom. I kicked the door shut as I leaned over the toilet bowl and purged the remaining liquor still sitting in my stomach.

When the dry heaves subsided, I stepped inside the shower, leaning against the cool wall as the warm water drifted over me. It was a good ten minutes before I forced myself to wash my hair and get out. Stepping out, wrapping in a towel, I grinned at seeing my overnight bag sitting on the counter. I grabbed my toothbrush and scrubbed my teeth, tongue and roof of my mouth, before dressing in a clean set of clothes.

Walking out of the bathroom, several grinning faces stood waiting for me. Katie handed me a cup of coffee, Bones slid the aspirin down the counter to me, and Maggie walked over with a plain bagel.

I accepted all three.

"Is Wayne alive?" I asked, taking a seat at the kitchen table.

"Last time I checked," one of the guys chuckled.

"You Ryan?" I asked.

"Yup," he said saluting his coffee cup to me. "Wayne was lucky enough to puke last night. He asked me to protect him from the witches before he passed out in the hammock in the backyard."

"How much Irish do you have in you?" Tech asked.

"I'm a mutt just like everyone else. Why?"

"Because I didn't know that you sang Irish ditties," Tech grinned.

"Oh no," I slumped my head into my hands.

Everyone started singing *'what should we do with a drunken sailor...'* and I bailed through the foyer and out the door. Wayne was walking up the porch steps and stopped when he heard the singing. He shook his head and continued walking into the house. Soon following, everyone started singing a new song, *'hang down your head Tom Dooly..'*

I laughed and sat at one of the patio tables to nibble on my dry bagel.

Eric showed up, joining me at the patio table. I looked around to make sure we were alone.

"You need to go to Michigan or Texas. Take your pick," I said.

"You talked to Layla," Eric grumbled. "I'm not running because of some fortune teller nonsense."

"It might be bizarre, unscientific, weird as hell, but it's not nonsense, and you know it. Layla says you have to run from your fate lines, so let's book you a flight and get your ass out of here. If something happened to you because of me… damn Eric—I can't even think about it."

"And, if it were you? Would you run?"

"If I had a choice, yes, I would. If it meant protecting my son, yes. I would run like hell."

"So if you knew you were going to die next week, you'd run?"

"No. I said if I had a choice. I don't have a choice, Eric. My son needs me to get Nola and protect him from her. But you do have a choice. I have plenty of other people here to keep me out of trouble. Go, Eric. Before it's too late."

"What about the boat?"

"Who cares about the damn boat! This is your life we are talking about!"

"So that's it. I just run and hide?"

"Nicholas and Charlie would love to see you. Just think of it as a vacation," I grinned.

"Please tell me that he's going to Texas," Wayne grinned, walking out the door.

"You believe all that shit too?" Eric asked Wayne.

"My ass would be long gone," Wayne nodded.

Everyone else started meandering out of the house, and we ended our conversation. Eric got up, kissed me on the cheek and left. I knew he would be calling Charlie and getting a flight out. Wayne patted my shoulder in support.

"Tell me that neither of us drove," I sighed.

"You drunk dialed Grady, and he called us," Katie grinned, filling up my coffee cup from a carafe. "Tech tracked the GPS on the truck, and we picked you both up and drove the other SUV back."

"I don't remember calling Grady," I said looking down at my phone.

"You sent him a video, actually," Tech grinned.

"Oh no," I said panicking looking at Wayne.

We both were thinking of the video at the witch's house.

"Wayne was singing karaoke, really badly, and you recorded it and sent it to Grady," Maggie laughed.

"We were at a karaoke bar?" I asked.

"No," Bones laughed. "You were in a biker bar."

"What did I sing?" Wayne asked, thumping his head on the table.

I pulled up the video files and selected the last one recorded. Wayne was standing on a chair in the middle of the bar, obviously smashed, surrounded by bikers in leather cheering him on and taking pictures as he sang '*I want to know what love is*' by Foreigner.

"Holy shit," I laughed.

"No…" Wayne moaned beside me.

"Afraid so, my friend," I grinned.

I stopped the video and checked my history log to make sure I didn't do anything other than sending the video to Grady. "Oh shit!" I said, reading my sent text messages.

"Too late," Anne snapped, walking up the driveway toward us.

She walked over and propelled me up and away from the patio table and back down the driveway to the roadside. She dragged me halfway down the road before she turned to face me.

I looked down and was surprised to see that I still had a cup of coffee in one hand and my phone in the other. I grinned and sipped my coffee.

"You going to tell me what the hell the doomsday text messages were about last night?"

"Um, I was drunk?" I grinned.

"That was obvious. But you get more talkative when you're drunk. What I want to know is what was all the—if something happens to me take care of the family—shit about? Spill. What's going on?"

"Anne, I'm sorry that I freaked you out, but everything is fine."

"You're lying. You're scared," Anne crossed her arms and started pacing in front of me. She kicked a pebble across the road before turning her laser beam death glare back on me. "You weren't scared when fifty bikers declared war on us. Or when you ran out of a building with a bomb. So, tell me what the hell is going on before I go back up to the house and tell everyone that you're hiding something!"

"Damn it."

I sat on the curb and took another drink of my coffee. It was getting below the halfway mark, which could become an issue if I didn't hurry up and get this over with.

"A fortune teller told me that Nola was going to capture me and torture me. But she didn't say I was going to die, so maybe it all works out."

"A fortune teller?" Anne glared.

"Anne, if I told you the truth, you wouldn't believe me," I said shaking my head.

"Kelsey, you're honest and loyal down to your bone marrow. If you tell me something happened, I'll believe you," Anne said, joining me on the curb.

So, I told her. I told her exactly what happened at the witch's house with Layla, getting drunk at the bar, and sending Eric to Texas this morning.

Anne was quiet for a long time, staring at the asphalt.

"What if they drugged you somehow, and it was all just some type of hallucination?" she asked.

I opened the video file and passed the phone to Anne. She watched the video from the beginning to end, and tears streamed down her cheeks when she finally handed it back.

"So you run like Eric did. You try to avoid it," Anne said.

"It's not that simple. I didn't see myself die."

"What the hell does that have to do with anything?"

"What if I find a way to stop her? Even if she tortures me first, I have to protect my son. Can you honestly say you wouldn't do the same for Sara?"

"Shit," she said. "There has to be a better way."

"I have to protect my son, Anne. I have to do whatever it takes to keep her away from him. And, you can't tell the others. They're not parents. They wouldn't understand."

Anne nodded, still crying. "I don't like this, but I won't stop you."

Everyone stood silently watching from the patio tables as Anne walked up the porch stairs and into the house. I was almost to the porch when my phone rang. I answered it, seeing that it was Grady.

"Morning," I smiled. "Thanks for sending the troops to pick us up last night."

"How's the hangover?"

"Non-existent. Between the aspirin, coffee and purging out my innards at early dawns light, I feel pretty good."

"Seems Anne and Whiskey left in the middle of the night to head your way. Pops is convinced you're in trouble."

"Nope, all is well. Anne's here, and we talked."

"Nice try. Now the truth," Grady sighed.

"Shit. I have way too many meddlers in my life," I grumbled walking further away from any eavesdroppers. "I'm fine. I just have some future plans that have the potential to backfire on my ass. And, I'm not telling you this, so you follow Anne's lead and jump States. I'm telling you because if something happens to me, I need you to help Charlie protect Nicholas. Don't let Nola near him."

"What are your odds for these future plans?" Grady asked.

"As good as they're going to get," I sighed. "Look, I'll take every precaution I can, but we both know going to war with Nola always posed a threat to my life. I need your word that my son will be your priority."

"I can help."

"By keeping my son safe, yes. But there isn't anything you can do for me here." I disconnected the call and walked around to the living room deck entrance to avoid the watching eyes in the yard.

In the kitchen, I refilled my coffee cup and caught up with Genie, Carl, and Tech in the living room. Carl was wearing skin tight Spiderman pajamas.

"Nice PJ's, Carl," I smirked.

"Genie got me these," Carl grinned, standing up to twirl around so I could get the full effect. His hippy long gray hair was even gathered together with a webbed black band.

"Super cool," I laughed, taking a seat.

"Anything on that Harbor cop, Officer Parsons?" I asked Genie.

"Nothing solid. He worked some questionable cases where evidence went missing. He also has a few harassment claims against him by the less fortunate women in the area."

"So he preys on prostitutes. Nice."

Genie slid me a file, and I flipped through it, but nothing stood out. I tossed the file back on the table and turned my attention to the three boxes stacked along the wall.

"Kierson sent those," Genie said. "He'll be here later today if he can but sent those ahead so that you could take a look."

I opened the top box, but it was filled with documents from some of my investment companies. I set it aside and opened the next box. On top of the stack of folders was a plain white envelope with my name printed on the face of it. I opened the envelope finding several sheets of paper with a handwritten note.

> *Kelsey–*
> *I'm sorry that I betrayed you. I tried to get my family safe, but she found them. I would never have betrayed you otherwise.*
> *Find her Kelsey. Find her before she destroys everyone you love. If anyone can beat her, it's you.*
> *Ethan*

"You okay," Tech asked, as I stared at the note in my shaking hands.

"Yeah," I nodded, passing him the note and looking at the other pieces of paper that were in the envelope. "He was on our side. I just wish he knew he could've told me. I would've helped."

The next few pages were highlighted shipping schedules from Mayfair Shipping from Miami, Panama City, and Bay St. Louis. I handed them to Maggie, who was now sitting next to me.

The last piece of paper was a list of phone numbers without any names next to them. I handed the list to Genie. She glanced at the list, raised an eyebrow and started typing furiously on her laptop.

"We already found the shipping information for Miami and Bay St Louis," Maggie said moving further down the table and opening her laptop. "But I'll start digging back through the records and look at these shipments from Panama City."

"These numbers all appear to be burner phones that were bought in various locations. Some of them are still active, though," Genie said.

"How many are active?" I asked.

"Twelve," Genie sighed. "And, they're all pinging off towers in or near New Orleans."

I turned to Bones, and he nodded.

I ran upstairs and put on a shoulder holster and retrieved my Glock from my shoulder bag. I found a lightweight blazer to hide the gun and threw my shoulder bag over my head. Chances were slim that one of those phones was being carried by Nola, but it was the only lead we had at the moment.

Chapter Twenty-Nine

It was a long day, and by the time we returned to the house that night, I was exhausted. We had managed to track down eleven of the twelve phones in a city full of tourists. Half of the phones had been given to homeless men, who were told to use them until the minutes ran out. The other half were various sketchy types that after being properly pressured, admitted that Nola had given them the phone. None of them knew where she was at, or if she would be returning to New Orleans. The twelfth phone had been turned off shortly after we left the marina and was never turned back on during the remainder of the day.

I changed into a comfy extra-long t-shirt and curled up in bed. My brain was still rolling over all the information that we had gathered, hoping that I had missed an angle, something else we could track down. But, there was nothing there. Our last lead would be the sting at the shipyard tomorrow. After that, I wasn't sure where to look next for Nola and would have to rely on the new contacts that Eric and I had established to report in if they sighted her.

Anne came up the stairs and sat on the end of my bed. She tossed a small plastic bag at me.

"I did some laundry today and found all of this wadded up in one of your duffle bags. Why do you have some man's wallet?"

I sat up and turned on the bedside lamp. Overturning the bag, I emptied the contents onto the bedspread. "Larry," I said, more to myself than to Anne.

"Do you know Larry?" Anne asked.

"No. He was the man that was in charge of Nicholas over the years. Nola killed him when he tried to protect Nicholas. I dragged his body out of the burning house and then relieved him of everything in his pockets," I admitted. "I forgot all about this stuff."

"You robbed a dead guy?" Anne said, shaking her head.

"I was in a hurry," I chuckled, flipping through the wallet.

The poor guy had no pictures, a couple fraudulent credit cards, an expired driver's license, and a very old condom with the foil starting to tear.

"How sad," I said, tossing the aged condom in the trash.

"What about this pen?" Anne asked, holding up a pen with the logo and name of a delivery company on it. "Is this a clue?"

"Probably not," I chuckled. "Have the brainiacs look it up in the morning to be sure."

I picked up some type of trading chip and looked at the stamped logo: Bloody Knuckles, New Orleans.

A flash of a memory crossed my vision, and the air smelled strongly of perfume. I looked back at the chip in my hand, and got out of bed, dressing quickly.

"I have to run back to New Orleans and check something out," I told Anne as I secured my shoulder holster.

"Where are you going this late at night?"

"Bars are open a lot later here than they are in Michigan," I grinned and started moving down the stairs.

Anne followed me down the stairs, and Katie looked up from the couch.

"You're about to do something stupid, aren't you?" Katie yawned.

"Yes. But I have to," I said hugging her, followed by hugging Anne and walking out of the house.

On the front porch stood Bones, Ryan, and Wayne, arms crossed over their chests and giving me the official 'you've been busted' stare down.

"Fine, you guys can go, but we have to hurry," I said dodging around them and getting behind the wheel of the SUV.

By the time the last door closed, I was already driving out via the front lawn and turning toward the highway.

"What happened?" Bones asked.

"Nothing happened. I just remembered there's a bar I was supposed to check out. One of my tips told me to look into it," I answered.

Bones knew I was lying, but didn't force the issue. I saw Wayne roll his eyes in the backseat and check his gun clip.

"What kind of bar are we going to?" Bones asked.

"Um, well…" I delayed. "I think it's a vampire bar."

"A what?" Bones chuckled.

I shrugged and plugged my phone into the car. "Call Baker," I commanded the phone.

"It's after two a.m.," Bones reminded me.

I just grinned as the phone rang.

"Baker," a stern voice answered.

"It's Kelsey. Do you know anything about a bar in New Orleans called the Bloody Knuckles?"

"Shit, really? How in the hell do you get yourself into this crap?" Baker asked.

"PS: you're on speaker phone, and I'm not alone. So, tell me about the bar," I ordered.

"Fine. It's a goth and vamp mix with a bit of S&M. Dress in minimal clothes, leather, color your hair black and no one will notice you."

"Peachy, but my plan is to be noticed. What else?"

"I don't know who owns the place. But the security guys are thugs for hire and the club has a bad reputation for violence and drugs."

"So it caters to a troubled clientele, some of whom wouldn't be noticed if they disappear off the face of the earth?"

"Yeah, could be," Baker admitted.

"Thanks, Baker. I have to go."

I pressed the button to disconnect the call and took a deep breath. So, the bar could be linked to human trafficking—not good.

I drove in silence to New Orleans and skirted the city to an almost abandoned business district. The only lights in the vicinity were from the red glowing logo of the Bloody Knuckles.

"What a stupid name for a bar," I complained, pulling into the lot and parking.

"How did you know how to get here?" Bones asked.

"I have no idea. I just knew."

"Is this the place you saw?" Wayne asked.

I nodded.

"We should think about this. There's no reason it has to be tonight."

"It's time to finish this," I said getting out of the car.

I walked up to the front doors, passing all the goth creatures waiting in line and approached the doorman.

"What do you want?" the bouncer glared down at me.

"Get out of my way before I have my friends rearrange your appendages," I sneered back in his face.

The bouncer looked behind me before quickly stepping back and opening the door for us.

Bones grinned. "What's the plan?"

I handed him the SUV keys. If my vision came true, they would need the car to get home.

"Spread out, and try to keep eyes on me," I gripped Bones' wrist. "Don't feel bad if you lose sight of me."

I ducked into the thick crowd before he could argue or question me.

By the time I had circled the room three times, I was getting discouraged. I was asked to dance twice, asked to bark like a dog, and offered a line of coke.

I moved over to the stairway in the back of the room so I would have a better view. Someone bumped into me from behind, and I was too late to notice the quick stinging bite of a needle sinking into my skin. I turned to fight, but my limbs gave out, and I crumbled toward the floor. I felt myself being lifted. I forced my eyes open one more time and wished I hadn't. Officer Parsons was the one carrying me down the back hallway. My eyes drifted closed.

Chapter Thirty

I couldn't count the number of days, the number of weeks, the number of months, that I was held in a dark, dank, cinderblock cell.

The first time they dragged me into the room, the smell of blood, sweat, and urine gagged me. Now the surrounding oxygen was poisoned by my own bodily fluids.

And, suffering pain had become as natural as breathing the wretched air. The only part of my body that wasn't damaged was my face. Nola wouldn't let them touch my face. It was my screams, my tears, and the fear in my eyes that she enjoyed the most. She eagerly watched from one of the corners of the room while I was tortured, her twisted grin widening as the pain escalated.

And, two days ago, the last piece of Layla's fated vision was fulfilled when I was horsewhipped until a thick layer of blood coated my entire back and the backs of my legs. Nola full-out smiled that day.

And, with sections of infected and split skin across my body, I knew—already dehydrated and weakened from a lack of food—that without treatment, I was going to die.

These were the thoughts running through my mind as the thick haze pulled me back under to sleep.

A bucket of cold water was thrown at me. I tried to suck as much of it as I could through my crusty dried lips before it ran in rivulets along the floor to the drain.

I struggled to force my head up, seeing Nola standing in the center of the room in an expensive business suit and heels. Next to her was the personal guard that never left her side.

"Time to wake up," Nola grinned.

"Go to hell," I sneered in a hoarse voice I barely recognized.

The snide remark was about as much energy as I could manage, and my head slumped of its own accord back between my shoulders. I hung limply from the chains that secured me to the wall. I no longer had the arm strength to pull myself up, and I was reserving what little energy I had left in my damaged legs.

"We have visitors coming and need to get you cleaned up," Nola said.

I felt the guard unchain one of my arms and then step to the other side to work the other chain. As soon as it released, gravity dropped me to the floor.

"You're starting to disappoint me, Officer Harrison. I expected you to be much more entertaining," Nola complained.

I laid on the muddy cool cement floor and closed my eyes. I felt the guard drag me up from the ground, half carrying me, over to a washtub, dumping my dead weight into the lukewarm water.

I sat up seizing in instant pain. The water was filled with a heavy solution of bleach that burned into the gashes on my back. I barely managed to keep my right hand submerged under the water. In my hand, I had palmed the knife that the guard always wore on his belt.

Nola leered over the side of the tub, crouching down to watch my face. She could see the nerves twitching, the tears glistening just behind my lids, and my chapped lips quivering as I tried to mask it all. Tried to hide the fact that after weeks and weeks of torture, she had finally managed to do the one thing I had vowed never to let her do.

Win.

She had finally won. She had broken me.

I knew that I was going to die in this room. I had accepted it. But before I died, I would try one more time to take her with me.

I turned to look at Nola. She seemed so pleased with herself. She started to smile, but then she stopped. She must have sensed that I had one more fight left inside me.

As she tried to propel herself away from the washtub, I threw myself over the edge, landing on top of her. I plunged the knife into her chest, using my body weight to sink it deep.

I laid on top of her, soaking her fine suit with the bloody filthy water that ran off my naked body. Staring her in the eyes, I turned the blade that was still embedded in her chest.

She gurgled and gasped, thrashing beneath me, as her eyes clouded over, staring past me.

It was over. Nola was finally dead.

The guard pulled me off Nola and looked down in shock at her corpse. He stood there as I laid naked on the floor watching him.

Finally coming to his senses, he leaned down and pulled the knife from Nola's body and stepped over to me. When he went to move the knife to my throat, I wrapped my legs around his head and threw him to the ground. Sitting up, I kept my legs locked and rotated my whole body the other direction. His neck snapped between my thighs.

I laid back on the muddy floor and quietly laughed. I didn't have the energy to do anything else, and yet, it felt good. It felt good to know that I beat Nola. That even if I died, I took the bitch out first.

I closed my eyes. I just need to rest for a bit.

Somewhere in my mind, I heard Grady's voice. He was calling to me. *Get up, Kelsey. They're coming. You have to fight. Get up!*

"I can't, Grady," I answered back.

You have to. Nicholas needs you. Get up, Kelsey!

"Ok, Ok," I agreed trying to open heavy eyelids. "You're so damn bossy."

Rolling over, I looked around the darkened room. The small window near the ceiling no longer carried small beams of sunshine. I must have fallen asleep.

I dragged myself over to the dead guard. Searching him, I pulled the keys from his pants pocket and picked up the knife that laid beside him. Using the side of the tub as a crutch, I pushed myself up to stand. Three steps toward the door, my body bounced into the cement block wall as my vision faded in and out and my sense of balance went askew. I followed the wall, holding it to stay upright, as I neared the door.

Sharp pains ripped through my biceps and shoulder as I held my arms up high enough to fight to unlock the door but by the third time, the lock released and the door opened. A guard was standing on the other side of the door, looking curiously back at me. I watched in slow motion as realization crossed his face. I stepped forward and plunged the knife into his stomach. Using my body weight as leverage, I leaned to the side, dragging the knife with me as it tore through him.

He stared in horror at himself as he dropped to the floor, blood spilling out of open gash.

Holding the wall for balance with one hand, I leaned over and pulled his gun from its holster. I heard a noise to the side and realized that four cages filled with women and children were placed along the far wall. I searched the man again and slid a phone across the floor. One of the women grabbed the phone, looking up at me.

I climbed the stairs—and killed everyone that crossed my path.

Grabbing a coat that hung on a hook in the kitchen, I tied the front of it closed and grabbed a set of keys hanging beside the door. A Prada purse sat on the counter. It was the last thing I grabbed as I stumbled outside. After hitting the unlock button on the key chain, the lights flashed on a dusty blue convertible that sat in the driveway.

I slid behind the wheel, immediately noticing the blood staining the pure white interior as I started up the engine and drove away. A few miles down the road, several police cars and ambulances were heading in the direction of the house. I kept driving.

Chapter Thirty-One

I chose East. When I had started out, I needed a direction to go, and East seemed just as likely to gain me distance from that house as North, South or West, so I chose East.

Every fork in the road, every intersection, every sign I passed, I kept choosing East. I could barely keep my eyes open, no understanding of my current location or my destination, so I focused all my energy on heading East.

What seemed like hours passed. Unable to drive anymore, I pulled behind a cheap motel and reclined the driver's seat. I passed out as the moon watched over me.

****

I heard the loud rumble of a diesel truck and felt the car jerk with a loud metal clank, but I couldn't open my eyes. I drifted back into unconsciousness.

****

The sun was setting when I forced my body upright to take in my surroundings. I heard voices speaking in another language, maybe Spanish. I looked out to see rows and rows of cars and trucks, and beyond that stood a perimeter of 8-foot metal fencing. I wasn't in the motel parking lot anymore.

Turning to the voices about fifteen feet away from my car, two men argued in rapid Spanish, while a third man stood back and rolled his eyes at them. I reached into the Prada purse for the berretta that I had stashed inside. I slowly slid out of the car, turning the gun to the three men as they silently turned to watch me.

"Where am I?" I asked.

"We didn't see you, Miss. We didn't mean to tow you along with the car," the bigger of the three men said.

"Where-am-I?" I asked again.

"You're in our tow lot. We were called to tow the car from the motel. We brought you here by mistake," the same man answered.

"Did anyone run the plate on the car?"

"No," one of the other men answered.

My vision was blurring, and my balance swayed as I stepped back to lean against the car. The man that had been watching the earlier argument stepped slowly toward me.

"Don't!" I warned, raising the gun back to his chest.

His movements stopped, but my attention turned to the logo on his leather vest: Demon Slayers.

"Do you know Renato Gonzallez?" I asked.

I tried to keep the hope that stirred within me smothered, but hot unwelcomed tears streamed down the side of my face.

"Yes."

"Call him. Tell him Kelsey needs his help."

The man nodded and slowly pulled out his cell phone. He made the call, speaking in rapid Spanish. After a few breaks in conversation, the phone was put on speaker mode.

"Kelsey?" Renato's voice called out.

"Renato, it's me. I need protection for 24 hours. No more. I just need to sleep and clean my wounds. Can you help?"

"Do you want me to contact your family?"

"No. I don't want anyone to know where I am."

I shook my head adamantly back and forth though he couldn't see that over the phone.

"They're worried, Kelsey. They've been looking for you for months," Renato said.

"I said no. Can you get me protection for 24 hours or not?"

"Si," Renato said before he started to speak in Spanish again.

The call was disconnected, and the man walked up and lowered my arm holding the gun. He then helped me to the passenger side before he slipped behind the driver's seat and started the car. Exhaustion pulled me back into the blackness.

Chapter Thirty-Two

Searing pain shocked me awake, and I fought back before my eyes were even open. Throwing a kick and a punch gained me enough space to throw my back against a wall and observe my surroundings. A Hispanic man covered a young crying woman's body at the foot of the bed. Beside her lay white rags, bandages, and an upturned bowl of bloody water. They were trying to help, and I hurt them.

"Sorry. I'm so sorry. Please, I didn't mean to," I whispered to them. "Are you hurt?" I asked as I moved away from the wall toward them.

The man helped the woman up, and she skidded away from me and out the door. She had a red mark forming on her cheek.

"I didn't mean to hurt her. I wasn't awake," I tried to explain.

"You scared her more than anything. Renato warned us not to approach you if you were asleep, but your wounds were getting infected," the young man said.

He paced two steps one direction, then two steps the other. The room was too small to allow any more steps. "I thought I could protect her if you woke."

"You can't. I've been trained to fight."

I looked about and realized belatedly that I was naked. I grabbed the blood-soaked coat from the floor and wrapped it around me.

"Is there a bathroom where I can shower and clean my wounds?"

"Si, but you need stitches. Some of the wounds are too big," he answered, but led me to the small bathroom.

"Do you have access to a doctor that I can pay when I get my money?"

He nodded and left without saying anything. I slipped into the bathroom and turned on the water in the compact shower stall. Preparing myself for the pain, I stepped in and gritted my teeth as the hot water hit the open wounds on my back, stomach, and legs. The water running off my body was a mixture of black filth and bright red blood, swirling beneath my feet.

Clean towels and clothes had been set on the sink. I dried off the best I could without aggravating the wounds but then chose to only slip on the panties before wrapping the now blood stained towels around me to cover my body. I threw the bloody coat in the trash can and left the rest of the clothes on the sink.

In the living room, the young Hispanic couple stood with an older man. I apologized again to the young woman for hurting her before I turned into the small bedroom that I had been sleeping in. The older man that I assumed was a doctor, and the young woman followed me in.

"It wasn't your fault. Ricky warned me about helping you, but I was worried about your cuts getting infected," the woman said as she set some supplies beside the bed.

"Are you the doctor?" I asked the older man.

"Sort of. You can call me Brian. I was told you needed stitches, but from the bruising I can see, I think you should go to the hospital for some x-rays," Brian said.

"No hospitals. If you can stitch up my back, I can stitch some of the front wounds."

"That's not necessary," Brian said.

"Maybe not for you, but it will go faster for me," I answered pulling some of the supplies out from the bag that he set on the end of the bed. I sat with my back facing him and dropped the towel. I heard him hiss between his teeth, but I focused on threading a needle.

"I have a pain killer that will put you to sleep, while I stitch these wounds. It'll be easier for you," Brian said.

"But more dangerous for everyone else," I answered. "No, we'll work together and get it over with."

The young woman started to clean and bandage some of the smaller wounds. I wanted to tell her not to bother, but she seemed to need to help in some way, so I left her alone. Using some white tape, I pulled sections of the skin on my thigh together before I started to weave the thread through my skin. My entire thigh burned in pain, but it was a pleasant distraction to the movement on my back where every small touch was like a hot poker.

"What's your name?" I asked the young woman, distracting myself.

"Annamarie," she answered quietly. "I'm Ricky's sister."

"That's a pretty name. I'm Kelsey," I smiled gently at her. "Thank you for your hospitality."

"My uncle owed you a debt, and I owed my uncle a debt, so it was my pleasure. Did you really beat up men to protect my cousin?"

She was referring to a bar fight last winter where two young Hispanic women were being harassed by some drunk rednecks. I only learned after I taught the rednecks a lesson in manners that one of the women was the daughter of a local biker.

"I just explained they needed to leave your cousin and her friend alone."

"Ha," she laughed. "Uncle Renato said that you knocked out all of one man's teeth."

"I think it was closer to five teeth, and the barstool did most of the work," I grinned.

"What about the man that hurt you?" she asked, nodding to my current wounds.

"Most of them are dead," I shrugged, taping up the center gash on my ribs so I could sew it next.

My answer seemed to spook her a bit, and I felt the doctor pause in his work on my back.

"Don't waste any energy worrying about them. If you saw their other victims, you'd have killed them yourself, Doc."

"I'm not actually a doctor. I was a medic in the service. Though compared to the botched-up stitch-work you're doing, I look like a freaking plastic surgeon. You need to stop and leave that one for me," Brian grumbled.

"It's fine. I'm just going to throw enough stitches to hold it together and let the rest heal on its own."

Brian leaned over and took a closer look at the wound on my side that I was sewing.

"Was there a tattoo there?" he asked pressing the skin over.

"Before they slit it to pieces with a serrated blade, yes."

"Shit. What was the tattoo?"

"It was a vow of justice," I answered truthfully.

"And, did you find it?" Annemarie whispered.

"Yes, but the price was high," I answered glancing away.

Images of the past few weeks pushed forward, and I forcefully pushed them back into the box in my head where they needed to be packed away.

"What day is it?" I asked to change the subject.

"Thursday," Brian asked.

"No, what month and day?" I asked.

Brian paused in his work.

"Were you unconscious? Do you have memory loss?"

"I don't know how long they kept me before I escaped."

"It's June 14th," Annemarie answered. "When were you taken?"

I couldn't breathe.

I kept trying to catch air in my lungs, but they wouldn't fill.

I gasped and gasped, but nothing happened. I jerked up the towel and stepped over to the wall, placing my back on the cool surface as I struggled.

"Small breaths. Count backward, 99, 98, slowly, 97, 96, 95… slow, easy, long breaths. In… Out…," Brian coached. "That's it. In… Out…"

He stepped over slowly and raised his hands to my shoulders, but I flinched back. He stepped back and moved Annemarie over to the far wall.

"Try to sit down and keep focusing on your breathing."

I moved back to the bed and lowered my head between my knees. The stitches on my back pulled and strained, but I ignored it as I focused on getting a full breath in my lungs, only to be replaced by the next.

When I had my breathing under control, I nodded to them.

"I'm sorry. I didn't mean to upset you," Annemarie cried.

"It's not your fault."

"Do you know how long you were gone?" Brian asked cautiously watching my reaction.

I nodded my head. "They took me in January."

"Shit," Brian cursed.

"Which is why your family is so fucking freaked out right now," Renato said from the doorway.

I raised the towel to cover my breasts and turned to face him.

"How did you get here so quickly?" I asked.

"I was in Biloxi, helping look for you. You look like shit," Renato sternly informed me.

"I feel like shit too," I grinned. "I would hug you right now, but I might hurt myself."

"Stay put. I'll send in Nightcrawler. Looks like you could use another set of hands to patch you up."

"Did you tell them?" I asked before he could leave.

"No," he sighed. "But you should. They're worried sick."

"I have a way to let them know I'm okay. But I need someone to make a road trip for me."

"Where to?" Renato asked.

"That depends. Where the hell am I?" I asked.

"Mobile, Alabama," Renato answered with a raised eyebrow.

"Then you're in luck. I have a storage unit on the north side of Mobile. Inside is an SUV, money and some supplies. Can you get someone there? I can pay them when they return."

"Write down the details. I'll take Ricky with me to retrieve whatever you need," he nodded and walked out.

A few minutes later, Nightcrawler sauntered into the room.

"Are they dead?" Nightcrawler gritted between clenched teeth.

"Most of them. Nola was the first to leave this world, and I twisted the knife just to be sure."

• • •

"Good. Let me know when it's time to round up the rest of the bastards. I'll be sure to bring a whip," he growled.

"Looks that bad, aye?"

"Shit, Kelsey. Renato warned me, but shit."

"Suck it up, and start stitching," I sighed, turning to sew another section on my hip. "I'm losing my patience with all the poking and prodding and just want this over with."

We all worked quietly, stitching and cleaning the wounds on my body before Nightcrawler eventually caved and broke the silence.

"Tech and Bones are still in Biloxi looking for you," Nightcrawler said as he stitched the back of my arm. "Katie went back to Michigan with James. She's still teaching the girls to fight."

"They getting any good at it, or just playing around?" I grinned.

"Trinity sucks. She's still worried about her manicure. Katie would've quit a long time ago if it weren't for the other girls trying so hard."

"Good. Maybe Katie is learning some patience during the process."

"Is that the woman that kicked Ricky's ass last month when he was in Michigan?" Annemarie asked as she helped me drink some chicken broth.

"I warned him not to mess with her," Nightcrawler laughed.

"Ok, so maybe she's not learning any patience," I smiled.

"They're all strung pretty tight these days. They haven't heard from you in months. We've been taking turns coming to Biloxi to help with the search."

"Yeah, I really fucked up."

"It's already on the news," Nightcrawler said, referring to Nola's death.

I nodded, looking away at the far wall.

"I threw a cell phone to one of the other prisoners on my way out. I just didn't have the strength to do more than keep shooting as I walked away."

"The news reported eight dead bodies and nine victims rescued. The FBI is involved."

"I left enough DNA behind that the FBI will know it was me."

"The club isn't going to want that kind of attention," Nightcrawler warned.

"And, they won't get it. I plan on leaving as soon as I'm patched up. Nothing will come back to the club."

"You can't drive until you heal some," Brian interrupted. "And, you need some sleep."

"He's right. You can sleep here tonight. I'll keep watch. Then tomorrow, I can drive you wherever you need to go," Nightcrawler said.

"Can I go too?" Annemarie asked.

"No," I answered, patting her hand. "It's not safe."

"I have the worst of your back sewn. I need you to lay down on your stomach so I can sew the back of your legs," Brian said. "And, I'm going to give you a shot in the ass of antibiotics so don't freak out on me."

"Do your thing," I said laying down.

After the shot had been injected, I drifted off to sleep, barely noticing the stitches being threaded through my thighs.

Chapter Thirty-Three

"You Drugged Me!" I yelled at Brian.

"No, he didn't," Nightcrawler said stepping into the room. "I did."

"You had no right!"

"Like I care," Nightcrawler snorted. "You were exhausted, twitchy, and in pain. I made a decision. You can be as pissed at me as you want. Now finish getting dressed so we can get the fuck out of here."

Nightcrawler clomped out of the room in his heavy biker boots as Annemarie helped me pull a second tank top down over my shoulders and back.

I stood, still fuming as we worked together to pull the sweat pants up. They kept trying to snag on all the stitches.

"I picked up some antibiotics. You need to take them all, and if any of the wounds get infected, you need to go to a real doctor for something stronger," Brian said.

"Thanks," I grumbled.

Annemarie snickered.

"Sorry," I said turning to face him "I meant, thank you, Brian, for helping me."

"Sure you did," he grinned back.

Annemarie snickered again.

In the living room, I found Ricky, Renato, and Nightcrawler sitting around and enjoying a few beers. Still pissed at Nightcrawler, I confiscated his beer and walked over to where my bags were stacked. Taking a small sip first, I set the bottle down and opened the first bag. Pulling an envelope from an inside pouch, I tossed it to Renato.

He caught the envelope and looked inside. "This is too much. I'll get the balance to Katie."

"Not necessary. I have plenty, so make sure everyone profits a bit."

I pulled a hip harness out and attached it to the side of my sweat pants. It wasn't ideal, but I knew my back couldn't handle a shoulder harness. Loading a clip in my Glock, I secured it into the harness. I had nowhere to hide my switchblades, so I kept them inside the bag.

"What happened to the car I arrived in?" I asked.

"It's in my garage," Ricky answered. "A Porsche 911 gets too much attention in this neighborhood, so I had to hide it."

"Did you bring the vehicle from my storage unit?" I asked Renato.

"The Escalade is at the tow lot. It had 300 miles on it when I picked it up," he said, shaking his head.

"Do what you want with the Porsche, but the FBI is probably keeping an eye out for it."

Annemarie walked back in and handed me the Prada purse I had when I arrived. Inside the purse, laid the gun that I had stolen from Nola's guard.

"Did anyone get their prints on this gun?" I asked Ricky.

"No. I had gloves on when I unloaded it."

"Good," I nodded, setting the gun aside and pulling out everything else that was in the purse.

Nola had fake ids and a pile of cash along with some type of small ledger book. I stuffed the ledger book inside one of my bags and threw the cash on the coffee table. I stuffed the fake ids back inside the purse and asked Annemarie for a plastic bag.

"Can you get this stuff to Katie or the Devil's Players? They can get it to the FBI," I asked Renato after I stuffed the purse and gun into the plastic bag.

Renato nodded, and I set it all on the coffee table. I picked up the beer from the side table and took another small sip. I could see the sun streaming through the front windows between the pulled curtains. I sat on the couch beside Nightcrawler, reaching out to steal a cigarette from his pack on the coffee table.

I was as antsy to stay as I was in a hurry to leave. I felt safe in this little house, but the longer I stayed, the less safe I was. It was time to run and run far.

"Nightcrawler has decided he's going with you," Renato said.

"I know, but it's better if I go alone. I have places I can stay, and enough cash to cover my expenses. I'll be alright."

"It wasn't up for debate. I'm going with you," Nightcrawler said.

I looked to Renato, but he just grinned.

I smoked in silence for several minutes before I spoke.

"I can't afford for anyone to track me down. You'll only put me in danger."

"I've got no one I need to call or keep in touch with," Nightcrawler added throwing his cell phone to Renato. "And, you need someone to watch your back, literally. Those wounds need to be treated and monitored. And, I can help remove the stitches when it's time. There's no point in arguing."

"Shit. You bikers are all controlling pricks," I grumbled.

Secretly, I was glad Nightcrawler agreed to come along. I could use the help. I was physically too weak to handle everything. I could always ditch him later on if I needed some space.

"I'm sure my family will suspect you stepped in to help me," I said to Renato. "Knowing them, they'll clone or bug your phone, hoping to find me."

"I'd expect nothing less of Tech and Katie," Renato grinned.

I took another deep inhale of the cigarette before stubbing it out in the overcrowded ashtray. I looked about the room. Brian and Annemarie stood off to the side. Renato looked at the worn carpet. Ricky and Nightcrawler openly watched me.

"I don't know how to thank everyone for what you did for me."

"Yeah, well, if Zach hadn't accidentally towed you along with the car, then I'm not sure we would have found you, so it was all dumb luck," Ricky grinned.

"How exactly does that happen, anyway?" Renato asked.

"He says he was so focused on the Porsche itself, he never even looked inside," Ricky grinned.

"He a prospect?" I asked.

Ricky nodded. "And, he'll continue to be one for a long time."

I grinned, not feeling sorry for the damn kid. Prospects had to prove responsible, and it sounded like this one might not make the cut.

I moved to pick up a duffle bag, and Nightcrawler actually growled at me. He set me carefully aside and grabbed all three duffle bags and carried them in one load.

Brian helped me down the stairs, across the yard and into the van. Renato got behind the wheel to drive us to the tow lot. I settled in the backseat and looked at my surroundings. Kids played soccer on the street as mothers sat on front porches watching over them. Husbands and brothers gathered near bikes and cars in garages. It was a family neighborhood. Their happiness looked so foreign to me. Would my son and I ever know this kind of peace?

I shook the thoughts away and focused on the street signs.

Chapter Thirty-Four

"Where to?" Nightcrawler asked as he approached the highway, driving my Escalade.

"Atlanta," I answered. "I have a place we can hide out that nobody knows about."

I pulled a laptop out of the duffle bag at my feet and plugged in a burner phone to use for an internet connection. The Escalade had wifi, but I wasn't sure if it could be traced. I moved to the cloud drive that Tech and I shared to communicate and scanned through the posts.

The older ones were short and sweet—Call home. The ones in the last twenty-four hours were a bit more dramatic.

Nola's body found, assuming it was you. Get in touch.

Are you safe? Are you hurt? Where are you? Call home or leave a post.

Katie is calling me every hour -hurry up and reach out.

Maggie says you are wanted for questioning, but there's enough evidence to prove it was self-defense. What did you do?

I typed a message back to Tech: *Alive. Safe. Need to hide for a few weeks. I have a friend helping me. I need some time, Tech. Respect that. I can't come home just yet. Love to all...*

I closed out of the cloud drive and did a search on Google. The information I was looking for was the third link down, and I clicked on it and started reading. Step

One—get my strength back. Step Two—know your enemy.

We had been driving for hours when Nightcrawler drove through a McDonald's and ordered us food, but ten minutes later he was pulling over so I could puke it back up alongside the highway.

"Fuck," Nightcrawler cursed, running around to my side of the truck to help hold me up. "How long has it been since you ate?"

"Yesterday's broth was the only food I can remember eating in a while," I admitted, spitting out the acidic bile. "I'm still getting used to drinking water."

"You should have said something."

He shuffled me back in the truck and dug out a paper bag for me to use in case I got sick again. He exited at the next turnoff and pulled into a gas station. I couldn't imagine anything in the store agreeing with my stomach. I leaned back and closed my eyes as I waited for him.

I must have drifted off to sleep because the next thing I knew, Nightcrawler was pulling into another gas station and pulling up to the pump to get gas.

"Sorry, I didn't want to wake you, but we were down to fumes," he grinned. "Here," he said, handing me a thermos. "It's tomato soup. Don't eat a lot, just sip it and try to eat a few crackers."

He pulled a package of crackers up onto my lap as I tried to twist the lid off the thermos. He took the thermos and poured some in the cup before resealing it and handing me the cup. I was too embarrassed by how weak I was to even thank him.

"You lived. Don't forget that. I don't know many people that could have survived what you went through," he said before sliding out of the truck to pump the gas.

I managed to eat two crackers and three swallows of soup before I felt my stomach rolling. Nightcrawler poured the rest of the soup back in the thermos and tucked it near my feet.

"We're just outside of Atlanta. Where am I going?"

"Take the 285 to 20 East, then follow it into Covington."

"Easy enough. I can wake you when we get close to Covington if you want to go back to sleep."

"It will be good for me to stay awake for a while," I yawned.

"Did you reach out to your family on your laptop?"

"I let Tech know I was safe," I nodded. "He'll spread the word."

"If Nola's dead, why are you hiding?"

"I can't let my family see me like this," I said, looking out the window. "I can't let my son see me like this."

"I get that. It's not easy for me to see you like this, and we barely know each other. Is that the only reason?"

I looked out the window absorbing my surroundings before I answered. "I need to kill someone before he kills me."

Nightcrawler looked over at me but didn't ask any more questions as he took the ramp for 20 East.

I directed him to the house, surprising myself that I remembered how to get there after so many years. He followed the long drive back to the pale yellow house with white trim. It was a good size house, nestled just behind a light stretch of trees.

Nightcrawler parked in the open carport. By the time I was able to release my seatbelt, open my door, and slide myself out of the truck to stand, Nightcrawler had all of our bags and the thermos in one hand, and another arm held out to help brace me, helping me from the truck to the front door.

"The key is behind the mailbox. Just slide the box to the side."

Nightcrawler slid the box aside and flipped the hidden door open, pulling out the keys. He nodded, impressed, but didn't say anything as he unlocked the door with one hand and tossed the keys in so he could free the hand to help brace me up the last step inside.

He guided me to the long rustic dining room table and helped me settle onto one of the four long benches. The main room was an open layout with the kitchen and dining room on one side and the living room taking up the large space on the other side.

"Damn," Nightcrawler said, setting the bags down and walking around the living room stripping the furniture of the sheets that protected them. "You own this place?"

"Yeah. I have the deed under an old acquaintance's name, but since they aren't aware it even exists, it can't be traced back to me."

• • •

"Is that legal?"

"Not really," I shrugged. "The worst that would happen is that I'd have to let her keep the property, and I might get my hand slapped with some type of fraud charges."

"What about the utilities, taxes, yard care expenses?"

"They are automatically paid from a shell company account under her name as well. The company files taxes separately."

"So, tax fraud?"

"Doubtful. All the expenses are legit, and the taxes are paid."

Nightcrawler pulled the sheet down from over the fireplace and grinned. It was a big screen TV. He walked off down the hall, and I carefully made my way into the kitchen to check supplies. I had stocked the cupboards with food, but most of the cans had expired years ago, and some of the dried goods were questionable. I plugged in the refrigerator before starting a grocery list.

Nightcrawler came back out to the kitchen and rolled his eyes. He led me over to one of the barstools to sit down.

"Where's the other bedroom?" he asked.

"Three bedrooms aren't enough for you?"

He glared at me, and I laughed. "Push the second wall sconce in the hallway up about six inches."

He went back down the hall and soon after, I heard him yell 'Holy Shit.' He returned a few minutes later grinning. "Why do you have this house?"

"Because I needed a safe place to hide Nicholas if Nola wasn't caught. I needed to be able to protect him," I shrugged. "It's been two years since I've been here, though. We need some groceries."

"I'll go shopping while you take a nap."

"Deal. Grab some cash out of my duffle bag. Keep enough on you to cover expenses and get out of dodge money at all times. I'll do the same. If we get split up, you'll need it."

I started down the hallway as Nightcrawler mumbled, 'Holy Shit.' He must have found the money bag.

I passed the War Room that was equipped with large touch screen monitors and laptops still in the box. I continued down the hall to the room I had clothes already stashed in. I pulled back the dust cover and even though it was still daylight, I turned on the lamp on the bedside table. I curled up on top of the comforter, falling fast asleep.

* * *

Chapter Thirty-Five

When I woke the next morning, I vaguely remembered Nightcrawler waking me throughout the night and having me eat, drink and take pills. Other than that, I slept like the dead and felt better for it this morning. At least I think it's morning, I thought, looking out the window again. Yup. The sun was rising in the East.

I dragged myself into the private bath and started up the shower. The hot water stung my back, but it wasn't as bad as the last time I showered. I heard the bathroom door open.

"You shouldn't be getting those stitches wet," Nightcrawler scolded.

"I went months without being allowed to shower. The closest I got was being tossed in a washtub of bleach. I don't give a fuck if you think I shouldn't get my stitches wet."

"Fair enough. Yell if you need help," he said before closing the door.

It took a long time to get dressed, but I finally managed to get some loose cotton pajama pants on and double up on tank tops again. The stitches were snagging on everything. I meandered down the hall and into the kitchen. Nightcrawler had a place set for me next to him at the breakfast bar. Taking my seat, I observed the plate of scrambled eggs, toast, some fruit, and a selection of glasses of different beverages, including a small teacup of coffee. I looked over at his oversized coffee cup.

"Is there a reason you're bogarting the coffee?"

"You're too weak to have much. The caffeine will send your nerves spinning. Concentrate on the food and other beverages, and as you build up to a whole meal, we can increase your coffee intake. Until then, you get a teacup, and only a teacup," Nightcrawler grinned.

"If I would've known you were this big of an ass, I would've never allowed you to come with me," I sighed.

I managed to eat half my eggs, a slice of toast and some fruit before I called it quits and drank my coffee. Nightcrawler grabbed a bottled water and steered me to the couch, handing me the bottle and the remote.

"I'm going to go for a run. Watch some TV or take a nap," he said before ruffling up my hair and heading out the front door.

I stared at the remote, trying to remember when the last time was that I watched TV. I couldn't. And, I honestly didn't miss it. I thought about turning on the national news, but I wasn't ready to know what was going on in the rest of the world yet. I tossed the remote on the coffee table, and despite my intentions not to, ended up falling back asleep.

An hour later, I woke when Nightcrawler was sneaking back in through the front door.

"Damn it," Nightcrawler chuckled. "I was trying not to wake you."

"I need to stop sleeping so much," I yawned.

"Actually, you need to get more sleep. It's part of the healing process."

"Well, I need to be on full meals and regular sleep patterns in the next few days."

"You can't rush this," Nightcrawler shook his head.

"I don't have a choice. I need to handle something, and I can't do that until I'm back on my feet," I said, pulling myself up with the armrest on the couch and walking into the kitchen.

I retrieved the leftover cut up fruit, nibbling on it as I drank a partial glass of milk. I took both into the War Room and started up the computers. It was time to get to work.

I had two of the new laptops setup and the laptop from my duffle bag setup. I didn't know how to connect them to the flat screen wall monitors, but I didn't really need to either. I didn't have enough information researched to bother displaying anything on the wall.

An hour into my work, I yawned and went to the kitchen to get a glass of juice. Nightcrawler was in the living room watching CNN with the volume turned low.

"And, in breaking news, the Miami DA's office announced that bail has been denied for veteran Grady Tanner for the murder of notorious Maxwell Lautner. Tanner will be remanded to Miami State Prison to await his trial. Jury selection is expected to begin sometime late

Fall of this year. If convicted, Grady Tanner could face the death penalty."

I dropped the glass I was holding to the floor, and it shattered around me.

"Shit," Nightcrawler said, running over to me. "I swear, I didn't know. No one back in Biloxi said a word about Grady being arrested." Picking me up, he placed me on the other side of the broken glass.

I stood frozen, staring at the TV screen, waiting for them to say that it was all a big mistake. That Grady wasn't really in Miami being charged with murder. A murder that was my fault.

I walked down the hall and into the War Room. Nightcrawler followed behind me and sat in the chair next to me. I closed the browser screen that I was on and pulled open the Skype service. I entered the number and hit send. Minutes later, Tech was staring at me over the screen.

"This isn't how it was supposed to go," I said, tears starting to well. "I thought I had more time to go after him. Why would he have gone after Grady? Why didn't you turn over the evidence to get him released? What the HELL is going on?"

"Kelsey, I don't know what you're talking about," Tech said calmly. "How are you?"

"Up until five minutes ago, she was getting better," Nightcrawler said. "She just saw on CNN that Grady was arrested for Max Lautner's murder."

"What? He wasn't even there," Tech said appearing dumbfounded. "Neither Donovan nor Bones has said a word to me about this. I swear, Kelsey. I would've called Maggie and turned over the evidence. I would've had Katie hire him a lawyer."

"Do it. Get ahold of Maggie. Get ahold of Katie. Tell Katie to contact Thomas Keegal and hire him to represent Grady. Shit," I said, getting up to pace. "I'm not strong enough yet."

"Kelsey, whatever's going on, we'll handle it," Tech said.

"You can't," I yelled at the computer. "No matter the reason that SOB started the case against Grady, he will hold him for as long as he can until I turn up."

"Who will hold Grady?" Nightcrawler asked.

I reached up to drag my hand through my hair, but a sharp pain ran through my shoulder. I cradled my arm into my chest as I tried to comprehend what was happening.

"Kelsey," Nightcrawler called my attention back. "Who is it? Who's coming after you?"

"The District Attorney," I answered him honestly.

"The Miami mother-fucking DA?" Tech yelled. "Why? What does he want?"

"I told him that I was going to kill him," I said before walking out of the room and to my bedroom.

I paced in the small space, but it only drove my anxiety up. Grady was suffering because of me. What had they done to him? What evidence did they have on him? Why didn't he reach out to Tech?

I knew the answer to the last question. He couldn't turn me in for Max's death. He was trying to protect me, even after I had disappeared off the face of the earth.

"Damn it, Grady! What the fuck were you thinking?" I screamed at the ceiling.

My hands shook, and my eyes were blinded by more tears. I grabbed a suitcase from the closet and started packing. I need to get to Miami. I need to save Grady.

Nightcrawler came in and placed his hands gently on my shoulders, but I pulled away. I didn't want anyone touching me.

"Katie is working on getting Grady a lawyer, and Maggie is getting the FBI in Miami to pick up the evidence from your safe-house in Florida. Tech needs to talk to you though. You need to help them figure this out so they can help Grady."

I nodded, setting down the stack of clothes that I was sorting.

I took a deep breath and walked back into the War Room. Tech was on the large wall screen.

"I want to patch Katie, Maggie, and Genie in on the call if that's okay. Genie will be able to track you, but Maggie says you're not in any trouble."

"Do it," I nodded.

Nightcrawler sat at the laptop and accepted the Skype connections and soon everyone's faces were displayed on the two screens.

"I'm not sure what's going on, Kelsey, but we'll get to Florida and help Grady," Maggie said.

"You can't. You can get the evidence processed, but make sure you have tight records of everything first. Once the DA's office has access to it, it may disappear."

"What?" Maggie asked.

"District Attorney Aaron Chandler is not a good man. He's only going to drop the case against Grady if he can get me back in the city and under his thumb. He wants me dead. And, if he gets me arrested, then he has the power to make it happen."

"You can't go to Miami then," Tech insisted.

"I agree," Maggie said. "If Chandler is dirty, we'll get the evidence on him and have him arrested. We'll work on getting Grady out of prison too. You just stay wherever you are hiding and let us handle it."

"I can't. If I don't show up on Monday, he'll have Grady hurt, perhaps killed. I have to make the trade."

"And, what about Nicholas?" Katie asked. "What about all the rest of us that have been worried sick that we'd never see you again? Is it that easy just to give up?"

"Katie, I can't let Grady take the fall for any of this. And, that's what he's trying to do. He's trying to sacrifice his life for mine. I can't live with that."

She turned away from the lens and wiped her tears with the back of her hand before turning back and nodding at the screen. "What do you need?"

"I need the lawyer for Grady. Prep him to be ready with any and all information. He needs to prepare for every move the DA is going to make. I need the FBI to process the evidence. I also need someone to look at whatever the DA is using against Grady as evidence. Since I know he wasn't there when Max died, whatever they have against him has to be fabricated."

"I can get access to it," Genie nodded. "I can also make sure the crime techs retain custody of all the new evidence and copy me on everything."

"Genie, don't watch the video of Max's death," Tech grinned. "It's a bit gory."

"Did you kill him?" Maggie asked me.

"No. I may have kidnapped him for a boat ride, but he jumped in the water all on his own," I said. "And, the only reason the video is gory is because I tried to save him but only managed to pull an arm up into the boat."

Maggie thumped her head on her desk. Genie scrunched up her nose and looked like she might get sick. Tech and Katie laughed.

"Okay, so your lawyer will have to work on the kidnapping part. As long as he can get you bail, it will give us time to gather evidence against Chandler. What is this guy capable of?" Maggie asked.

I looked at Nightcrawler, and he nodded. I turned my back to the laptop, and Nightcrawler helped to lift my tank tops to show them my injuries.

"I'll kill the motherfucker," Tech growled.

"Oh my god," Genie cried.

Maggie and Katie were silent. I think they knew that anything they said would just hurt worse. Nightcrawler helped to pull the tank tops back down over my stitches.

"Kelsey, you can't go to Miami with injuries that bad. If the DA does manage to get you locked up, how are you going to defend yourself?" Maggie asked.

"I'll do what I have to do. Can you meet me at the house in Miami tonight? And, can you set up a meeting with Mickey through the warden? I don't want it getting back to the DA that I visited the prison."

"I'll set it up. How far out are you?"

I checked the clock. "I can be there by six tonight."

I disconnected the line and walked back to my bedroom to finish packing. By the time I came out, Nightcrawler had all the rest of the bags, including some groceries loaded into the car. He picked up my suitcase and helped me lock up the house.

Chapter Thirty-Six

I asked Nightcrawler to stop at a rest stop just inside the Florida border. I got out of the SUV and found a clean patch of grass to sit on. Stretching left and then to the right, I worked as many muscles in my arms and back as I could. From there, I stood and stretched my calves and thighs until I felt them resisting.

"That's enough," Nightcrawler said. "You don't want to overdo it. Here, eat some food. I packed turkey sandwiches. They'll be a little dry, but they shouldn't upset your stomach."

Sitting down again, I took another solid drink of water before eating half of my sandwich. When Nightcrawler realized that I was trying to force myself to eat the rest of it, he took it away and threw it in the trash.

"You can't get up, can you?" he grinned down at me.

"I think I overdid it."

Grabbing me under my armpits, he helped to pull me up and held an arm out for me to grab onto if I needed help on the way back to the SUV.

"I'm impressed. Another week and you'll be fit to take on an eighty-year-old woman."

"Shut up and drive."

We pulled in the back driveway around 5:30. I wasn't surprised to see multiple vehicles parked in the back lot. I took a deep breath to prepare myself. As I opened the screen door and stepped into the kitchen, I could hear Katie yelling, followed by Bones yelling back at her.

"It's not about what you want or what you need, Bones," Katie yelled. "It's about what Kelsey needs."

"She needs me to get her the hell out of town is what she needs. I'll fly her out on my grandfather's jet until this all blows over," Bones yelled.

"You think that she'll just be okay with that?"

"I wasn't planning on giving her a choice. She could get killed."

"And, so could Grady," I said from the doorway. "Is that acceptable to you, Bones? To trade your friend's life so easily?"

"Kelsey," Bones said, reaching out for me.

I jumped back behind Nightcrawler. Nightcrawler held his hands out for everyone to stop their approach.

"Kelsey," Nightcrawler coaxed.

I peeked my head around his shoulder and saw everyone was frozen in their place. I looked at Katie and then to Maggie. Maggie nodded.

"Everyone," Maggie called, getting them all to turn to her. "You need to give Kelsey some space. She's not going to be comfortable with people hugging her or unexpectedly touching her. So, let's just back up. Bones, you too."

Bones eyes were locked on mine, but he stepped back and leaned against the living room entranceway. I slowly followed Nightcrawler into the room, remaining for the most part in his shadow. The door to the War Room was open, but the wall-mounted TV screens were now along the living room wall and the living room furniture had been moved to fit a large folding table and chairs.

As Nightcrawler led us to the center of the room, I became overwhelmed with the number of people. My heart raced, and I stepped further away from the crowd. Nightcrawler held his hand out, palm open, in front of me. I looked at the hand, then at him. He patiently waited until I took his hand before leading me over to the far wall to sit on the sofa. He sat a few feet away, but on the edge, positioned to stop anyone from getting too close to me. I had to blink fast, to prevent myself from crying.

"We have a meeting at the prison at 10:00 tonight. Are you sure you don't want me to go alone?" Maggie asked.

"No. I need to talk to Mickey. He won't help if you ask him. Hell, he might not help if I ask him." I looked over at Wild Card. "Is Nicholas safe?"

"He has Charlie, Reggie, Jackson and Pops on him at all times. I'm surprised they even let him go to the bathroom by himself. And at night, Donovan has a full security crew watching the ranches."

I turned to Donovan, "Lisa?"

"Eight months pregnant and counting," Donovan grinned. "She's good. She told me to give you a hug and a kiss, but she'll forgive me if it's not what you need right now," he shrugged. "And, thanks for coming to help Grady. He didn't tell anyone the mess he was in."

"That's just Grady," I smiled. "I'll get him out, Donovan. No matter what, I'll get him out."

• • •

Donovan nodded before turning away. He loved Grady like a brother and me as a sister. Chances were good that he would lose one of us.

"Genie, Tech, do you guys have anything yet?"

"Curiosity got the best of Genie, and she decided to watch the death of Maxwell Lautner against our recommendations. So, she spent the last hour in the bathroom throwing up while I had to do most of the research," Tech grinned.

Little tiny Genie in all her quiet, giggly, happy-go-lucky-personality, hauled off and slugged Tech in the arm hard enough to knock him out of the metal chair he was sitting on.

Everyone laughed at the shocked look on Tech's face and the superior grin on Genie's face. I held my ribs and tried to hold my laughter in because it hurt too much.

"Broken or bruised?" a voice to my right asked.

"Doc," I grinned. "Just bruised."

"And, the shoulder?" he grinned back with a raised eyebrow.

"It was dislocated a few weeks ago, and I had to pop it back into place," I frowned.

"So it could be fractured?"

"Doubtful," I said shaking my head. "I think I'd know."

"No, you wouldn't," Nightcrawler said. "Today was the first day you've been even able to walk across a room by yourself. Let the Doc check you out."

"Fine, but I'm not going to the hospital," I insisted, pointing a finger at Doc.

"Didn't figure you would, Dear," Doc grinned and followed me into the back bedroom.

Once in the back room, Doc closed the door, and my hands started to shake. "Doc, I can't," I admitted, shaking my head.

"It's alright. Let me just take a look at your shoulder and ribs. You don't have to get undressed. Do you need antibiotics?"

"A medic gave me some. Nightcrawler has them and gives them to me. I don't know what kind they are."

"Sit. Let me look at your shoulder first," Doc insisted and came over to run his hand around my collar bone and shoulder joint. "Your collar has a knot in it. Was it broken too?"

"Fractured, but it's getting better. It was a couple of months ago."

"And, how long ago was it that your shoulder was dislocated?"

"I don't know," I sighed.

"Well, the bones feel like they're in all the right places, so if it's anything at all, it's a fracture, but I think it's more likely a pinched nerve or tendon. Could even be just cramped muscles. I'm going to check out your ribs, but you can leave your tank tops on."

Doc quickly and efficiently checked my ribs, first on one side, then on the other. I was shaking by the time he was done, and he stepped back and leaned against the wall to give me some space.

"I don't think anything is broken. I'll check the medication and make sure it's strong enough. Do you need anything else?"

Still trying to calm myself, I was unable to talk but managed to shake my head no.

I sat on the bed for a long time, trying to get my hands to stop shaking. Every time I thought about walking back down the hall and into the living room, they just shook harder.

Wild Card stepped into the doorway and without meaning to, I cringed back.

"You're okay," he assured me. "We need your help out there, though. Nightcrawler is talking to Doc, so why don't you let me be your bodyguard for a little while."

I looked up at him, and he stepped back and turned toward the living room. I got up and walked near him, and when I was just two feet behind him, he started moving forward. He was letting me be his shadow, just like Nightcrawler had. He led me over to the same spot on the sofa, and I pinched my shaking hands between my knees as he sat a few feet away from me, pitched forward to stop anyone from getting too close. Again, I had to blink back the tears. How was I going to help Grady if I was afraid to be in a room with friends and family?

"So, I wasn't able to get a copy of the video that the DA has as evidence against Grady, but somehow—and I don't want to know how—Carl obtained a copy," Genie grinned.

I winked at Carl, "Thank you, Carl."

"I wanted to help Grady," he grinned back at me.

"I'm glad, but next time check with Tech first, okay?"

"Okay," he smiled before turning back to his laptop.

Tech shook his head. "I have the video ready to play if you're ready."

I nodded, and Tech pulled it up on the center screen. Donovan closed the curtains to darken the room, and I tensed up. Wild Card held an open palm in front of me, and I grabbed his hand as if my life depended on it.

The video showed a boat crossing the water before it stopped. It was similar to the speedboat that I had borrowed from Lenny but a different model. Lenny's had dual engines. This boat was only a single engine. I didn't recognize the area. The video was from a buoy recording, though, one that was North of the warehouse district, not South, where I took Max.

Two men were in the boat, and I was surprised to see the one in the back was Max. The one in the front had a mask on, but when he pulled off the mask, it appeared to be Grady. I looked confused back at Genie and Tech. Genie had her hands over her eyes and Tech just shrugged that he didn't know why the video showed Max and Grady.

Something about the man with Max's face seemed familiar, though. Something about how he moved. Then the man with Grady's face pulled out a knife and slashed Max's throat. He then grabbed Max as he was falling and shoved him over the side of the boat. I sat there, stunned, and confused. Tech stopped the video and nudged Genie that she could uncover her eyes.

"It's obviously fake, but how do you prove it?" I asked.

"We can't. Not without the original footage," Genie shrugged. "The video has been spliced and then flattened, so we can't pull apart the layers. I did find some traces where the pixels don't line up well, and it might be enough to prove to a jury that it has been tampered with, but it's not much to go on."

"And, if I can get you in to see the original footage?" I asked.

"Then game on," Genie grinned.

Nightcrawler walked over and set my duffle bag by my feet before stepping back. I pulled out my phone and called Uncle Hank.

"Hello," he barked into the phone.

"Still haven't learned phone etiquette?" I asked.

"It's easier to scare the telemarketers off if you're mean from the start," he chuckled. "Can't talk at the moment, though. Should I head your way?"

"Sounds good. You need an escort? I know you're getting old, and it's going to be dark soon."

Uncle Hank grunted and hung up on me.

"That's not good," I said staring at my phone.

"What's wrong?" Maggie asked.

"Uncle Hank didn't want to talk on the phone. He's coming over."

"Shit. If he's nervous…"

"Yeah, not good," I repeated. "Tech, rewind the video to when the pretend Max stands. Can you slow down the video to about half speed?"

"Sure. Did you see something?" he asked as he started it back up.

I was watching the screen and stood. I was about to walk closer when I realized that Donovan and Bones were standing nearby. I took a step back. Wild Card stepped around me and held his palm out. I took his hand, and he led me closer to the screen. Something about the fake Max was unnervingly familiar.

"Play it again."

Tech went back to the same mark and replayed the piece at an even slower speed.

And, that's when I saw it.

All the air left my lungs as my chest started seizing and I dropped to the floor. I was still tightly gripping Wild Card's hand as he kneeled in front of me and called for Nightcrawler. Nightcrawler pushed him out of the way and forced me up, and into the corner of the room. He yelled for the curtains and blinds to be opened as he held me up by my shoulders. I could see him counting out breaths but as the pounding of my heart got louder, I could no longer hear him.

I saw Bones approach and my lungs seized tighter.

I watched as Donovan, and Wild Card dragged Bones out of the living room and Genie and Maggie encourage everyone else outside.

Doc stepped in and held up a syringe. I shook my head and focused back on Nightcrawler.

I still couldn't hear him, but I watched his lips count out breathes. In… 1,2,3. Out… 1, 2, 3... In… 1… 2… 3… out… 1…..2…..3…

"There you go...," I heard him finally. "Breathe in, slowly, now out, slowly, keep it slow. Close your eyes, relax. Breathe in and... out. You okay now?"

I nodded and continued focusing on my breathing for a few more minutes before I was okay enough to open my eyes.

"That was embarrassing," I said.

"I'm going to leave a couple sedatives with Nightcrawler and Wild Card," Doc insisted. "If those panic attacks get any worse, they are to inject your ass. Got it."

"Yup," I grinned.

"Can you tell me what happened?" Maggie asked nodding at the video.

I heard the screen door open, and everyone slowly walked back in but kept to the other side of the living room.

"Where was Eric when the boat from Max's real death was retrieved?"

"I'm not sure. His deputy went out with us to unlock the boat shed. He said that Eric was on leave," Maggie answered.

Tears slid down my face as I walked over and picked up a throw pillow, gripping it tightly to my chest as I sat on the end of the couch.

"Kelsey?" Katie asked.

"It's Eric. The man that was killed in the video. It was Eric."

I sat on the couch, staring at the floor for a long time. Tears streamed down my face as I looked up to face the crowded but eerily quiet room.

"I did this. My friend is dead because of me. You all need to leave before it's too late. You need to save yourselves and everyone you love."

"You did not do this," Aunt Suzanne said, bulldozing herself past everyone.

She sat on her knees a few feet in front of me, careful not to reach out. "You look at me, and you listen up, Kelsey Harrison. There are evil people in this world, and you have always been brave enough to stand up to them. Eric was a good cop. His death wasn't just about protecting you. It was about protecting the rest of the world against the bad guys. Don't you steal that from him in death."

I nodded, wanting to reach out but unable to.

"Kelsey," Maggie interrupted. "How do you know the man in the video is Eric?"

"He worked his shirt up on his arm so that I could see part of his tattoo." My hands shook as I pointed to the inside of my own forearm.

"A small panther, just above his left wrist," Wayne said, walking over to the TV screen. Tech adjusted the video to zoom in on Eric's arm. "I remember seeing the tattoo and wondering what it meant."

"He got the tattoo years ago," Aunt Suzanne said. "Eric fell in love with Kelsey, but they were too different to make it work."

"My lion," I smiled at Aunt Suzanne.

"Destined to want the Panther," Aunt Suzanne grinned.

"Lion? Panther?" Donovan asked.

"Their friend Carly is a bit of a hippy spiritualist," Aunt Suzanne laughed. "She told him that he and Kelsey could never be life partners because he was a lion and she was a panther. He got a tattoo of a panther on his wrist and told Kelsey he'd always love her."

Donovan, Ryan, and Wild Card were watching Bones. He was tense, fists tightly clenched, and looking out the window.

"Eric knew he was going to die," Wayne said. "He knew it just as certainly as you knew that you were going to be kidnapped."

"So, why then? Why didn't he stay in Texas? If he would've just stayed there like I asked him…"

"A man like Eric can't hide, Kelsey," Uncle Hank said. "It's just not in him."

I looked down at the floor and watched tears drip off my face and onto the carpet. Aunt Suzanne handed a tissue to me, and I wiped my face.

"Did you love him?" Genie asked in her innocent way.

"As much as I could," I nodded. "If my life would have been simpler, he would have been the perfect man for me. But I grew up learning how to fight my own battles, and he wanted someone to protect."

It was silent for a long time until Uncle Hank cleared his throat.

"We can mourn Eric later, Kel. We need to talk," Uncle Hank insisted.

I nodded. "Speak freely."

He started walking over to me, and I involuntarily flinched. He stopped and pulled out a chair a few feet away.

"I'm going to make some fresh coffee," Aunt Suzanne said, climbing up from the floor.

"Kelsey can't have coffee. Can you see if there's any tea?" Nightcrawler said.

Several sets of eyes turned to me in shock.

I turned to Nightcrawler and stuck my tongue out at him as he chuckled and took residence in the bodyguard seat to my left on the sofa.

"Tea with a dash of honey I think would be best," Aunt Suzanne smirked, walking into the kitchen. "I'll see what I can whip up for snacks too."

I turned to Uncle Hank.

"I remembered Charlie telling me about your friend Grady. When he was arrested, it seemed—off. I did a little digging. The DA's office ran their own investigation and issued the warrant for his arrest. There was never a police file. When I met up with my buddy who works at the Center where the buoy data is stored, he told me I needed a warrant and then he got up and walked away without another word. The next day, I noticed I had a tail. Yesterday, I found a tracker on my caddy. I pulled it off before coming over tonight. I'm not sure what I walked into, but I don't want your Aunt around it."

"Genie, Maggie, can you guys see if you can get a federal warrant for the video files?"

"Tech, Bones, inspect the Caddy to make sure that nothing else was missed."

Bones and Tech walked out. Tech carried with him a bag that I knew had scanning devices. Carl tilted his head and followed Tech outside.

A piercing noise split the air in two. I jumped onto the back of the couch and covered my head. My body shook as I waited for the impending pain.

Nothing happened.

I looked carefully through a gap between my arms as Nightcrawler stood protectively in front of me and Uncle Hank bowed his head.

"Shit," I whispered, slipping off the top edge of the couch back onto the seat. "I'm sorry. I'll try to get it together."

"Kelsey Harrison, I was in that house. I saw where that bitch kept you. I can't imagine what she did to you, so you act as looney as you need to act for as long as you need to," Maggie said, before turning and walking out of the house.

"Kierson had to drag her out," Genie whispered. "He was crying and wouldn't let me go in."

"I lived," I whispered.

I looked at Nightcrawler, and he grinned down at me.

"I lived," I said louder, and we both smiled.

"I killed the bitch. And, I escaped. I will get through this too," I nodded to myself. "And, yeah, I'm probably going to do some looney shit for a while, but I lived."

"Damn straight," Nightcrawler laughed.

"That's my girl," Aunt Suzanne grinned, handing me a cup of tea. "But I think the next time I make you tea I'll use the microwave instead of the tea kettle," she winked before returning to the kitchen.

"If you're going to the prison tonight, you need a nap first," Nightcrawler said.

"I'm not a child," I glared.

"Either take a nap, or you don't go. You're jumpy when you're tired, and it's going to be hard enough for you to get through security to get inside the prison, not to mention all the doors and noises. Drink your damn tea and then go take a nap."

I glared at Nightcrawler, and got up, walking a wide circle around everyone as I escaped down the hall to the back bedroom. It was starting to get dark out, so I turned on the closet light and a side table lamp. I took a drink of my tea before laying down.

Wild Card stepped in and sat down on the floor near the bedroom door. He winked at me, and I grinned. He wasn't guarding my door because I was in any danger. He was guarding it because he knew that was what I needed. I closed my eyes and fell fast asleep.

Chapter Thirty-Seven

I dreamt that I heard Grady's voice calling out to me.

I turned to listen in the blackness that surrounded me. *"Grady?"*

"Did you make it out?" Grady's voice asked.

I couldn't see him, but I could hear him as if he was only a few feet away, hidden behind the black fog, just out of reach. I stepped forward, into the darkness, feeling the temperature drop.

"No—Don't follow me. Stay in the light," Grady's voice called.

"But where are you?"

"Are you safe? Did you make it out?"

"Yes."

"Then run, Kelsey. Run!"

I woke with a start, sitting up in bed, covered in sweat. Throwing myself backward into the headboard, I scrambled up on my feet on top of the bed, my back braced against the wall.

My abrupt waking startled Wild Card, causing him to jump up in a panic near the doorway.

"I'm okay," I gasped, controlling my breathing.

I closed my eyes and counted it out.

"It was Grady. He told me to run. My God that sounds so nuts, even to me."

I ran my hands through my hair, pulling the strands tight to my scalp.

"That doesn't sound nuts at all," Wayne chuckled from the doorway, standing behind an alert Wild Card. "Grady dreamt that you were talking to him all the time."

"That's too weird," I laughed.

"He would've sold his soul to get you back. Grady and Eric believed me when I told them about the fortune teller and the vision. It somehow made sense to them. As for me, I can't figure out why you did it. Why you let Nola kidnap you."

"Because in the vision, I didn't die," I answered honestly. "And, if I didn't die, then there was a chance, albeit a small chance, that I could take down Nola. She wasn't going to stop. She was going to keep coming after my family until blood was spilled."

"You had to fight your demons," Wild Card whispered.

I nodded.

I looked at the clock. I had two more hours before we had to be at the prison and it was a half an hour drive. I maneuvered around Wild Card and Wayne and cautiously walked down the hallway. Tech and Genie were working away on their laptops in the war room. Maggie was looking out the front bay window in the living room, talking on the phone.

I peeked into the kitchen to find Ryan and Uncle Hank sitting at the small table and Aunt Suzanne fiddling around in the kitchen. Ryan waved, Uncle Hank winked, and Aunt

Suzanne rolled her eyes and poured me a half a cup of coffee.

I sat at the bar to enjoy the cup, and she slid a plate with a boring turkey sandwich with lettuce and tomato toward me. I pouted but took several bites before I pushed it away and turned back to my coffee.

I enjoyed two whole sips before Nightcrawler came in and took the cup away. He pushed the sandwich plate back in front of me and strolled into the living room.

I threw my best glare at his back before I forced myself to eat the rest of at least one-half of the sandwich. Aunt Suzanne put the other half in the refrigerator. *Yeah. Something to look forward too.*

I walked over to the kitchen door and started to step outside, wanting a smoke. I stopped myself when I realized the outside lights were off.

"Tyler's out there," Ryan said. "Turn on the light and call out."

I flipped the switch, and the porch and driveway lit up. I saw a figure on the edge of the lawn.

"Tyler?" I called through the screen.

"Yeah," he answered hurrying up the porch steps to stand in the light. "Come on out. We have three guys out patrolling, and I've vetted them all," he grinned.

"Thank you," I smiled and stepped out on the deck.

He pulled a cigarette and his lighter out and handed them off to me. Tyler loved me, I thought as I inhaled deeply.

I heard the screen door behind me and jumped. Turning, I saw that it was only Nightcrawler. He shook his head at the cigarette I was smoking.

"Hey, it's all part of my relaxation program," I grinned.

"At least it's not coffee," he said, lighting up a cigarette for himself.

Nightcrawler stood tense, looking about the yard. He took a deep breath and opened his mouth to say something, but then stopped himself. He looked down at the porch.

"Spit it out," I said. "Whatever you need to say, just say it."

"I don't think you should go to the prison tonight," he sighed. "It's too much for you right now."

"I don't have a choice. I need to set up protection for Grady and a phone call won't cut it."

"We can't send a bodyguard in with you," Nightcrawler said.

"Maggie will be with me. Maybe they'll let her take a taser in with her, so if I lose my shit, she can zap me," I grinned.

Nightcrawler rolled his eyes and walked off into the dark yard.

"Anything special you need me to do?" Tyler asked after Nightcrawler was out of sight.

"Not at the moment. If Genie gets a warrant to pull some security videos, she might need to take Tech with her. If that happens, can you babysit Carl?"

"I shouldn't have asked," Tyler laughed. "Yeah, I'll have him rewire something to keep him out of trouble."

"How's your training going?" I asked.

"It's not. It's been too busy with everything going on for Bones to work with me. I'm going to have to start from scratch again. But, I've been running and lifting weights."

"I'll talk to the guys and see if we can get a rotation of trainers set up. I would work with you, but Nightcrawler says that I'm comparable to an eighty-year-old woman right now."

"Should I pick you up a walker?" Tyler chuckled.

"Being you're not trained, I think that even my eighty-year-old self could get a few solid moves in, so I'd watch it," I grinned.

Donovan stepped out onto the porch as I was lighting up a second cigarette.

"Maggie wants to leave early, so you'll have plenty of time to get through security," Donovan said.

"In other words, she wants plenty of time for a few panic attacks along the way."

"It could happen. Those metal gates and cell doors might be a problem for you. Doc is sending a sedative with her, just in case."

"Smart. But I'm going to go in all Zen-like and channel my nervous issues into positive thinking," I grinned.

"To have a sit down with a cop killer and drug dealer?"

"Mickey isn't as bad as people make him out to be. On the inside, he's a complete marshmallow."

Maggie snorted, stepping out onto the deck. "Oh, yeah. That's why I almost peed my pants the first time you dragged me with you to visit him."

The last time Maggie and I had visited Mickey, it was to tell him his daughter was murdered by a man named Darrien Pasco. It had been an intense meeting.

"Pasco dead yet?" I asked, cringing.

"He's been hospitalized four times, but he's still alive," Maggie shivered.

"Only six more trips to go," I sighed.

Donovan raised an eyebrow not understanding. I turned to Tyler, who was grinning. Mickey had a rule, that if you hurt someone he cared about, you'd get it back tenfold. Pasco tortured and killed his only daughter and was locked up in the same prison. He had a lot more suffering to endure.

I channeled as much Zen as I could muster, but by the time we finally reached the holding cell that they would bring Mickey into, I was ready to jump out of my skin. Every time the cell doors buzzed and slammed shut, I either jumped back into Maggie or jumped forward into the warden. He looked ready to drag me back out by the time we got to the room.

"Shit, that was a long trip," Maggie sighed. "You are so damn twitchy."

"Sorry," I said, leaning over to put my hands on my knees and take several deep breaths. "Nightcrawler tried to warn me, but I had to come."

"We have about ten minutes before they bring Mickey in, so sit and relax."

I tried to relax, but every time I heard one of the doors open and slam close, no matter how far away, I jumped. I stood back up, pacing, and unfortunately, all the movement was pulling at my stitches. The loose-fitting blouse I had worn had spots of blood already dotting my sleeve.

By the time they led Mickey in, I was beyond tense. The sound of his chains caused me to move to the back wall and lean my forehead on the cool cement. I focused on my breathing but still jumped when the guard slammed the door shut.

"Try not to move your chains," Maggie said to Mickey as I continued to count out my breathing.

By the time I turned around, both of them were intently watching me. Mickey had his fingers interlaced, and the chains tucked under his wrists.

"You're not well," Mickey said.

"That's an understatement," I chuckled humorlessly.

I pulled the chair on my side of the table out and sat a few feet away from the table.

"Are you scared of me?" Mickey asked.

"No. I'm scared of everything," I said shaking my head. "But, I'll get past it."

"You've been missing for months. I heard on the news that Nola was dead. Was that you?"

"She had me until a couple days ago," I nodded. "She got what she deserved in the end."

Mickey looked at my hands and then at the small area of my neck that was exposed.

"How bad off are you?"

"Bad," Maggie answered for me. "She should be in a hospital on a morphine drip, but she insisted she needed to speak to you."

I looked up at the camera and watched until the light went from green to red. Mickey glanced up and grinned.

"Why me?" Mickey asked me.

"I need your help. And, I know it's going to cost me, but I have to ask for it anyway. There's a man in here, Grady Tanner. He's a friend of mine. I'm trying to get him out, but he'll need protection until I do. I'm hoping to have him out Monday or Tuesday. But as soon as I put my plan in motion, my enemies are going to go after him."

Mickey looked up at the camera and then shifted back to look at the door. When he did so, his chains rattled, and I jumped.

"Nola chained you?"

I nodded.

Mickey was silent for several echoing strikes of the clock. He sat there intently watching me, inspecting my reactions, studying my breathing. I closed my eyes and waited for him to speak.

"Tanner's already been marked. The guards roughed him up and encouraged a few inmates to lean on him as well. I've been watching because it doesn't make sense. Who painted a target on his back? He's not a cop. And, he's not from around here."

"The DA."

"Chandler?"

"The one and only. He wants me in Miami so he can drum up charges against me. He'll put me in the women's prison as quickly as he can."

"Why?" Mickey asked, leaning forward, careful not to jangle his shackles.

"He's one of the men that Nola brought in to hurt me. But, it's more than that. He was so eager to hurt me that it was more like revenge for something that I did. I haven't figured it all out yet."

"He was the prosecutor on my case when he was just an assistant DA."

"I know. But he's mine," I said, looking up at him and forcing myself to make eye contact. "I need to do this my way."

Mickey nodded. He looked back up at the camera confirming the light was still red.

"I'll agree to protect your friend if you pull my file and research something for me," Mickey said.

"Research?"

"The cop who was murdered, Derek Iverson, I didn't kill him, Kelsey."

I studied Mickey. His cold eyes stared back.

"Did you know him?"

Mickey nodded. "Derek was a rookie on my block when he first started. One night, I was walking by when I noticed a standoff between Derek and a robber at the corner liquor store. Derek was alone and in over his head. His hands were shaking."

Mickey looked away and stared at the wall before continuing.

"The woman behind the counter was crying, and the guy with the gun was ready to shoot. I walked in and walked up to the gunman. I didn't know his name, but I recognized him, and he recognized me. I held out my hand for the gun, and he handed it over. I set the gun on the shelf near the door and walked out."

"That was kind of stupid," I laughed.

Mickey shrugged.

"As the years passed, Derek and I would exchange the occasional head nods, but we never spoke. One night I was at Sully's when Derek walked in. He walked right up to me and shook my hand. His wife had given birth to their first son, and he wanted to let me know they named him Michael and would be calling him Mickey as a nickname.

"I sat there, stunned. I looked at him and said 'but you're a cop'. Derek just laughed and said there's good and bad in everyone." Mickey shook his head grinning. "He was a good man."

"Was that the last time you saw him?"

Mickey nodded. "He was found dead later that night in his apartment. His wife and son were still staying in the hospital."

I continued to study Mickey. I knew the basics of the case. They said Mickey followed Derek home and killed him. Witnesses testified that he had threatened Derek in the bar.

"Who testified against you?"

"Sully, for one," Mickey chuckled. "I could've put him six feet under, but what was the point? I don't think any of the other witnesses were even at the bar that night. I was setup."

"Who was at the bar that night?"

"It was a long time ago, Kelsey."

"Think Mickey. Think about the room. You would've looked around. Who else was there?"

"Kelsey?" Maggie asked. "What are you thinking?"

I held up a hand for her to wait as Mickey furrowed his brows concentrating.

"I had my usual guards with me. I sat at the end of the bar, but there were three booths behind me. My guard was in charge of watching my back, but you're right, I would've looked for myself. Only a few tables toward the front had customers, and some of them left when I showed up."

Mickey turned his head, thinking hard on something.

"What is it?" I asked.

"Derek went to wave at someone but stopped. I had just offered to buy him a celebratory beer, but he said he had to go."

"Which direction was he looking when he was going to wave?"

"The back booth. I looked that direction, but the guy facing me had his head ducked down, and the other guy had his back to me."

Mickey turned back to me and shrugged.

"I'll look into it, but if I decide you're guilty, I quit. I won't help a cop killer beat the charges."

"Wouldn't expect you to," Mickey grinned. "For years, I didn't care. I was going to be in here, regardless, so what did it matter."

"But when Molly died, you remembered Derek had a kid."

"I don't want that kid growing up thinking I killed his old man. I've done a lot of bad things, but Derek was a good man that I respected. He didn't deserve to go down like that."

"It's almost time," Maggie warned, looking up at the camera.

"You'll have Grady's back in here?"

"I'll put the word out. Anyone messes with him, they'll have to answer to me."

"Thank you, Mickey."

"You know, his tattoo makes me think of you," Mickey grinned at me.

"I didn't know he had a tattoo," I said surprised.

"He has a tat on his back of a panther climbing a cliff," Mickey nodded. "In prison, tats say a lot about a convict. We used them as a guide to see if someone is affiliated with anyone. But when I saw his, I thought of you for some reason."

"A panther?" Maggie broke out laughing. "Oh my god, it's fate."

"Shut up," I grinned.

Mickey looked confused, but the guard came in and said it was time to leave. I jumped again from the sounds of the chains.

"One more thing, Kelsey," Mickey said, turning back to face me as the guard jerked on his arm. "Don't let the fear in—Stay angry. If you end up on the other side of the barbwire fence, you're going to need that anger to survive."

The guard roughly pulled his arm again, moving Mickey out the door.

I sat there and let Mickey's words sink in. He was right. I could be afraid, or I could get angry and fight back. I chose to fight.

Chapter Thirty-Eight

By the time we got back to the house, I was wired. It was almost midnight, but I had somewhere I needed to be. I walked into the kitchen and grinned at Uncle Hank.

"Want to go ruffle some feathers at Sully's?" I grinned.

"Beats anything else I have planned," Uncle Hank grinned back.

"Eat the other half of your sandwich first," Aunt Suzanne ordered, pointing her authoritative finger at me before she kissed Uncle Hank on the cheek and walked down the hall.

"We doing something fun?" Wild Card asked.

"Could be interesting," I shrugged, grabbing the half sandwich from the refrigerator. "Anybody that wants to go, get some Kevlar on and load up."

"About fucking time we get to do something," Wayne grinned, and fist bumped with Ryan.

Bones grinned, leaning against the wall, watching me.

Tyler looked bummed.

"Tyler, you can go too. Stay behind me and follow my lead. We'll consider it part of your training."

"I don't have a vest," Tyler said.

"She's got a shit load of equipment in the war room," Tech called out.

"I think Genie and I will call it a night," Maggie said. "We have warrants to serve in the morning for the videos you need."

"Probably for the best," Donovan chuckled, pulling on a bullet proof vest.

Nightcrawler helped me carefully strap on a vest, and Wild Card brought me a hip holster to clip on.

"So what's the goal tonight?" Uncle Hank asked.

"To find out why Sully and everyone else lied about Mickey killing that cop," I answered as I walked outside.

"He didn't do it?" Uncle Hank asked.

"Nope. But Derek saw someone that night at the bar and didn't live through the night to tell anyone," I answered, pulling the driver's door open and getting behind the wheel.

"You sure you don't want me to drive?" Uncle Hank asked.

"I'm sure," I grinned.

He ran around to the other side and commandeered the shotgun seat. Wild Card and Nightcrawler climbed in the back. Bones, Ryan, Wayne, Donovan and Tyler squeezed into the other SUV.

I threw the truck in reverse and hit the gas, driving around the other SUV in the curved driveway and into the road before slamming the truck into drive, and squealing my tires down the road. The guys in the other SUV caught up to me three blocks away.

"Shit," Nightcrawler said. "You *do* know how to drive in reverse."

"Only when she's pissed," Uncle Hank grinned, holding the 'oh-shit' ceiling bar.

I pulled up behind Sully's and stepped out of the SUV. Popping the back hatch, I flipped the hidden switch and grabbed a double barrel shotgun.

"I don't think so. Your arms are too weak to hold it. You're likely to drop it and shoot one of us in the ass," Nightcrawler said, taking the gun away.

"Fine. But we go in fully armed, and I take the lead. Sully won't shoot me," I said, moving toward the back door.

He was right, and I wasn't really angry with him for pointing it out. I was angry because I was so weak.

"On my six, Tyler!" I called out.

"Yes, ma'am," he answered coming up behind me.

I walked through the door into the dimly lit bar with heavily armed men following in behind me.

"S-U-L-L-Y...," I called as I made my way down the hall into the main room.

I spotted Sully behind the bar in his usual spot. He froze momentarily before he made a step further down the bar.

"You blink the wrong way, and this all goes to hell. Step away from the bar," I warned.

Sully stepped back, away from the bar and kept his eyes glued to me.

"Ladies and gentleman, the bar is closed. Make your way to the exits and don't forget to leave a tip," I yelled out, and the guys laughed.

Uncle Hank strolled behind the bar and passed Sully's revolver and shotgun off to Tyler. Customers casually exited the restaurant. No one seemed too concerned about why we walked in armed to talk to Sully. In this neighborhood, someone storming in shooting was the standard.

"What can I do for you, Officer Harrison?" Sully asked.

"It's just Harrison. Or if you're lucky, maybe someday you can call me Kelsey, but let's stick to Harrison for right now, shall we?" I grinned.

I motioned for Uncle Hank to haul him around the bar and to one of the tables.

"Check the rooms, make sure everyone cleared out," I ordered to the rest of the guys.

Half of them split off to check the back office and the bathrooms. The other half covered the doors.

I wandered around the bar's seating area, looking at various pictures until everyone reported back that the rooms were clear. I then moved behind the bar-top and set up a long row of shot glasses down the bar-top. I handed a top of the line vodka to Nightcrawler, and he happily started filling the glasses.

"So, Sully," I paused to down a shot. The hot liquor burned my throat, but the heat was welcomingly familiar. "I had a nice chat with Mickey tonight. Seems he's no longer willing to accept the blame for a cop's death. He wants me to find out who really killed Officer Derek Iverson. He told me to come talk to you."

"Ah, shit," Sully whimpered. "They'll kill me. Look, Kelsey, I'll visit Mickey. I'll make it up to him somehow."

"It's Harrison, remember? We're not friends, Sully," I shook my head. "And, Mickey has no interest in anything but clearing his conscience on this one. His only kid is dead. He's facing a long lonely stretch in prison for something he didn't do."

"I can't help you! I never wanted to set Mickey up. He's like a brother to me," Sully whined.

"A brother," I laughed. "Did you hear that, guys? Sully considers Mickey to be like a brother, and yet he still set him up for murdering a cop."

A room of heavily armed men glared at Sully.

"Donovan?"

"Yeah," Donovan said leaving his post at the front door.

Ryan rotated in to cover his post.

"There's a trap door in the floor behind the bar. I suspect that's where the security feeds lead. He has a video with audio for the main bar," I nodded up at the camera, "but he also has video recordings rigged in the wall panels at all the booths. I want everything," I grinned.

Donovan circled behind the bar and found the access door. He started down the ladder. Wayne and Nightcrawler followed him.

"Jackpot," Nightcrawler called up.

"Harrison, please," Sully cried. "They'll kill me."

I walked over to the booth and slid into the seat across from him. I waited for him to look up at me before I spoke.

"There are much worse fates-than death. Believe me," I said.

Sully brought his elbows up on the table and cried into is hands.

I pulled my gun out of its harness and racked the slide, before laying it on the table, pointed directly at him. I rested my hand on the handle, with my point finger extended out past the trigger. Sully quit crying.

"Why was the cop killed?"

"I don't know, I swear I don't," Sully shook his head, staring at the gun.

"Tell me what happened that night."

"Mickey was in with his usual bodyguards. He was surly—got into some argument with his daughter. Then the cop comes in and shakes Mickey's hand. Tells Mickey, he just named his first born after him on account of him saving his life when he was a rookie. Mickey seemed happy. He even smiled. He offered to buy the cop a beer, but the cop left. Mickey stayed for a few more rounds before leaving. Probably left two hours after the kid left."

"Who approached you about lying about that night?"

"Some city lawyer. Came in with a couple cops. Roughed me up real good and did a number on the bar. Broke every bottle in the place. Said if I needed further encouragement, I had better invest in a bullet proof vest."

"What cops?" I asked.

"Your old boss and a couple of his guys," Sully nodded.

Red flags were waving inside my head. "And, the city lawyer?"

"At the time he was just an assistant DA," Sully said in a shaky voice.

"His name?"

"Aaron Chandler."

"And, what else should I know Sully?"

Sully gulped, looking around the room before turning his attention back to me.

"Chandler was in the back booth with some other guy the night that cop died."

We walked through the kitchen door and found Katie and Tech were still up, seated at the breakfast bar drinking coffee. The men started hauling in all the video and audio recordings. Tech looked overwhelmed by the amount of data that moved past him and into the living room.

"Relax," I grinned. "We only need whatever's available for the night a cop was killed. The rest I had them take because it freaked Sully out."

Tech nodded, walking into the living room to start sorting out the mess.

"Why do you look so defeated?" I asked Katie.

"I can't get that damn lawyer on the line," Katie snapped. "Thomas Keegal seems to always be in a meeting, and he's not very attentive to returning phone messages. His secretary told me that the soonest he could meet with me was Monday."

I called Baker.

"I heard you were alive. You okay?" he asked answering the phone.

"I will be. Is Keegal still our attorney?"

"Yeah, though he's not as effective as he used to be. He's gotten pretty high and mighty. I was thinking of switching to a guy named Brackins. He has a small office, but he's sharp."

"Criminal work?"

"Some litigation, some criminal," Baker answered. "This about your friend Grady?"

"Yeah."

"Keegal has more experience, but if he half-asses the situation, then it could hurt Grady. I'd go with Brackins if it was my ass sitting in a cell. But I can drop a call to either one of them."

"Set up a meeting with both of them for 9:00 a.m. at the country club. And, meet me there."

"You got it, partner," he said before disconnecting.

"I know Thomas Keegal," Bones said stepping into the kitchen. "He handles our Florida legal work for Barrister Industries."

"Call your sister. See if she can catch a ride tonight on the company jet and meet me for breakfast." I grinned. "Tell Rebecca to leave your grandfather at home, though."

Bones grinned and stepped into the living room to make the call.

"Oh, this is going to be fun," Katie laughed.

● ● ●

Chapter Thirty-Nine

It was Saturday morning, and everybody who was anybody in Miami was at the Country Club rubbing elbows or snubbing the hired help. I walked in with Katie by my side. Both of us wore elegant but simple business dresses and high heels. My dress was a simple long sheath design and felt more comfortable than having pants rubbing on my waistline. Unfortunately, the outfit required a bra, so I was cautious when I moved to minimize the friction on my back.

The maitre'd recognized me immediately and greeted me accordingly. I asked if Baker had arrived yet and I was informed that he had and that my table was waiting. Donovan and Wayne followed us at a distance, but it was obvious to all the surrounding patrons, that the men, finely dressed in navy suits, were part of our security detail.

Entering the private room that had been reserved for us, Baker stood and walked over to kiss my cheek and greet me. I braced myself for the familiar act, but he noticed me tense up. He nodded and stepped back.

"Kelsey, what a pleasure it is to see you again," Rebecca greeted and started to stand.

I held a hand up for her to stay seated, before greeting her back. "Rebecca, thank you for coming on such short notice."

"May I introduce Thomas Keegal and Cameron Brackins –," Baker said, gesturing to each man.

"A pleasure to meet you, Ms. Harrison," Cameron Brackins said. Having stood when we entered, he extended a hand across the table.

I accepted the handshake and turned to greet Keegal, but he was too busy to be bothered as he was rudely informing the waitress that she shorted him on his scotch.

I grinned at the waitress as she passed by. She was one of the kids that I had mentored when I lived in Miami. "Jenny, right?"

"Yes, Ms. Harrison. I'm surprised you remember me," she nodded her head and smiled.

"Of course I remember you. How's your sister, Sawyer?"

"Well, thank you. She'll graduate high school next year."

"And, you? Still going to college?"

"Yes, ma'am. Third-year law student," she grinned proudly.

"Baker, can you give Jenny one of your business cards? She's going to be an excellent resource some day. I want to be sure she calls us and lets us know where she settles."

Baker walked over and handed Jenny his card. Rebecca surprised me by walking over and handing Jenny her card as well.

"If Kelsey Harrison is betting on you, then I'm willing to do the same," Rebecca grinned. "Stay in touch and let me know if you need anything."

"Baker," Keegal interrupted. "No offense man, but I thought you needed to meet on business. I'm not in the habit of listening to a bunch of housewives chit chat when I could be out golfing."

"Jenny, can you excuse us and come back in about ten minutes?"

"Yes, ma'am," she agreed and hurried from the room.

"I, of course, meant no offense to you, Ms. Hartwood," Keegal said, nodding to Rebecca. "When I heard that your grandfather was kind enough to give you the CEO chair of Barristers, I was quite agreeable to working with you closer."

Rebecca fumed and stepped back to the table. Palms flat on the table, she leaned over and glared down at Keegal.

"Please, Rebecca, allow me?" I asked.

She looked over at me before taking her seat again. Cameron Brackins was still standing but moved back to lean against the wall. I light smile tickled the corners of his mouth.

"Donovan, can you ask the maitre'd to come in for a moment?" I asked as I sat in the chair that Baker held out for me.

A moment later, Donovan followed the maitre'd into the room. The man nodded his head forward and awaited my request.

"I would like Mr. Keegal to leave the club. After today, his influence in Miami will be taking a downward spiral. He will no longer be the type of guest that should be allowed entry."

The maitre'd nodded at me and stepped back, motioning Mr. Keegal toward the door.

Mr. Keegal laughed. "Do you know who I am, little girl?"

"You're the lawyer that before this meeting, ignored several calls regarding an important case. I came here this morning, with the intention of hearing you out before I decided what my next move would be. But after witnessing your behavior, I don't need any more time to think about it. You're fired, Mr. Keegal. You are no longer the litigation attorney for KNC Enterprise, Mayfair Shipping or The Other Layer."

"You have to be a client to fire me, Ms. Harrison," he chuckled.

"This is fun. We should have recorded this," Baker laughed beside me.

"I am recording it," Katie said.

Everyone turned to see her with her smartphone pointed at our table.

"What? This is a golden Kelsey moment," she grinned.

"You see, Thomas," Baker grinned. "Kelsey is the majority owner of all those companies."

"She's also a major investor in Barrister Industries," Rebecca grinned, sipping her mimosa. "You're officially fired by my company too."

Keegal was no longer laughing.

"But, surely, you aren't serious about firing me? I'm the best attorney in Miami," he choked out.

"Were," Baker shook his head. "Even before you pissed off Kelsey I was planning on hiring Mr. Brackins and firing you."

"But I have represented your companies for years," he tried to back pedal.

"You need to leave, Mr. Keegal. This isn't up for discussion. You're fired. Now get out, or I will request security to drag you out."

Keegal slammed the French door into the wall as he stormed out. The maitre'd ducked his head, attempting to hide his grin, and quickly followed him.

"What a fun breakfast," Rebecca laughed. "We should do this more often."

Katie walked around the table and took the chair that had previously been Keegal's.

"Permission to close the blinds, Ms. Harrison?" Wayne asked from his position near the door.

"Yes, please. I feel like a sitting duck in front of all these windows," I sighed.

Jenny stepped back in the room, looking nervous and carrying a tray of beverages.

"My apologies, Ms. Harrison," Jenny nodded.

"You are old enough now to call me Kelsey," I grinned. "What's all this?"

"A gentleman called and asked to speak to whoever was serving you. I took the call, and the man said I was not to serve you coffee but to give you chamomile tea. And, he said you had to eat a veggie omelet with wheat toast. I really didn't know what to make of it, so I brought you tea and coffee."

Wayne and Donovan laughed. Donovan took the tea from the serving tray, setting it in front of me. Then he stole the coffee for himself.

"Jenny, it's fine. He's sort of my physical therapist, you might say. I'll drink the damn tea, but if he calls again, feel free to tell him to go to hell," I grinned. "Now, do you have other tables to work, or are you at our disposal?"

"I was scheduled off today, but they called me in when you reserved the room. I'm all yours."

"Good. Let's get a food order placed and then I want you to come back in and join us. And, I'll order the damn omelet."

She grinned and pulled out an order pad.

Jenny rushed off to the kitchen to place our orders, and I turned back to Cameron Brackins who was now seated next to Katie across the table.

"First, I want you to hire Jenny. She will be your paid intern for the rest of the summer and then she will work part time while she finishes law school. I'm confident that you will want to retain her when she graduates."

"Done," Cameron agreed.

"Next, I need you to clear your calendar. Grady Tanner has been charged with the murder of Max Lautner. He didn't do it. I want him released of all charges by Monday."

"I'm not familiar with the case beyond what the news has reported. Is there any evidence to dismiss the case?"

Jenny came back and joined us at the table. Everyone smiled a welcoming smile at her, and I pulled a check out of my shoulder bag and handed it to Cameron.

"Will this be enough for a retainer to get started?"

"Uhh, yes," Cameron said, clearing his throat. "This should cover any expenses. I take it money is not an object in this case?"

"Money is always a consideration," Rebecca said. "But Grady is innocent, and he's a friend of Ms. Harrison's and mine. His expenses will be taken care of without hesitation."

Cameron nodded and turned to Jenny.

"I've been asked to hire you. You'll be a paid intern while you finish law school. We can draw up a Non-disclosure later, but if you accept the job, then you can stay in this room. Otherwise, as Ms. Harrison's lawyer, I'd have to insist that you leave."

"You'll hire me?" Jenny asked, shocked.

"My dear," Rebecca grinned. "If Kelsey is vouching for you, we all want to hire you. But working for Mr. Brackins makes the most sense for your future."

"Yes, yes!" she grinned. "I would very much like to work for your firm Mr. Brackins. I've followed your cases and find your work to be impeccable."

"That's settled then," I interrupted. "You can sort the details later. Now the case—Yes, we have enough evidence to get the case dismissed."

"It's tricky, though. As soon as you get Grady released, they're going to arrest Kelsey," Katie interrupted.

Baker, Rebecca, Cameron, and Jenny all looked up at me in shock.

"I didn't murder him!" I exclaimed throwing my hands up in exasperation.

Chapter Forty

It took three hours to get Cameron up to speed. Jenny was pulling her weight already by suggesting different motions that they could file. She also wanted to review the evidence records with the FBI first hand. It was obvious that Cameron was impressed with her.

She excused herself on occasion to pick up our food order or to refresh our drinks but never missed a beat, keeping up with strategies and case references. I asked her to get the manager of the club for me and she hurried out of the room.

"What's her story?" Baker asked.

"Sucky parents, but she has a lot of brains and determination. I helped her get custody of her younger sister, Sawyer, and she's been raising her on her own while working and putting herself through school."

"Hell, even if she's only available to work weekends, she'll be worth every penny," Cameron grinned.

"How's she affording law school?" Rebecca asked.

"I tried to pay, but instead she negotiated a loan with me. Interest-free for the first three years out of law school and then an aggressive repayment plan at a reasonable percentage. It was a very detailed loan agreement," I smirked. "But she would only take the money for law school. She pays for everything else herself."

"Damn," Wayne said.

"Yeah," I grinned.

Jenny returned with Mrs. Ellison, the manager of the club. I explained how Jenny's future had dramatically changed, and it would be quite impossible as one of her benefactors for me to grant her the option of providing notice. And, though it was poor form, that Jenny should not be held accountable because of the situation.

Mrs. Ellison was excited for Jenny and wished her well before excusing herself.

"I feel bad," Jenny said looking toward the door. "She's always been so good to me."

"You don't have time to feel bad," Cameron smirked. "It's going to be a long day. Feel free to bring your sister into the office. She can watch tv or use one of the computers."

"Are you sure? She is a teenager, you know." Jenny looked skeptical.

"It will be fine. I promise," Cameron laughed as he gathered his notepads. "I'll reach out to Katie and keep her up to date," Cameron said to me. "We'll plan on being at the courthouse first thing Monday morning with dismissal filings. I'll try to keep you out of jail as well, but they may take you in for questioning. They can hold you up to 24-hours without charging you."

"I'll be arrested immediately. It's the time between booking and a bail hearing that I'll have to be ready for. I have a plan for that, though," I grinned.

"I'm sure you do. You seem to be a resourceful woman," Cameron grinned.

* * *

"Her devious mind doesn't hurt either," Donovan chuckled.

"Cameron, when Grady and Kelsey are in the clear,"—Rebecca handed her business card over to him—"you'll need to reach out to Baker and me to start setting up meetings to take on our business interests. But they're secondary until then."

Baker handed Cameron a business card as well.

"Look, Jenny, I got their cards too," he grinned at her.

She rolled her eyes and grabbed the rest of the notebooks. "I'll make you proud, Ms. Harrison."

"You made me proud years ago," I smiled as we parted ways.

Twenty minutes later the guys carried the takeout bags into the kitchen, and I went to the living room for an update.

"What are we doing?" I asked.

A dozen people were scattered around the house, each with a pile of DVD's stacked next to them and earphones plugged into laptops. Some were set up at the dining room table, a few more in the War room while others stretched out in recliners or curled up on the couches to work. Everyone was intently glued to their assigned laptops.

"Those videos you, um, *borrowed*," Tech said, glancing over at Maggie, "They revealed two other hidden cameras inside the bar. We're trying to catalog everyone who met with the DA."

"I'm trying to ignore all the other juicy bits since I can't use any of it in court," Maggie grumbled. "We've already found several recordings of the DA meeting with your old boss, Trevor. And, then we have some meetings with another guy that we haven't identified yet."

"So it was payback?" I asked.

"What?" Tech asked.

"When Chandler was torturing me, he seemed so angry with me. I didn't understand. But, if he had been working with Trevor and Feona, that would explain why."

"You shut down not only a source of income but also his supply of girls," Maggie nodded.

I followed Tech into the war room, and he played one of the videos on the larger screen.

"This is the night the cop was killed. We don't have audio, but do you recognize the man that is meeting with the DA? We can't get a clear shot of him," Tech asked.

I didn't need a better angle to recognize the man in the still shot. Turning away, I started grabbing the piles of DVD's and carrying them into the living room. I dumped them into one of the boxes and started taking the other stacks and adding them to the box.

"What's up?" Katie asked.

"Everyone needs to stop watching these," I answered taking the laptop that Bones was using and ejecting the DVD. I tossed the DVD across the room at a box.

"We might not be able to use them in court, but it could still help," Maggie said.

"I said STOP watching them!" I yelled, throwing the laptop across the room at the wall near the boxes. Small pieces of plastic flew back, and I watched the laptop screen snap to a blank black screen.

Everyone in the room was silent and either watching me or staring at the demolished laptop.

"Ok. You heard her," Katie said, getting up.

Everyone moved around me gathering up the DVD's and tossing them back into the boxes.

"I need these videos to disappear. Permanently," I said, still staring at the broken laptop.

"I'll get rid of them," Ryan offered.

Ryan and Wayne began carrying the boxes out.

"Burn them. Make sure there isn't a single copy."

"Consider it done," Ryan nodded.

"Am I the only one that doesn't understand what is happening right now?" Maggie asked.

"No. None of us understand," Katie answered. "But those videos have Kelsey scared. And, if she says they need to be destroyed, then that's what the fuck is going to happen."

"Kelsey, you don't have anything to be afraid of," Bones said, stepping up beside me.

He placed a hand on my arm.

I stepped away from him, looking up at him. A humorless laugh escaped.

I looked around the room at all the faces, trying to reassure me that I was safe, and laughed harder.

"Nothing to be scared of? Oh, Bones, if you only knew," I shook my head. "I've handled Pasco, a biker gang, gun runners, and drug dealers. And, I wasn't afraid. Nervous, yes. Not overly optimistic about my odds of living, yes. But I wasn't filled with a fear so dark that it makes me consider putting a bullet through my head!"

Wayne and Ryan had walked back inside the house and froze in place along with everyone else. They watched me intently as I paced around looking at all of them.

"Kelsey? What are you saying?" Uncle Hank asked.

"I'm saying that if anyone finds out about those videos, we're all dead. They'll come after our families, our friends, everyone. Everyone you know and love will be in danger."

I watched everyone's faces whiten, their eyes open wider and saw the fear reflected back in their expressions when they realized I wasn't joking.

"Bonfire, now," Donovan called out.

Everyone started hauling out the boxes. Tech and Genie started to wipe the hard drives on the computers clean.

"What about Mickey?" Maggie asked after we had torched everything.

"We can have the witnesses recant their statements to give Mickey an alibi. Other than that, we'll need to review the evidence as if it were any other cold case. Uncle Hank, will you help Maggie work the case?"

"I already made some notes of things to check out," Uncle Hank nodded.

"Bet you that it was either the DA or the guy that was meeting with him, that killed the cop," Katie said.

"Follow the evidence," I nodded. "I'm betting the DA is our guilty party. If it leads to the other man we saw in the video, then we'll drop the investigation, and I'll talk to Mickey."

"Kelsey, who is this guy?" Tech asked.

"You don't want to know," I answered, turning to walk down the hallway.

I must have fallen asleep. I opened my eyes to a room dimmed in partial darkness. The bedroom door was open, though, preventing complete blackness.

Sitting in the doorway, leaned against the doorjamb, Wild Card watched me.

"How long have I been asleep?" I asked, carefully sitting up. My muscles protested any movement, and I forced myself to stretch my arms and back.

"About six hours. I was going to wake you soon. You okay?"

"No," I shook my head. "No, I am not okay."

"Talk to me."

"I can't. More importantly, I don't want to."

I slid out of bed and went into the private bathroom, closing the door behind me.

After I had washed my face and calmed my nerves, I was sitting on the back porch in one of the Adirondack chairs. Everyone else was inside, filling their dinner plates, so I Skype Nicholas.

"Hey Mom," Nicholas said while moving himself and the laptop over to his bed.

"Wow, you're getting so big," my voice shook as I looked at him on my laptop screen. "Hard to believe that it's been almost six months since I saw you."

"You okay?" Nicholas asked looking scared.

"I have a few bumps and bruises, but I'm okay. How about you? You having fun with Aunt Charlie and all your uncles?"

"I've gotten really good a riding and roping. And, Pops is teaching me how to wrangle cattle," he grinned a toothy grin.

"Sounds like fun. I wish I was there."

"Are you coming home soon?"

"I can't just yet. Grady is in trouble, and he needs my help."

I touched my fingertips to the screen, trying to push the lock of hair away from his forehead.

"Mom?"

"Hmm?"

"Is Nola really dead?" Nicholas asked, looking down.

The lock of hair fell forward covering up part of his face.

"Yes. She's dead. You're safe now," I said.

"Are you safe?" he asked.

"Why would you ask something like that?" I asked worriedly.

"You didn't come to see me. And, the security guards are still posted at the gates."

"I'm just being careful, Nick. But I won't lie to you. There's a good chance that I'm going to be arrested. I already have a lawyer working on it, and I'm innocent, so they can't keep me. I just didn't want you to see something on the news and worry."

"I should be with you."

"No," I said, shaking my head at the image of him on the screen. "Never again will I allow you to be in harm's way."

"But Mom —,"

"No." I sighed and rubbed my forehead.

Bones stepped out of the house with a pile of folders.

"Nick, I have to go. Be good for Aunt Charlie and all your Uncles. I love you."

"I love you too, Mom," he said, as we both closed our laptops.

"Katie asked me to give these to you," Bones said, handing me the folders and sitting in the Adirondack chair next to me.

"Thanks."

I set my laptop aside and started flipping through the folders. The first two were of Mickey's trial. The rest of the folders contained the background searches that I had asked Katie to run. Harbor Officer Parsons, the man responsible for drugging me and taking me to Nola, was one of the men I had ran. The report indicated that he lived in an apartment, alone, in one of the suburbs of New Orleans. No wife. No kids. He would be easy to get to when the time was right.

"Are you ever going to forgive me?" Bones asked, breaking the silence that hung between us.

"There's nothing to forgive, Bones. You were angry and said a lot of things. Some of them were cruel, but some of them were the truth too."

"And you and I?"

"No. There's never going to be a 'You and I'," I admitted, looking up at him. "I'm not the person you thought I was. I'm not the innocent, naïve woman I was pretending to be. Hell, I'm not even the person I was pretending not to be, anymore."

Bones leaned forward, elbows on knees, clasping his hands.

"No. I guess you're not," he sighed. "Eric and Grady kept trying to get me to understand, but I didn't want to see it."

"I didn't mean to deceive you. I didn't mean to drag you or anyone else into this mess either."

"You were protecting your son. I get that."

In our silence, the laughter and talking inside the house seemed to grow.

"And, Grady? After this mess is settled, will you work things out with Grady?"

I laughed. "Nothing ever happened between Grady and I. But, no, I'm not looking to be in a relationship with anyone. I need time. I need space."

"I think that's a mistake," Bones said turning to me. "I might be jealous as hell, but Grady's good for you. And, you're good for him. The two of you look at each other, and it's as if a thousand words are spoken. It's intense. And, I hate it. But, it's not something to throw away."

"I have a son that I have seen once in 3 years. I have a back full of stitches and a bum shoulder. I have multiple businesses that I haven't looked at the books in months. And, I have a lot of evil shit going on inside my head. The last thing I need right now is a man in my life."

"Too late," Wild Card chuckled, stepping out of the house.

Wayne, Ryan, Donovan, and Nightcrawler followed him onto the porch.

"You have a whole house full of them," Wild Card said.

"But we're bored. You got anything you need us to do?" Wayne asked.

"I have some recon work that needs to be handled," I nodded, grabbing three of the folders from the stand. "I need more details on these three men, but keep a low profile and don't get caught."

"What kind of details?"

"Movements. Friends. Neighborhood details. How accessible they are. Anything will help."

"Sounds boring," Ryan said, taking the folders. "Can't we just beat the shit out of them?"

"Maybe later," I grinned.

Chapter Forty-One

I woke to the sound of birds singing nearby. I opened my eyes, looking at my surroundings, surprised to find that I was in my room in the Miami safe house. The window next to the bed was partially open and the morning sun streamed in along with the songbirds' twirls.

Wild Card sat on the floor, stationed at the doorway. His head was leaned back into the door jamb as he slept.

"Quit staring at me," he grinned without opening his eyes.

"How did I end up in bed?"

"You fell asleep in the War Room with your head on a laptop. I carried you in and dumped you in bed," he said while getting up and stretching his muscles. "And, we need to either drag a cot in here or you need to share the bed because I can't keep sleeping in the doorway."

"I think I'll be okay without a bodyguard now," I grinned, crawling out of bed.

I looked down at the pajamas I was wearing. They consisted of a pink t-shirt and matching sleeping shorts. I looked at Wild Card, but he just grinned and shrugged.

I decided I didn't want to know the details of how I came to be in the pajamas and instead I grabbed a change of clothes and went into the bathroom to shower. By the time I was dressed and ready, I found a large cup of coffee on the dresser waiting for me.

I drank my coffee as I walked down the hall and into the main rooms. Genie, Carl, and Tech were in the war room, but they looked bored. Maggie and Wild Card were in the living room drinking coffee and chatting. Aunt Suzanne was cooking up a storm and Bones, Uncle Hank, Wayne, Donovan and Ryan sat around the kitchen table. I nodded to everyone and stepped out onto the porch to snitch a cigarette from Tyler.

Nightcrawler and Tyler were standing in the driveway talking. They grinned at me as I walked toward them, both pulling out a pack of cigarettes and offering me one.

"You look better," Nightcrawler nodded.

"I feel better," I admitted. "After a light breakfast, I'm going to make a run to a local gym. You guys want to go?"

"Hell yes," Tyler grinned.

"Me too," Katie giggled coming out to join us. "It's been a whole week since I've had a chance to kick anyone's ass."

"You hear anything from the lawyer?"

"Cameron called last night and said that all the evidence and the motions to dismiss were looking good. He didn't see a problem with getting Grady out, even if it was a release on bail until they cleared all the charges. He said they'd need you there, though."

"I know."

"This DA will be waiting for you, won't he?" Nightcrawler asked.

I nodded and took a hit off my cigarette.

"As soon as Grady's in the clear, get him out of town. Send him home."

"And, if he doesn't go along with that plan?" Bones asked, walking out with everyone else.

"Make him. He can't stay in Florida. Figure it out," I said.

"Yeah, that sounds simple enough," Donovan said, rolling his eyes.

"Donovan, tell him that you need help to protect everyone in Michigan since Lisa's close to her due date. Fly back with him and just make it seem like I'll be flying out a couple hours later. Tell him my lawyer has it all worked out."

Bones snorted, and Tech laughed.

"It's close to the truth," I shrugged.

"Yeah, about as close as the Sun and the Moon," Katie grinned.

"Wild Card, I need you to head back to Texas."

"No."

"What do you mean, No?"

"As in we're not married and I don't have to follow your orders. I'm staying until you're in the clear. Reggie, Jackson, Charlie, and Pops, along with an array of security guards, have the ranches covered. I'm staying."

"I'll fly back to Texas," Wayne nodded.

"Thank you, Wayne. At least someone can be agreeable around here."

"Ha. He has a thing for a rancher's daughter that lives nearby," Wild Card smirked.

I looked at Wayne, but he only grinned back. Whatever. I just needed to thin the herd in Miami, so I didn't care what his reasons were.

"Uncle Hank, I need to talk to the Commander. Can you set something up?" I asked.

"Sure," Uncle Hank nodded.

"Katie, book the flights to get Grady, Donovan, Wayne and Ryan out of town as soon as Grady is cleared of the charges. And, Wild Card, please head home. If there's any blowback, I'll want you in Texas protecting my family."

"No," Wild Card shook his head. "I know what you're doing, and you're not doing it alone."

"You have no idea what I'm doing," I said, looking away as I took a long drag off my cigarette.

"The recon assignments yesterday—did you really think that we wouldn't figure out that they're somehow linked to when Nola had you?" he asked, stepping up close to me and gently holding my shoulders.

"It's not your fight," I whispered, trying to control the tears that threatened just behind the surface.

"And, you didn't start this war, Kelsey," he said. "You were a good cop, doing her job and ran into some sick fuckers who turned your life upside down. It's not your fault." He gently wrapped his arms around me and tucked my head into his shoulder. Leaning in, he whispered quiet enough for only me to hear, "Give me a list, and I'll kill them all."

I pulled away and looked up at Wild Card. "And, then what? What kind of person will I be when it's all over? What kind of mother?"

I looked around at everyone on the porch. Hank and Maggie must have slipped back inside. Only Wild Card, Bones, Donovan, Nightcrawler, Katie and Wayne remained.

"Don't get me wrong, I want blood. I want them to die. But what does that make me?"

"She's right," Katie sighed. "She'll feel guilty as hell and never forgive herself."

"They need to die," Donovan sighed. "You know they'll hurt other women."

"They need to be stopped. But death?" I said, shaking my head. "No, that's too easy. I need a few of them to suffer like I suffered. I need to find a way to get revenge and still be able to look in the mirror when it's all over. Because, right now, I'm on a ledge. One misstep and I'll become someone that I'll end up hating."

Everyone but Bones looked away. Bones stared at me, reading my face.

"Then we do it your way," Bones said. "We take them down, one by one. We find their weakness and destroy them."

"I'd rather just kill them," Nightcrawler said.

"Me too," Wayne chuckled. "But, we'll do it Kelsey's way."

Katie just grinned and bounced up and down, looking excited.

"I'll try it your way," Wild Card nodded. "But if it doesn't work—,"

"Then we do it our way," Bones grinned.

Donovan nodded as the other men chuckled.

"Okay, then. Who's our first target?" Wayne asked.

"Our first priority is to get Grady out of prison, but we can't do anything about that until tomorrow. So, I plan on eating breakfast and then going to the gym," I said, tossing my cigarette into the driveway.

Donovan laughed. "Everybody eat fast. Kelsey's up to something."

"I have no idea what you're talking about," I winked at Donovan.

After scarfing down a quick breakfast, everyone crammed into two SUVs, and we drove to a gym in a seedier section of the city. Bones grinned at me as we walked up.

"This place like Calvin's?"

Our mutual friend Calvin ran a gym that Bones and I frequented in Michigan.

"Not even close," I said, turning my head to yell at everyone else. "Heads up! Watch your back in this place," I grinned.

Everyone grinned as they followed me inside.

The gym didn't smell all that great, which was the first thing I noticed. The second thing I noticed was one of the gym managers yelling at a man on the third mat to quit beating the shit out of the other guy who was unconscious at his feet. The man doing the ass kicking seemed to be having a hearing problem and didn't stop. I recognized the unconscious guy as Little Joe, so when Donovan made a move to walk over, I grabbed him by the arm and shook my head.

Little Joe enjoyed getting his girls hooked on H, turning them out to work the streets and then beat the shit out of them if they didn't bring back enough profits. It wouldn't be a loss if he left in a body bag.

I continued looking around the gym and found my mark. He was warming up on mat six, getting ready to square off with a fighter that I didn't recognize.

Wayne saw where I was looking and grinned. "He's one of the guys you had us follow yesterday."

I had read through the recon notes late last night and smiled when I saw that Badger still frequented Mickey's gym. The location was perfect for what I had planned.

"Today's all about multitasking Wayne. I needed to exercise, and at the same time, I'll be sending a message to a friend," I grinned, walking over and without asking, sliding between the ropes.

"Mind if I cut in?" I asked glaring at Badger, the man that I had targeted.

The other fighter looked between us, as we glared at one another, and bailed off the mat.

"You look like shit, Harrison," Badger sneered at me.

"I think I look pretty good for being a '*dead bitch*,' Booger," I grinned.

"It's not Booger. My name's Badger," he snarled.

"No. No. I'm sure I have it right, Booger," I grinned.

I turned to Katie, and she tossed me bindings for my hands. Booger was gloved up, but I couldn't street fight in boxing gloves. He realized what I was doing and pulled off his gloves, tossing them out of the ring.

I stepped a few feet away from him and finished wrapping my hands before tossing the remaining binding back to Katie. The rest of our group had spaced out around the ring, stretching and watching the room as they kept one eye on me at all times.

"So you think you can kick my ass?" Badger laughed. "If memory serves, you were nothing but idle threats the last time we talked."

"If memory serves, I was chained to a fucking stone wall the last time we spoke," I glared back as I circled the mat with him. "And, this time, I'm going to fuck you up. But don't worry—I'll let you live—at least today."

I easily blocked his first swing, ducking behind him, throwing a jab to his kidneys. He staggered forward before spinning around. I didn't hesitate as I threw a knuckle strike to the throat. I grinned as he gagged and grabbed his throat. I slammed an elbow into his face and laughed when the blood gushed from his nose.

I was full-out giddy as I continued my assault—a solid punch to the ribs, a knee to the balls, a sidekick to his kneecap. Each strike was calculated and timed so he would feel each injury. His piss poor attempt to defend himself proved futile, and he was soon laying in a bloody ball on the mat floor.

Sliding back through the ropes, I walked away.

Badger was still alive, but he was now a marked man. Before the end of the day, anyone that knew me would know that Badger was one of the men that hurt me.

I took up a jump rope and started working the rope as my muscles stretched and burned. I knew that some of my stitches were pulled out, but they didn't hurt. Nothing hurt anymore. I didn't feel anything but ice cold hatred for the men that had tortured me.

"Explain to me again why we're not killing him?" Wild Card asked.

"Because his cousin and I are allies," I laughed.

"Who's the cousin?"

"Mickey McNabe."

Everyone grinned, knowing that Mickey was already in the process of torturing one bad guy.

"Mickey owns the gym and will hear about today. And, believe me, he'll be very creative when he deals with laying out a punishment for Badger."

"You worried about so many witnesses around here?" Donovan asked.

"No. This gym has warning signs posted all over that you fight at your own risk. There's usually a few fatalities a year so no one would think anything of a fight getting out of hand. That's why they come here."

"Nice," Nightcrawler grinned. "If only fights could be arranged here."

"Who says they aren't?"

"As in death fights?" Katie asked. "And, the police don't shut it down?"

"Why? It's criminal against criminal. If the bad guys want to kill each other off—why should the police care?

At least they're not shooting each other on the streets where innocent people get hurt in the process."

"Cool," Wayne nodded.

I wasn't really sure if I would consider it cool, but it was definitely not worth my time and energy worrying about it, which I knew first hand was how most of the Miami cops felt about the gym.

Tiring out before everyone else, I toweled off and walked a circle around the gym. The gym manager was still standing next to Little Joe's unmoving body.

"He dead?" I asked.

"Hell if I know," the manager shrugged. "It's not worth the risk catching a disease to check for a pulse."

"Smart," I nodded. "You call an ambulance?"

"Yeah. I warned them to wear double layered gloves," he grinned. "You get things settled with Badger?"

"No, I wouldn't say we're settled. But Mickey should get the message and things will be figured out from there."

He nodded. "Probably best to let Mickey decide. I wasn't able to hear anything that was said, but between the look on your face and the look on the men's faces that came in with you, I would guess that Badger's days are numbered. And, good riddance." He spat on the cement floor, but forgot about Little Joe's body at his feet and ended up spitting on his head. "Oops," he chuckled.

I finished circling the gym and rejoined our group as they were packing up. I turned Tyler's face to the side and inspected the bruise that was forming.

"I know, I know, never let your guard down," he chuckled.

"But will you remember the next time?" I grinned back.

We walked out the same way we entered, and I felt a little like a street banger running his crew. I chuckled at the thought as a familiar caddy drove by and parked. I gestured for the driver to wait and I asked everyone to meet me back at the house.

Katie looked over at the caddy and grinned. "Kelsey will be fine, boys. Let's go."

I walked over to the caddy and slid into the backseat. Uncle Hank pulled out of the lot, just as the ambulance was arriving, lights off.

"Another dirtbag dead?" the Commander asked from the front passenger seat.

"Not sure," I chuckled. "It was Little Joe, and nobody wanted to touch him to see if he had a pulse."

"No wonder the ambulance has its lights off. They're probably hoping that if they stall long enough, he'll die for sure," Uncle Hank grunted.

"We thought we got rid of him last winter. He OD'd in his apartment. Unfortunately, they got there in time to revive him. The paramedics took a lot of ribbing for that one."

"Huh," I grinned. I had been in Miami last winter and had encouraged the prostitutes to inject him while he was unconscious. "Anything interesting happen after that?"

"Heard all his girls moved two streets over and signed up under a different pimp. One of Mickey's crew. A couple even got dried out from what I hear."

"Except the one that was beaten to death last week. What was her name? You know her, Kelsey. You turned her daughter over to social services."

"Kara?"

"Yeah, that's her. She went back to Little Joe for the drugs. He beat her to death and left her body on the street."

"Don't feel too bad. She had a number of chances to get out. She knew he was going to kill her someday."

Uncle Hank turned into a community park and pulled to the far end where we would have the most privacy. We all slid out of the hot car and moved over to a nearby picnic table.

"So, what do you need?" the Commander asked.

"Time, just time," I grinned.

It took about an hour to explain everything that had happened to the commander and what I needed him to do. He was pissed as hell, but not at me, and easily agreed to help where he could. We both knew there was a limit to what he could do though.

Uncle Hank stayed quiet while we talked. The cop in him understood. The man that considered me part of his family struggled with the thought of losing me.

The commander's wife pulled up, and he left with her. We didn't want too many people seeing him with Hank right now.

"Stop worrying, Uncle Hank," I nudged his side. "I've been in trickier situations than this and walked out just fine."

"You've never walked in when you're already hurt, though. You can't hide those bruises and cuts with baggy clothes. You go into that prison injured, with both guards and prisoners gunning for you, and—." He couldn't finish the sentence and just shook his head looking far off.

"I'll live as long as I can," I said. "That's all I can promise. What else can I do?"

"Run."

"I can't. I won't. Grady shouldn't be in prison. The DA will hold him until he can get his hands on me."

"Damn it, Kelsey. You can't always be the sacrificial lamb!"

"I can when I'm the reason Grady's in there in the first place. Come on," I nudged him again. "If it was Aunt Suzanne?"

"It's not the same."

"Are you sure? This all started because I was a cop. And now someone close to me is in danger because of it. It's that simple. It's my fight, not Grady's."

"And what do I tell Aunt Suzanne, and Charlie, and Nicholas,… when you come out of that prison in a body bag? What do I tell them then, huh?"

"You remind them that I died the way I lived. We all know that when the time comes, whether it's next week or next year, I'll die fighting for something I believe in."

Uncle Hank nodded as he looked across the park, blinking rapidly to clear his eyes.

"And if it's next week," Uncle Hank sighed, calming his emotions. "Is there anything you need me to take care of?"

"Two things. And, if I live, then you have to forget you ever heard about the second one."

He nodded but didn't look back to face me.

"First, don't let Charlie cut you and Aunt Suzanne out of her life. You two have been the closest thing to parents that girl has ever had. She'll need you."

"I'll keep track of her," Uncle Hank nodded.

"The second thing is that you'll need to ask Nightcrawler to take you to my hidden house. He knows where it's at, but nobody else does, not even Charlie. In the house, under the bed, there is a loose floorboard. Under the floorboard, there is an old videotape and some files. Get them and keep them hidden. Don't ever let Charlie see them."

"What are you talking about? You don't keep secrets from Charlie," Uncle Hank said, turning to face me.

"This one thing, she can't know about. It would crush her, Uncle Hank."

"Charlie's strong and a tough cop. I'm sure she can handle whatever it is your hiding."

"No," I said shaking my head.

I got up from the picnic table and looked around to make sure no one was able to hear us. The park remained relatively empty except some kids playing on the other side.

"When we were kids, I had to do some horrible things to get Charlie out. I had to blackmail the sheriff with incriminating evidence. Evidence of something that happened between him and I. And, I had to blackmail our parents for the murder of our grandparents. I can't stand the thought of Charlie finding out about any of it. She'll blame herself."

Uncle Hank watched me closely.

"Dear lord, you were only a kid," he said.

We stared at each other, both of us with tears streaming down our cheeks.

"And, Charlie's father was beginning to look at her like a young woman instead of a twelve-year-old girl. I couldn't wait any longer," I admitted. "I had to do something."

"Oh my God," Uncle Hank said as he pulled me into him and held me while we both cried.

We were at the park longer than we planned, but eventually, we wiped our tears and pulled on our cop faces. We got back into the Caddy and drove to the safe house.

"I'll keep your secret, Kelsey. But you and I both know that eventually, you have to deal with the monsters in your past. You and Charlie both need to face them down. Charlie needs to face her father, and you need to face that Sheriff. And, when that time comes, I want to be there."

I had so many demons in my life that my childhood seemed like a distant memory most days. And, I knew with certainty that now wasn't the time to dwell on it. If I was going to survive the next week, I had to bury everything else and keep my head in the game.

Chapter Forty-Two

I woke hours before the alarm clock went off, covered in sweat. I didn't even try to go back to sleep, but pulled myself from the bed and stretched my sore muscles, careful not to pull the hundreds of stitches that ran across my back and legs.

Today was the day. Today was the day that I would walk into the courtroom in Miami and face off with one of my biggest enemies: District Attorney Aaron Chandler—the man responsible for so many of the stitches that held the skin on my back together after he had whipped me until my blood coated the floor.

I could still smell the copper that burned my senses. I could still hear the crack of the whip. I could still feel the slice of what felt like a scalding knife slicing my skin apart.

And, as badly as I wanted to run and wait until I was fully recovered to face him, I couldn't leave Grady in prison to suffer. And, the DA knew it. He knew that I was here. He knew that I would trade my life for Grady's.

I'd done everything I could to prepare. Only one task remained: Live. But was I strong enough to stay alive until the lawyers got me out?

I was about to find out.

I pulled on sweat pants and carefully put on an oversized sports bra. While it didn't provide as much support, it sat looser on my back and would help with the rubbing. Tucking my hair into a messy bun, secured with a hair band, I snuck out the hidden doorway in the bedroom and out into the side yard. I set out for a jog down the empty streets as the sun was just starting to peek out over the horizon.

****

"Good news," Cameron Brackins greeted us just inside the courthouse. "I was able to run into Judge Lampton yesterday, and he promised to hear our motions this morning. He signed off on the prison transfer notice and Grady should be transferred here by mid-morning."

"That's good. Any sign of Chandler?" I asked.

"Not yet," Jenny answered. She was actively watching the hallways. "Notice was sent this morning to the DA's office, but I have a friend there that says that Chandler usually doesn't make it into the office until after 10:00. We might get lucky."

"Jenny," I patted her shoulder. "I'm prepared for whatever happens, and the DA will be here. He's been waiting for me."

"Well, we don't have to make it easy for him. I had security set aside a room for us. It's under my name, and nobody knows me, so you should be safe there until we need you. Let's go."

I grinned and looked at Cameron as we followed Jenny.

"She's amazing. She's barely slept in two days and shows no signs of slowing down," Cameron grinned.

"I'm glad. Just don't let her burn herself out. She has a teenager to raise for another year at least."

"Her sister Sawyer is a handful, but she's a good kid. I had them both stay over at my house over the weekend along with two other lawyers, a paralegal, and my mother. My mother was having a ball spoiling Sawyer and cooking for everyone. I have to admit that Sawyer is rooting against our case. She wants to stay longer," he chuckled.

I looked at Cameron and then back at Jenny as she turned to hold the door open. Cameron was older than Jenny, but now that I looked closer, their ages weren't all that far apart. Jenny was in her mid-twenties, and if I had to guess, Cameron was in his early thirties. Maybe it wasn't appropriate given their working relationship, but he would actually make a good man for her.

"Did I mention that two other lawyers, a paralegal, and my mother were there?" Cameron said grinning at me.

"Oh trust me, counselor, I didn't miss one speck of the information that you conveyed," I winked at him, walking into the small conference room.

"What are you two talking about?" Jenny asked.

"Sawyer," I smiled at Jenny. "I hear she's not on our side."

"Oh, you know she was just teasing, Cameron. Sawyer loves Kelsey," Jenny insisted.

"Relax," I chuckled. "I was just teasing too."

"Okay, good. I'm going to go monitor the hallways. Text me if I'm needed."

Donovan, Katie, Maggie, Tech and Genie all pulled out chairs at one side of the table, making themselves comfortable as Cameron reviewed what he had gathered to fight my case when an arrest happened. He had some strong motions to keep me out of jail, but unfortunately, they wouldn't be helpful until my bail hearing. A lot could happen in the gap between an arrest and bail hearing.

About an hour later Cameron's phone chirped, and he read the text. "Grady's here. I have to go talk to him and get some signatures. We'll be in courtroom 302. Maggie, Tech and Genie, I need the three of you in there waiting for us. Donovan, it would help to speed up the process with Grady if you were with me. He's more likely to trust me if he sees you there." Cameron gathered up his files and briefcase before turning back to me. "Hide in here until one of us comes to get you. Don't even pee without our permission, got it?"

"Yes, sir," I grinned.

"He's kind of hot," Katie giggled before Cameron was even out of the room.

Tech growled and tugged on the back of her hair, getting her attention. "Behave," he ordered.

"Sure, babe," she grinned and kissed him quickly before he walked out.

The small room seemed bigger with just Katie and I waiting alone. The ticking of the clock as the second hand moved slowly around was the only sound we could hear. We were in a distant part of the courthouse, and it was unlikely that anything exciting would happen.

"Why is it that as soon as you aren't allowed to pee, you have to go," I grumbled.

Katie slid her empty water bottle down the table at me.

"No thanks," I laughed and pushed it back at her. "So, are you and Tech going to be the next couple that takes the plunge into marriage?"

"Hell no," she said. "Tech knows that I'm not exclusive. He might not like it, but that's all there is to it."

"Who are you trying to fool? Him or yourself?"

Katie leaned back in her chair and grinned. "If only the sex wasn't so amazing –,"

"Stop, no. Don't tell me," I laughed, covering my ears.

"Seriously, he drives me nuts in every good way, but we're too different," she said shaking her head. "When we go to the bar, I order a gin and tonic, and he orders a root beer. A root beer. It's just too strange."

"I don't know. I would think having a permanent designated driver would be kind of nice. And, considering your history with your mom's drinking issues, it should put Tech further in the pro column, not on the cons list."

"It just seems immature somehow," she shrugged.

"Yeah, because a biker who also happens to be a computer genius working for a security company, just screams immature."

"Oh shut it. Whose side are you on anyway?" she laughed.

"Yours. You just haven't figured it out yet," I grinned.

"I have to pee. Stay here," Katie grinned getting up to walk out of the room.

"Oh, that's evil," I laughed and threw the empty water bottle at her.

"I know," she said as the door swung shut.

My phone rang, and I answered it seeing it was Wild Card.

"DA just got here. He parked in the North parking lot and has one security detail with him. Shit," Wild Card said startled.

"What's wrong?"

"Nothing, sorry. Kid on a skateboard almost ran me over. Oh, shit—,"

"Now what?" I sighed.

"She just blasted into the DA and threw her coffee all over him. It's one of those fancy coffees too. He has foam dripping down the front of his suit."

I didn't say anything, I just sat in silence, cringing.

"Damn, he's got her by the arm and is yelling at her. A woman is running up to them. She got him to release the girl and now the woman and the DA are yelling at each other."

"Where did the girl go?"

"She ran the opposite direction and around the back of the building."

I placed my head on the conference table and just listened.

"What the hell? The girl just came out around the far side of the building and got in the woman's car. She's hiding in the back seat."

"Is Chandler still yelling at the woman?"

"No, she's walking back to her car. Chandler is walking into the courthouse."

"Is the woman close enough that you can talk to her?"

"Hang on, ma'am –,"

"Ask her if she is Cameron's mom?"

I heard him ask, but then there was silence.

"She's not answering, but based on the shocked look on her face, I'm guessing she is," Wild Card chuckled.

"Tell her to take Sawyer's ass back to Cameron's house and stay there until she hears from him."

He relayed the message. "Man, she squealed the tires and everything. She's three shades of white and completely freaked that she got caught."

"I have a feeling that Cameron's mom is a lot like Dallas," I sighed.

"Poor guy. Where do you need me now that the DA is in the building?"

"I need you guys to stay outside. Grady will need coverage if we get him released."

"Got it. We'll make sure he gets out okay."

"Appreciate it," I said hanging up.

Katie stepped back into the conference room and seconds later Jenny came flying in through the door.

"The DA and Cameron are arguing on the third floor."

"Good, where's the bathroom?" I asked.

"Right across the hall, but hurry," Jenny said.

I quickly peed, washed my hands and walked back to the conference room.

"I'm going to head back upstairs. Chandler is in a really bad mood and Cameron might need the support."

"Does his bad mood have anything to do with a latte covering the front of his expensive suit?" I asked as I was sitting back down.

Jenny spun around and looked at me in shock.

"Oh, no. It wasn't me. But I did have a message delivered to Cameron's mother to get Sawyer and go straight to Cameron's house and wait for him."

"I'm going to box their ears!" Jenny growled as she clenched her fists.

"And, they deserve it, but it can wait. Get back up there," I nodded to the ceiling.

Jenny spun around and left.

Chapter Forty-Three

It wasn't until 10:30 that Donovan came down and escorted Katie and I up to the courtroom. Two court security guards trailed behind us. I looked sideways at Donovan.

"It's okay, they're guarding you," Donovan grinned.

"Until the tide changes," I said grimly.

Stepping into the courtroom, I immediately noticed Grady. He had a swollen eye, and his nose appeared to be broken. He was also keeping one arm pinned up to his ribs. He briefly glanced at me before glaring at Donovan.

My heart twisted. I wanted to run over and talk to him. I wanted to explain. I wanted to apologize to him for dragging him into my mess. Instead, it took all of my control to keep walking forward.

"He's not happy about any of this," Donovan whispered. "He wanted me to drug you and hide you somewhere until all this was over."

"Well, tough," I whispered back.

I was so focused on Grady that I didn't notice DA Aaron Chandler until I was standing right in front of him. He smiled an evil smile at me before turning his attention back to the judge.

"Your Honor, as District Attorney I have requested that Kelsey Harrison be placed under arrest. I have already called officers to the courthouse to escort her out."

"Not so fast, Mr. Chandler," the Judge ordered. "I want to hear her statements regarding Mr. Grady Tanner first. Ms. Harrison, will you take the stand?"

I walked to the side chair, and after swearing to tell the truth, I sat down. The judge addressed his questions directly to me.

"I have just seen evidence that shows that you were with Maxwell Lautner when his death occurred. Can you validate that evidence?"

"If you are referring to the video showing Max jumping into the ocean, followed by a shark attack—then yes, I was there, and that was Max Lautner."

"And the other video showing Mr. Grady Tanner murdering Maxwell Lautner? It is my understanding that you can identify the true victim of that crime?"

"I can, Your Honor. Both in that manipulated video and in the additional videos that I watched of buoy camera surveillance, I identified Sheriff Eric Hawkins as the victim. In the manipulated video, I was only able to identify him by a tattoo on his inside left wrist. It is a black panther. I can also state that the attacker in that video could not be Mr. Grady Tanner. Eric was taller than Grady. In the video, the Eric is shorter than the attacker. Additionally, the attacker is right handed. Grady is left handed."

"Do you know Grady Tanner personally?"

"I do, Your Honor. He was part of the task force team that helped raid the Pasco estate last winter with the Miami PD and the FBI. He also went on to assist me in rescuing my son, who had been kidnapped years ago. I would consider him to be an honorable man."

"Very well. I have heard enough. I'm ordering the immediate dismissal of this case. Mr. Grady Tanner is free to go." The judge slammed the gavel down with enough force to make me jump.

I started to walk back toward the defense table when Chandler grabbed my arm to stop me. I barely managed to stop myself from reacting and striking out against him. Grady, Wild Card and Donovan all stood, clenched, ready to snap.

"Your Honor, if I may," Cameron called out.

"What is it counselor?" the Judge asked.

"The DA's office has expressed the intent to arrest Ms. Harrison for her involvement in this case. I would like to go on the record with a statement before that happens."

The Judge nodded to the stenographer before telling Cameron to proceed.

"It is our belief, based on evidence in another matter, that District Attorney Aaron Chandler wishes to harm Ms. Harrison. We ask that he not be allowed direct access to her without her security detail or myself present. We also request that if she's arrested, she is mandated to either a precinct holding cell or the county jail, and not be allowed to be transferred to the State prison."

"I have with me a request for a restraining order specific to Aaron Chandler, Your Honor."

"I will agree to the restraining order, but I can't order Ms. Harrison's placement location until a bail hearing. It is on the record though that you have a concern for Ms. Harrison's life and I will go on the record as stating that the DA's office better be careful to ensure that Ms. Harrison is appropriately protected and not transferred to the state prison." The Judge signed the restraining order and handed it back to Cameron. "Is that all, ladies and gentlemen?"

"One more moment, Your Honor. If you can just bear witness," Cameron requested. "DA Chandler, please remove your hand from Ms. Harrison's arm."

"She is being taken into custody. I'll release her when she is formally arrested," Chandler snapped back.

"We have plenty of guards and law enforcement officers in this room, Mr. Chandler. Release your grip on her immediately," the Judge ordered.

Chandler released my arm with a shove.

"And what are the charges that the DA's office will be filing?" Cameron asked.

"She'll be charged with kidnapping in the first degree."

"Very well," Cameron said, unbuttoning his suit coat.

The Commander and two of his senior level officers stood up and walked our way.

"I took the liberty of canceling your officer request to arrest Ms. Harrison since we were already in the courtroom," the Commander said. "We will be happy to transport Ms. Harrison and have her booked on the charges."

* * *

I quickly walked up to the officers while Chandler was still in shock. I turned my back to the Commander while he carefully placed the cuffs on my wrists and escorted me out of the courtroom.

"Hurry," I said when we were out in the hall. "As soon as we are away from the Judge, he'll try to have me transferred to another precinct."

"Already thought of that," the Commander said as he and the two other officers raced beside me to the elevator that Uncle Hank was holding open. The door closed with us safely inside just as Chandler walked out into the hallway.

"When we get to the first floor, we need to hurry out the back door. We have a squad car waiting to transfer you in for booking. Then we'll move you to an interrogation room and hide you as long as we can stall."

"Just don't jeopardize your jobs. Any amount of time helps because Cameron's hands are tied until my bail hearing. But in the end, it's going to be up to me to stay alive."

"We'll protect you as long as we can," one of the other officers said.

"I always hated Chandler," the other officer grinned. "He's a self-important little prick."

Hours later, I sat in an interrogation room—my head spinning from everything that had happened since I had left the courthouse. The Commander had gone above and beyond simply trying to protect me. After transferring me to my old precinct, we ran through the booking process at lightning speed. From there I was moved to the county jail for processing and to change into the neon orange jumpsuit, before, like a revolving door, I was transferred out of county for supposed questioning at another precinct.

It was smart. The DA would spend most of the day following my paper trail. And, when he followed that trail to this precinct, one of the oldest and largest precincts in the city, he would have a hell of a time figuring out which room I was hidden away in. I didn't even know how many interrogation rooms were in this building – but was guessing it was a lot. I also knew a good number of the officers at this precinct that would do what they could to protect me.

The DA could stall up to 72 hours from my arrest until a bail hearing. If they managed to keep me hidden through the night, it would be one less day that I was exposed to whatever the DA had planned.

I pushed all the vending machine snacks out of the way with my right arm and leaned my head on the cool laminate table top. My left arm was secured by a chain and cuffs to the bracket in the center of the table. I closed my eyes to sleep.

Hours later, I woke to the sound of arguing outside the interrogation room. I recognized the voices. Agent Jimmy Kierson, a friend and FBI agent, was one of them. DA Aaron Chandler was the other. He had found me.

Blood and Tears – Kelsey's Burden Series

I glanced up at the clock and noted that it was after midnight. I smiled and nodded. The Commander had kept me safe longer than I expected.

The yelling outside subsided, and the door opened. I was surprised to see that it was Agent Kierson that entered and not the DA.

"Ms. Harrison," Kierson nodded formerly. "The FBI would like to get your statement on the matters involving the death of Nola Mason. It's my understanding that you're scheduled to be transported back to jail, but with your permission, I would rather get your statement before that happens. Is that acceptable to you?"

"Yes, of course. Anything that I can do to assist the FBI," I grinned.

DA Chandler had been standing in the doorway but was now steaming down the hall cursing loudly.

"Here," Kierson said, passing me a thick new notepad and pen. "Please write out as much as you can remember regarding your history with Ms. Nola Mason. Every last scrap of information may be important to the case, so please, take your time."

Kierson was grinning as he relaxed in the chair on the other side of the table and started picking through the snack options that were scattered about.

I laughed and picked up the pen and began writing. It was a good thing I had taken a nap. It was going to be a long night.

****

I had dragged out writing the saga between Nola and myself until mid-morning, but there was nothing else I could think of to write, and I was thoroughly exhausted. The DA was back and champing at the bit to have me transferred. Agent Kierson agreed to comply as soon as my statement was typed and signed so that it could be processed.

Next thing I knew, Genie was at the door delivering large grocery bags of breakfast and taking the statement to prepare it for signatures. I was sure that her typing skills were going to be at an all-time low.

I shook my head, grinning, as I dug through the bags with one hand to find Aunt Suzanne's famous homemade breakfast favorites. I filled a paper plate with fried potatoes and homemade biscuits and prayed this would not be my last meal.

Agent Kierson, the Commander, and a few other officers joined us in the interrogation room to fill up on all the food that Aunt Suzanne sent. There was enough for at least thirty people, but Agent Kierson was making a serious dent in the containers and the Commander did his fair share of damage too.

"I should arrest you more often," Kierson grinned, rubbing his stomach. "Now get some sleep. Genie's only going to be able to stall for a couple hours and then we are out of tricks. You'll need to be ready."

I agreed and laid my head back on the cool tabletop to nap until it was time to be moved.

Genie managed to stall until 2:00 before she woke me. I was asked then to take my time and read the statement carefully before signing, and we stretched it out for another hour. Then with a wink to Genie, I let her know that certain information was incorrect. She left with the notes to type the corrections, but we all knew that the gig was almost up.

At 4:30, I was transferred to the DA's custody by officers of his choice and transferred to County jail.

Chapter Forty-Four

"You're back," the female guard snorted as she escorted me through the halls, taking me deeper into the jail. She was the same guard that had processed me for intake yesterday. "You weren't here long enough yesterday to get your bunk assignment. Are you planning on staying longer this time?"

"If it's up to me, I'll be here until my bail hearing. Any word on when that will be?" I asked.

The guard looked at me strangely. "I figured that you already had your bail hearing. I don't have any orders to transfer you again."

"Not yet you don't. The DA will have something planned for me though."

She glanced at me again but didn't ask any questions. We arrived in a stockroom where she signed me out a toothbrush and bedding. I then carried the measly belongings as I followed her into an oversized room with metal bunk beds lining each long wall.

"You've been assigned to this block. Keep your head down. It gets a little rough in here," the guard whispered.

"I expected no less," I sighed. "Any recommendations of where I should bunk?"

"Wherever they let you," she whispered back, closing the door behind me.

About twenty women of various ages and sizes glared back at me. All of them had the same stone cold look on their faces.

"You're a cop," one woman said, walking from the back of the room forward.

"Used to be, years ago," I shrugged. "Now I'm just a pissed off mother."

"Harrison? Dat' you, girly?" Another voice asked, stepping around a bunk.

"Hey, Cotton," I nodded. "You still in here?"

"More like back. D'ay got me on some deal'n charge dis time. Punks. All bullshit if'n you ask me," Cotton snorted. "Bunk below me open. Park ya-self dare."

She pointed to the open bunk, and I walked past the other women who now looked a bit confused.

"Cotton—you good with this white bitch cop being in our block?" another woman asked.

"More d'an good. Harrison got my cousin Shauna off the streets. She da cop that took out dat crazy fucker Max too."

Nothing else was said as I made up one of the small beds before laying down to rest.

"Why you here, girly?" Cotton asked sitting at the end of the bed. Some of the other women moved forward, circling around.

"I'm in trouble, Cotton. The DA is gunning for me. He wants me dead."

I looked back at the block entrance, but the guard wasn't paying any attention.

"Who in here works for him?"

"Chandler? A couple of guards, I hear, do favors for him, but you can be protected in here," one of the other women said, sitting next to Cotton on the bed. "Now, if he gets you in the State prison, that's a different story. I have a sister there. She says he owns the guards and uses the prisoners as his personal sex slaves. That shit's not right."

"No, it's not."

"You gonna get out on bail?" Cotton asked.

"When and if I live long enough to get back to court, my lawyer has a plan that should work to get me out."

"Well, den you good. I got your back 'til tomorrow when you go to court."

"I have a feeling I won't be here that long."

"How's dat? He can't get ya transferred out yet tonight."

"If he wants her, he'll get her," the woman next to Cotton sighed.

"What's your name?" I asked her.

"Sammy."

"Sammy, can you reach out to your sister? Have her spread the word that if I can live long enough, I plan on taking down Chandler?"

"I can put out a call to my mom, but I'm not sure if she can get to the prison to see Tanalla tomorrow morning. She has a job and all."

"Write this number down. It's a friend on the outside. She can get your mom some money and get her to the prison in the morning." I gave her Katie's number, and she went to the guard and asked if she could make a phone call. I was surprised that he let her out to do so.

"Supper time, form a line," a guard ordered.

I followed the lead of the other inmates and stepped in line behind Cotton. She pulled me forward and placed me in front of her. "I got your back, girly," she whispered.

We walked in single file line down to the cafeteria where we stood and waited for our trays of questionable food. When it was my turn in line, the woman behind the counter stepped back and grabbed a tray that had been sitting on the far counter and passed it to me.

"What da hell, Mary?" Cotton asked the serving girl.

"Just doin as I been ordered," Mary replied, nodding her head to the far wall.

Two guards leaned against the wall, holding their expandable batons, watching us.

"It's fine," I said quietly. "Just keep moving."

"This isn't good," Cotton whispered as I followed her to a corner table.

"I ate two solid meals today," I grinned. "It wasn't that long ago that I couldn't remember when my last meal was, so I'll be fine." I tossed my napkin on top of my tray and pushed the tray to the center of the table.

"What do you think they did to it?" Sammy asked, inspecting the food on my tray.

"I think they drugged it," I shrugged. "It would be easier to sneak me out of the jail if I was drugged. A lot quieter too."

"Like sleeping drugs or as in let's get high drugs?" another woman asked, paying closer attention to the food.

"I don't know, but there's always the chance that Chandler's desperate enough to poison me to death too, so I would choose wisely ladies," I grinned.

The women lost interest in the tray and then surprised me by divvying up their own trays on an outstretched napkin for me.

"I'll be fine, really," I said.

"If you're right and they transfer you to the prison, you need to be at the top of your game. So, eat up," Sammy said.

I nodded and ate the food that they had gathered for me. When we were done, I dumped the full tray of food in the trash and walked with the women out into the courtyard. It was a small courtyard, filled with rough patches of grass and resin picnic tables. To the left, there was a small gravel jogging track.

"Cotton, will you keep an eye out while I go for a jog?"

"You want to run on dat dirt track?"

"I need to keep active," I nodded.

"Go den. We can laugh at ya from here," she chuckled as they gathered to sit on top of one of the resin tables.

I had run about three miles before I noticed the number of inmates in the courtyard was thinning out. I didn't want our group to be the last to go inside. I nodded to Cotton. She nodded in agreement, and we filed back inside.

"Everyone will be in the rec room to watch the news. We can go shower while it's quiet. Never go alone to the bathrooms and never shower without a group," Sammy advised as we followed her down the corridors to our block and then into the shower rooms.

We were each given a towel, and I selected a stall in the center with Sammy on one side and Cotton on the other. I had forgotten about my back when I took off the neon orange shirt.

"Holy mod'er," Cotton gasped.

"Compliments of my last visit with Chandler," I shrugged and stepped into the shower.

"You suppose to shower with all those stitches?" Sammy asked.

"Nope," I grinned. "You want to find out how bad my BO can be after days of running without a shower?"

"Not really," Sammy cringed. "But that shit got to hurt."

"What caused those marks?" another woman asked.

I looked back at her and saw tears forming in her eyes.

"I said, what caused those marks?" the woman asked again, stepping closer to me.

"A whip."

"My moms died in prison. She had marks like that on her body. This Chandler guy do that to my moms?"

"Most likely. He likes to chain his women up and whip them. He gets off on it."

"And, this Chandler guy—You going to make him pay for what he done to you?"

"If I can live long enough, yes. If I don't, I know that my friends will eventually take care of him."

The woman nodded and stepped into her own shower stall without another word. I stepped into mine and showered quickly.

The rec room consisted of TV areas in three of the four corners and a gaming area in the fourth. In one corner was a sitcom show. In another corner was Lifetime TV. And, in the third corner was CNN playing national news coverage. I started walking toward the CNN area which was mostly vacant except for a few older inmates.

"Oh, man. You going to make us watch this boring shit?" Cotton complained.

"It's good for you. But no, you don't have to stay. I'll put my back to the wall," nodding to the chair along the far wall.

"I don't mind staying," the woman from the shower room said, walking over to drag another chair over.

"I'll stay too," Sammy said grabbing a third chair.

Cotton sighed, but her and the rest of the women pulled up chairs and sat with us as we watched CNN. We were diligent about looking about the room and checking where the other inmates and guards were every few minutes.

"And, in other news, CNN correspondent Donna Jenkins is in Miami with new details on the murder of the notorious Max Lautner. Donna –,"

"Good evening, everyone. I am Donna Jenkins, and I am outside the Miami downtown courthouse where yesterday morning, all charges against veteran Grady Tanner were dropped for the murder of Maxwell Lautner, a well-known gangster and human trafficking criminal. Following his release, former officer, Kelsey Harrison was taken into custody for allegedly kidnapping Max Lautner which led to his untimely death.

"We have just received word that Kelsey Harrison is currently being held at the county jail and awaiting her bail hearing that has been scheduled for 1:00 tomorrow afternoon at this same courthouse."

I looked up at the clock and counted the hours. Eighteen hours and counting.

"We also have this statement from her defense attorney, Cameron Brackins—"

"It's a sad day," Cameron said into the microphone, "when one of Miami's finest former officers is taken into custody by a corrupt DA to face erroneous charges. The fact is that we have presented video evidence that Kelsey Harrison not only did not kill Max Lautner, a known violent criminal, but she even tried to save him from his own stupidity when he jumped into the ocean and was attacked by sharks."

Cameron shook his head in a dramatic pause.

"I can only hope," he continued, "that the citizens of this city will do everything in their power to help protect this woman, who has risked her life so many times protecting others. May God be with her."

Cameron stepped away from the mike and the camera followed his gallant decent down the courthouse stairs.

The women around me cheered and clapped.

"Well, done, Cameron," I grinned.

"Your lawyer's hot," Sammy grinned.

Several of the women nodded their agreement.

"So, Max was attacked by sharks?" Cotton asked.

"Yup. It was disgusting."

"I would've done a happy dance," Cotton said, getting up to demonstrate.

"Oh yeah," said one of the other women. "Dat man deserved those sharks shredding his ass." She joined the circle of happy dance demonstrations.

I rolled my eyes and leaned my head against the wall behind me. Eighteen hours, Kelsey, just eighteen more hours.

The rest of the news was interesting but wasn't related to anything I was involved with so I didn't pay much attention. At 8:00 we joined the movie room to watch a movie that I had seen last year. It was a good comedy, so I didn't mind watching it again.

By 10:00 we were all shuffled back to our block, and it was lights out by 10:30. It didn't take me long to fall asleep, but being a light sleeper, I wasn't surprised to wake up before the cell block lights came on sometime after midnight. This was it.

I slept in my clothes, including my shoes, so by the time the lights were turned on, I was standing at the end of the bunk in the main walkway facing the bars.

The female guard that checked me in seemed surprised that I was up and ready.

"Harrison, front and center. You have a visitor," she called out.

"Guard, you're not taking me to a visitor," I said loud enough for everyone to hear as I walked up to the bars and slid my hand through the opening to be cuffed. "You're taking me to an illegal transfer to the prison."

"I was told to take you to the private visitation room. That's all I know," the guard said as she snapped the cuffs in place.

"They're gonna kill her," Sammy called out from her bunk.

"She was one of you," another woman called out. "She was a cop."

"If that's true then she must've been a dirty cop to be locked up in here," the guard said as she opened the gate and pulled me out. The barred door slammed into a locked position behind me.

"Stay strong, girly," Cotton called out. "Don't let the bad man get ya."

The guard pulled me through the next door, a solid steel unit that dulled the yelling from the block behind us.

"I don't appreciate you getting the block all wound up," the guard said as she waited for the next door to be released.

"I don't appreciate you taking me to the executioner," I shrugged.

"Nonsense," the guard shook her head. "You're going to the visitor's room, not the guillotine."

"Then why are all the security cameras turned off?" I asked as we made our way through the next door and walked down the hallway.

The guard didn't say anything, but I felt her hand tense on my arm as she realized the lights on all the cameras were red, where they should be green flashing lights.

"What the hell is going on?" the guard whispered.

"I told you. They want me dead. The DA and his criminal friends," I whispered back. "If you have a moral bone in your body, call my lawyer and let him know that they transferred me."

"I can't do that," the guard said.

"Then I hope you can live with what happens next," I said as we turned the corner and the DA stood waiting with the two guards from the cafeteria.

"We'll take the prisoner from here. Thank you, guard," Chandler grinned at me.

The female guard hesitated, but I shook my head at her. "Go."

She turned and hurried back to the cell blocks.

Three more hallways, four steel doors, and a fenced gate with barbwire trimming, and I was loaded into a white van and driven away. I debated the entire time about fighting back, but Chandler could use it against me to keep my locked up longer. I would wait until I had no other choice.

We arrived at the prison an hour later. At the delivery docks, I was transferred over to two new guards, who pocketed the money that Chandler handed them. They hauled me through the doors, through several gates, and down even longer hallways.

I noticed on the trip that the camera lights here were still green. The hope that it gave me was short-lived when one of the guards noticed me looking at the cameras.

"Don't worry, sweet thing. My friend Pete is stationed to watch the monitors tonight. Those old things go haywire all the time and lose the footage. The state should really invest in some new equipment."

His laugh sent chills down my spine and distracted me from noticing that the next door I was led into was the boiler room. I tried to turn back, but it was too late. The door slammed shut, and the guards dragged me forward.

In the center of the room, hanging from an old cast-iron pipe, was a chain with a set of cuffs attached at the end.

Chapter Forty-Five

I fought, hard and fast, but between the two guards who escorted me into the room and the other two guards waiting for us inside, I was overpowered quickly

I did some damage, though, I grinned painfully to myself. I was sure that I cracked the one guard's ribs. And, after swiping his baton from him, I got a good strike across the face of another guard before I was hit from behind. I don't remember everything after that. All the kicks and hits blurred together.

I rolled onto my stomach on the warm cement floor. I was in the middle of the boiler room, covered in blood. All four guards had walked out laughing.

I was pretty sure my shoulder was dislocated again, but at the moment, I didn't care. I was just thankful they hadn't raped me. But the fact that they used their batons and boots to inflict the damage told me enough. They didn't want their DNA on my body when it left the prison in a body bag.

Hours passed, and I managed to slide myself over to a floor drain to relieve myself. It felt like I was pissing blood, but I refused to look. My whole body hurt. Several sections of stitches on my back had torn open.

After peeing, I crawled with the use of my good arm over to a support beam and leaned against it. I needed to realign my shoulder. Sitting up straighter, I braced my hold on the beam and threw my shoulder into it. I felt the bone snap back into the socket just before I passed out.

I was moving. No, I was being half carried, half dragged. Through my foggy brain, I opened a partial eye and saw them taking me down a long hall, then another. Several hallways and doors later, my toes dragged through gravel and dusty dirt, only to catch on the occasional clump of grass.

The guard carrying most of my weight hefted me up higher and kept dragging me. I could hear women's voices around me, slowly quieting as we passed. And, then I was unceremoniously dumped into the dusty dirt face first.

I laid there—waiting—waiting for the final blow.

"She doesn't come out of this yard alive!" the guard yelled as he walked away. "Or there will be hell to pay for all of you!"

Smart, I laughed to myself. It would be easy to blame my death on a yard fight. It would explain all the bruises. The fact that I used to be a cop made it all the more believable.

I rolled onto my back. A cloud of dust formed around me, making me cough. I didn't care though. The sun felt warm on my face and arms. If it was really time to die, it was a beautiful day at least.

No one moved toward me for a long time. They were probably waiting to see if I would die on my own. No such luck, ladies. You'll have to finish me yourselves.

When I did finally hear someone, a face leaned over me, blocking out the sunlight.

"I'm trying to get a tan here. Do you mind?" I coughed.

"Yup, you sure sound crazy enough to be the woman that my sister was talking about."

"You Sammy's sister? Tanalla?"

"That's me," she grinned sitting next to me in the dirt. "I have a few friends that agreed to help, but what can we do? If they want you dead, they'll get to you one way or another."

"I need you to help me hold them off," I coughed.

When I wiped my mouth, fresh blood coated the back of my hand. "Fuck," I grunted as I rolled over and up into a sitting position. "How many guard towers are behind us?"

"Shit," Tanalla grumbled. "Two, but only one of them has a guard. A young kid that still doesn't know the shit that goes down in here."

"Okay, so they can set snipers up on the roof and in both the towers. Is there a better place to take cover?"

"I didn't agree to get killed for your ass," she complained.

"I'm not asking you to," I said, looking up into the sky. "Is it close to noon yet?"

"Around 11:00," Tanalla nodded.

"If I'm not in court by 1:00, all hell will break loose. I just need to stay out here until then."

"And, then what? Superman coming to rescue you?"

"No," I chuckled but cringed when shooting sharp pains lanced up my chest. "Then the FBI comes in and gets me out."

"No shit?"

"No shit. They already know I'm here. I just have to get word to them that I'm in the courtyard."

Tanalla motioned one of the other women over, and soon a large group of women circled in, hiding us from the guards' view. Tanalla took a cell phone of all things from one of the women's socks and handed it to me.

"Not many minutes left on that phone, so make it quick."

I called the one number that I knew would always be answered.

"Tell me that's you," Tech answered.

"I'm alive, but not for long. I'm in the North courtyard, and the guards ordered the prisoners to kill me. I'm safe at the moment, but they want me dead, real quick."

"A guard in county called and told us that you were transferred in the middle of the night. Kierson and Maggie are at the prison, but the prison is reporting that you're not there."

"They didn't bring me in the front door, Tech. I won't be in their computer until I'm dead. Get a chopper in the air—film this shit and do it quick."

"We need to move over to the wall," Tanalla said, as she helped another woman pull me up. The phone in my hand disappeared as I was dragged over to the side.

"Tip the tables over on their sides to offer more protection," I coughed, trying to stand on my own, but if it weren't for the wall I was leaning against, I would have fallen.

"Hey, Tan. You sure about this? This woman could get us all killed," one of the women complained.

"Don't help if you're too big of a pussy. Personally, I like our odds. Who wants to be the next one that gets dragged down to the boiler room?"

"I'll get the bastard, I promise. Just help me get back to court," I coughed.

They didn't argue anymore as they tipped the tables over. I heard the chopper approaching as the four guards that beat me last night came running back out into the courtyard.

"What the fuck is going on?" one of the guards yelled. "I told you bitches to finish her off."

"We don't work for you today, Officer Quinn," Tanalla said, stepping in front of me.

"So you have a death wish, do you," the officer to the right said, stepping forward.

I pushed off the wall and stepped in front of Tanalla and some of the other women.

"Be aware, gentleman, that chopper filming us from the tree-line was sent by a friend of mine. Anything you do will be turned over to the police and the media. You're done. It's over."

"Chandler has a long reach, inmate. If he wants you dead, then that's what is going to happen."

I blocked the first blow, but the second one hit my cracked ribs. I dropped to one knee and tried to pull myself up as I saw the expandable baton coming downward toward my head.

Tanalla flew past me into the guard, knocking him and the baton away. Next thing I knew, the women attacked the four guards, and I was crawling through the dust and dirt to help them fight them off.

Shots fired nearby, forcing us all to freeze and put our hands in the air. We couldn't fight our way past bullets. I closed my eyes and rolled onto my back. Once again, waiting.

"You're a hard woman to track down, Harrison," Maggie's voice shouted from nearby.

"Well, when I realized you sucked at following breadcrumbs, I called for a chopper. Figured you needed bigger clues to follow," I grinned without opening my eyes.

"Who's-who out here?" Kierson asked.

"The women were all helping me. The four guards are on Chandler's payroll. I was delivered to them by Chandler personally in the middle of the night. Every injury I have was from them. They have a playroom set up in the boiler room. Should be plenty of DNA to collect. And, they had another guy, Pete, running the cameras."

"Send in the medics," Maggie called over her radio. "Alright, ladies, you're not in trouble, but if you can cooperate and move over and place your palms flat against the wall, this will go smoother."

"It's okay. They're the good guys," I called out.

* * *

"You sure? I've never known it to be a good time to turn my back on any cop, especially a Fed," Tanalla argued.

"If you want the guards gone, and me to be able to go solve that other problem, then they need to see that you're cooperating," I coughed, leaning over on my good arm. I spit fresh blood into the dirt below me.

"Okay, fine. Come on, Ho's. Let's line up and show 'em our booty," Tanalla said.

All the women moved over and followed orders. The medics came out and helped me on a gurney while the four guards were led out in cuffs.

"I need to go secure the boiler room. Anything else we need to know?" Kierson asked.

"Take Chandler down before he kills me. I won't live through another fight right now."

"I will," Kierson said, squeezing my good arm. "Get her to the hospital. Maggie, call Cameron and let him know she'll need surgery and won't make it back to the courthouse."

I stayed conscious through the first three long white hallways but drifted off after that.

Chapter Forty-Six

I heard the voices before I opened my eyes. Low whispering. My Nana always said that your ears burned when someone was talking about you. The voices must be arguing instead of talking because my whole body burned.

"You can't protect her on your own. She needs her family," Charlie argued.

"It's what she wanted. The place is safe. No one will find her," Nightcrawler argued.

"It's not up to either of you," Maggie said. "Kelsey's going to do whatever she wants."

"Hell, yes," I cackled on a dry throat.

Gasps of surprise replaced the arguing voices.

"Water... please."

"How are you feeling?" Maggie asked, filling a small plastic cup.

Charlie helped me sit up enough to drink as Maggie held the cup for me.

"I feel like four guards wearing steel-tipped boots and wielding wooden batons rearranged my body parts," I sighed, leaning back into the hospital bed.

"Fuckers," Tech grumbled from the corner of the room.

"Yeah, fuckers," Genie agreed, standing next to him with her arms crossed, mimicking his stance.

Everyone grinned at Genie except for Maggie who shook her head and rolled her eyes.

"Any permanent damage?" I asked.

"You've been here almost two weeks," Charlie said. "I signed for them to keep you under sedation. You had a rib pierce your lung. You'll have to stay for a couple more days for them to monitor you and then we have to decide where to move you. But, it will be months before you're back on your feet."

"The charges against me?" I asked.

"All the charges have been handled. You were officially charged with unlawfully detaining a suspect, but you were offered a plea deal of time served. Cameron still needs you to sign the agreement, but the new DA and the judge already signed off."

I nodded. It was a minor slap on the hand charge, and everyone knew it.

"Nicholas?" I asked Charlie.

"Safe. He's in Texas with Reggie, Jackson, Wayne and Pops. We can call him later, but let's stay off Skype until your face heals a bit."

"I can't go to Texas. I'll put Nicholas in danger," I told Charlie.

"There's no more danger. Chandler and the guards were arrested. We got everyone."

I turned to Maggie, dreading the question that I had to ask.

"Is Chandler still alive?"

Maggie looked quickly around the room, but everyone seemed spooked by the question. I closed my eyes and took a deep breath.

"How long ago was he killed?" I asked.

"Two days ago," Maggie said. "How did you know?"

"How was he taken out?" I asked.

"Sniper rifle at 300 yards. No trace of the shooter," Bones answered.

"The Harbor cop in New Orleans. Is he dead too?"

Genie opened her laptop and started typing. A few minutes later she looked up, her large eyes gave her answer away before she spoke.

"He was found dead in his apartment two days ago."

My body shook as I looked around at so many people that I cared about.

"Hey, there," Grady coaxed, walking up to the other side of my bed and cupping my face. "We're here. Tell us what's going on, so we can help."

"I'm next," I answered as the tears flowed down my cheeks. "He's cleaning house, and I'm on the list. We can't stop him."

Time stood still as Charlie stared at me. A slow tear streaked down her left cheek, and I placed my hand over hers. She leaned over, burying her face in my shoulder and cried. Her body trembled in unison with my own.

Nightcrawler stepped over to Charlie and after picking her up, carried her out of the room.

"Maggie, get the doctor and get the release papers signed. Katie, book a private plane to Texas," Grady said without ever looking away from me.

Grady pulled the bottom sheet over to the right side of the bed, moving my body with it. He walked over to the other side and climbed into the bed. Carefully lifting me, he settled me on top of his arm, nestled between his shoulder and neck.

"Sleep," he whispered, pushing my hair away from my face. "We'll keep everyone safe until you're ready to take charge again."

"And, what if I'm never ready," I whispered back.

"You will be," he said as he kissed my forehead.

My heavy eyelids closed, and I drifted off with one hand clutched tightly to the front of Grady's shirt.

Thank you for reading Blood and Tears, the fourth book in the Kelsey's Burden series. I originally intended for this to be the last book in this series—but there was too much left unsaid! I mean, what's going to happen with Grady? Who's coming after Kelsey? Will she ever be able to have a normal life without looking over her shoulder? Yikes! Read on to find out...

Book Five of the Kelsey's Burden Series:

Love and Rage

The choice was to run, living the rest of my life in hiding, or to fight back—hunting down those who hurt me in the worst of ways. After everything I survived, would I be strong enough to do either? Was I strong enough to walk away from the protection that my family offered? The loving arms of my only son? And, if I stayed to fight, already injured and barely holding on to reality, could I survive another war?

Her enemies are powerful, and they're currently holding all the cards. Either way, Kelsey must find a way to beat the odds before it's too late.

The final battle. Book Five of the Kelsey's Burden Series. Love and Rage.

About the Author

Even as a very young child, I loved everything that adults considered scary—fast roller coasters, tall heights, and especially horror films. I know—I know, children shouldn't be allowed to watch horror films. But my grandmother, bless her heart, kept catching me sneaking in to watch them, and later it became something we did together. We'd curl up on the velvet flowered couch, sharing a hand-crocheted blanket and a big bowl of popcorn while we watched with huge eyes the scariest of movies.

One night (way past my bedtime) we were watching the movie Carrie. You know the one—where the high school girl is bullied and turns out to have evil powers and torches the high school. Even as a kid I never found the movie itself all that scary. But at the very end of the movie, unbeknownst to us, a hand suddenly pops out of a grave.

When that hand popped up, grandma and I grabbed hold of each other, gripping the other as if our lives depended on it, and screamed bloody murder. In a flash, my grandparent's bedroom door flew open, and my grandpa came flying out, shotgun in hand, wearing plain white long johns and searching in every direction to determine where the danger was.

Grandma and I were dumbfounded. We just looked at each other. And, then we did what we always did after a good scare—we laughed until we cried. Big, loud, tummy-rolling laughter. Grandpa didn't find the situation quite as funny and stomped back to the bedroom muttering 'damn women', which only made us laugh harder.

I still love scary movies, scary books, tall heights, and fast roller coasters. And, I was blessed to have had a grandmother in my life that encouraged me to be adventurous and brave. A grandmother who bandaged my skinned-up knees, who walked me to the fair every year, and who would talk to me for hours as we sat in the strawberry patch eating until we had sour-stomachs.

Love always Grandma. You are missed more than you could ever imagine.

And, to my readers—thank you for all the reviews and supportive messages. My favorite pastime is reading the comments sent to me, so please keep posting reviews, ratings, and Facebook messages!

Best wishes to all,
Kaylie Hunter

Contact Information:
Email: AuthorKaylieHunter@gmail.com (Ask to join the mailing list for new book releases!)
Facebook: Author Kaylie Hunter
Amazon's Author Page: Kaylie Hunter
Twitter: @BooksByKaylie

Printed in Great Britain
by Amazon